A Tribute to Leather

First Edition

Published by The Nazca Plains Corporation
Las Vegas, Nevada
2009

ISBN: 978-1-934625-27-9

Published by

The Nazca Plains Corporation ®
4640 Paradise Rd, Suite 141
Las Vegas NV 89109-8000

PUBLISHER'S NOTE
A Tribute to Leather is a work of fiction created wholly by *Christopher Trevor's* imagination. All characters are fictional and any resemblance to any persons living or deceased is purely by accident. No portion of this book reflects any real person or events.

Cover Photo, IStockPhoto
Art Director, Blake Stephens

DEDICATION

This book is dedicated to the memory of "Larry Townsend",
October 27th, 1930 - July 29th, 2008
a true Leatherman, Pioneer and Outstanding Author of intense Leather tales...

A Tribute to Leather

First Edition

Christopher Trevor

CONTENTS

ROCK STAR ABDUCTION

by Christopher Trevor

"ARRRRRGGGGGHHH!!!!! *Fucking bastards, low lives!!!"* I raved miserably and in fury as the fifth guy who had paid for me took his turn plowing my poor over-used hole.

"Yeah, oh yeah, that's the word you handsome rock star, *fucking, fucking, and fucking some more,"* the guy laughed as he held my Goldtoe brand black socked ankles aloft (my socks rumpled down around my calves and ankles) and rammed hard into me over and over, harder and harder. "Fuck man, after I'm done reaming you and my good buddies here get their seconds I'm coming in for seconds and thirds at your sweet hole."

"AAARRRRRRRRR!!! Sw-sweet hole nothing you pervert," I seethed through clenched teeth. "After all the goddamned times I've been fucked all I got back there is a sloppy and sopped cunt hole! God, you perverts have ruined my poor asshole!"

"So glad you know it bud," the guy laughed and slid deeper yet into me, holding my socked ankles tighter as he lifted them higher.

"Seconds is going to cost you extra man," I heard one of the guys who'd abducted me say to the guy fucking me and fucking me.

"Uhhh yeah, fuck, it'll be worth it man," the guy with his cock in my hole said breathlessly, leering down at me, holding my ankles tighter and slamming into me with what felt like the force of a jackhammer. "It's the most handsome rock star of all time after all. Shit, I'll even pay for fourths and fifths if I can get it up for it! Fuck that, I'll pop a Spanish fly to get it up again for this sweet piece of asshole. Damn, I can fuck this handsome piece of ass all day.

1

He's even better looking than Elvis was."

That said he pulled one of my feet to his mouth and suckled one of my toes through my thin black sock and then announced that he was cumming, ready to fire bomb my shit chute with his hot creamy load. As he sucked my toe I could feel the sleazy sensations emanating up my muscular leg and into my cock.

"Ohhh yeah, fucking A man, totally fucking A," the big lug panted, his big thick meat stick spearing me deep, hard and awful.

"OHHH you bastard," I babbled and seethed, writhing miserably under him as he fucked me deeper, ready to spew his hearty mess inside me.

"Damn, I'm so fucking deep in him I can feel his shit with my cock," the guy panted and thrust like a madman. "I wouldn't be surprised if my cock slid up and out of his mouth, HAR, HAR, HAR for you rock star!"

After all the times I'd been fucked already I just couldn't get used to the awful feeling of it. Yet every time I was fucked my cock grew hard and my balls churned. The guy thrust so deep into me that I thought he was going to literally rip me in two or perhaps his monster-sized cock would indeed slide out of my mouth, as he had just said. He was of the jumbo-size when it came to cock. He filled me and stretched the walls of my shit chute like I could not believe. I then felt his hot slimy and thick juices flood my hole. The look on his face was one of pure and sheer sadistic ecstasy.

"OHHH yeah, yeah," he grunted, holding tighter and tighter to my socked calves and ankles.

"P-pervert!" I spat at him.

Again he slurped at my toes through my socks. The sensations in my cock were phenomenal. When he was done his spent manhood slid out of my totally stretched sopped anal canal. He lowered my feet to the bed I was tied to at the wrists and one of the guys who'd abducted me, the monster named Cleeve, quickly took position at the side of the bed. He slid the vibrator/butt-plug way up into my hole and turned it on full fucking blast.

"OHHH GOD," I seethed and squeezed my eyes shut for a second as the thing came to purring life deep inside me.

It sent chills through me and caused me to break out in goose flesh every time they wedged that fucking thing inside me. Cleeve lubricated my sore cock with a lotion of sorts that heated up when it touched flesh. He then began stroking me, a medium-sized clear vial held in his other hand near my gaping slit. As always I held my ass cheeks tightly around the vibrating butt-plug wedged up in my poor hole.

"AYYYYRRRRRR, GOD," I bellowed as the guy meanly stroked

me.

"Coming up, another good load of handsome rock star spunk for us to put on the market," Cleeve laughed as he meanly and unceremoniously jacked me off. "Fuck, but this heating lube, the plug in his hole and the aphrodisiac we're feeding him all combined really does the job of making him cum every time we want him to."

"Fuckers, not to mention how when my hole is used is humiliating," I panted.

"Well hurry it the fuck up and get his nut juice," one of the guys standing there with a gargantuan hard-on said in a pushy tone of voice. "I paid good fucking money to plow that rock star's hole, not to watch him be jacked off and enjoying himself. And fuck it man, *I'm better than ready.*"

"You know the rules bud, for every time this handsome stud takes it up the ass he owes us a vial of his jazz, followed by a vial of his piss," the guy stroking me said. "And when I say his jazz I'm not talking music here, HAR! Fuck man, when we're done here we'll make millions marketing his juices."

"OHHH fuuuuccccckkk, I-I'm cumming, *again you bastards, you kidnappers got me shooting my damned load,*" I grunted crazily.

The guy pumped my big tube steak with his hand, catching my spurts of jazz in the clear vial he was holding.

"AHHHRRRRRRR!!! Sleazy perverts!" I gasped, watching as my sexy mess was being deposited into the vial. "Stealing a guy's jazz has to be against the law."

"Yeah, and stealing a rock star has to be against the law too bud," but we sure as shit stole you, you handsome fuck," Cleeve mused as I spurted out the last of my mess into the vial.

"OHHH shhhiiiittt," I keened the pain in my hole immense now that I had shot my load and that thing was still purring away inside me. "Fuckers, stole me is half-right. You bastards carried me off like a sack of dirty laundry. OHHH GOD, my poor hole."

"Yeah, we don't like leaving it unoccupied you stud," Cleeve said, handing his partner the vial of my cum and placing another vial over my wide sexy cock slit. "That's why any time you're not being fucked and puckered we put that butt-plug inside you."

I had been there long enough at that point to know what the guy wanted next. I took a deep breath and did my best to piss as liberally as possible into the new vial. As I pissed in spurts into the vial I felt the mess of cum dripping from my poor hole under me. God almighty, how many times had I been fucked like some cheap whore on a Saturday night at that point? The room I was in smelled of sex. It smelled musty and sweaty, of man sex. Most of the smell though was coming from my sopped and sticky hole.

"Yeah, that's it bud, super rock star piss," Cleeve laughed. "Fuck it all, sleazy guys out there and even girls will pay through the nose and other parts for this."

"What a way to make a living," I said miserably.

"And everyone knows that after a guy shoots his load he always has to piss," Cleeve laughed. "So just keep this good stuff brewing for us you stud."

When I was done pissing Cleeve capped the vial and handed it to his partner as well, a burly looking guy named Otis. He stood up straight, reached down and slid the vibrating device out of my hole. It came out with the sounds of squishing emanating from my poor shit chute, followed by a loud, watery and smelly fart. All the men in the room laughed and guffawed meanly. Cleeve then looked at the guy who had complained of his payment for me a few minutes earlier. My captor gestured at him with a mean looking grin on his face. I gulped hard in total fear and held back another fart because I knew that that gesture from Cleeve always meant that I was about to be brutally butt fucked yet again. The next guy up, a guy who looked like he heaved wooden crates for a living climbed on the bed between my legs, hoisted my smelly socked feet to his broad muscular shoulders and entered my sopped cum soaked hole slowly…

"ARRRRRRRRR fuuuuccccckkk," I seethed anew as his thick meat stick filled my stretched, pussy hole…

My fans, my groupies, my friends, my family and the rest of the world thought that I was on a love retreat of sorts, a break after the long concert tour I had just been on…*fuck,* if the world only knew…

The two men who'd manufactured my abduction had planned it all down to the littlest detail.

They had newspaper and tabloid connections it seemed…

The headlines in the mainstream newspapers and the tabloid rags were all basically the same.

"Hunky and Handsome Rock Star Disappears For Secret Love Tryst."

"Handsome Rock Star Spotted in Miami Beach Florida with Latest Gal Pal."

"Rock Star Keeping In Secret Contact with Agents and Confidants about Love Nest."

"Handsome Latino Singer Disappears From Public Eye To Make Time With New Love Interest."

"Handsome Rock Star Vanishes After Final Show of Concert Tour to be with Secret Girlfriend."

None of the headlines were true. Shit, nothing they wrote even came near to the horrible truth of what had befallen me. Rock star, Latin heartthrob and idol of millions worldwide. If my fans knew the awful truth of what had happened to me they never would have believed it, let me tell you... *Fuck, I couldn't believe it myself!* Four days it had been so far that I had mysteriously disappeared from the face of the earth, or so it had seemed. Four days of being constantly fucked. Four days of living and fucking hell, literally fucking hell. Four days with practically no sleep, except for the few times I had passed out the pain from being fucked with huge cocks so awful. Four days that seemed more like four weeks...and things were just getting started, or so I was told...

In the afternoon of the fourth day things were going as they had been since I had been brought there, wherever there was...

"OHHH GOD almighty, no, no, *not again!!"* I sputtered madly, the pain intense and burning the walls of my hole.

"Yeah, that's it you handsome fucking rock star," the guy plowing me said mockingly, sliding in and out of my hole like crazy. "Sing for me bud. I wonder how all your fans would feel to see your sloppy squishy cunt hole eating up my big man meat. Fuck man, your shit chute is sucking me in further every time I plow you. Fuck, every time I saw you on TV or on stage I admit I had a fantasy of fucking the tar out of you man. And now look, my goddamned twisted fantasy has come true. OHHH yeah, yeah!!!"

Stretched out in a spread eagle position on a raised bed, wearing just my stinking black socks by Goldtoe, my wrists tied tight above me to the bed board I was being brutally butt-fucked for what seemed like the thousandth time. And every time following being fucked I was meanly milked and siphoned of my load, which as you already know was collected in a vial followed by a vial of my piss as well. The lubricant they used on my big uncut tube steak heated up when applied to the skin, thus causing my poor organ to feel sore and burnt, worse each time I was milked and forced to piss. God, every fucking time they touched my poor sore cock I nearly flew out of my socks. My creamy jazz and sour piss would be sold to the highest bidders. I wondered miserably how much my juices would go for on E-bay. The socks I was wearing, the same fucking pair I had on the day they captured me they planned to sell for at least five thousand dollars. The way those socks were scented at that point avid and sleazy foot fetishists out there would bid like crazy for them. A plastic zip-lock bag was already labeled with my name and the caption under it, which read, "Rock Star's Smelly Socks. Worn with his designer outfits during his final concert while on recent tour." During the night when not being fucked, which was not that often I was made to wear and sweat in white briefs, them also to be sold to the highest bidders. Watching those guys take turns sliding the briefs on me was embarrassing beyond words. God, also while not being fucked and to really get me sweating in the under shorts they kept a big fat latex vibrating butt-plug wedged deep in my poor hole. The feeling was astronomical, that fucking thing purring away deep inside me, tickling my innards in a way. And for whatever the reason having my butt hole firmly, tightly plugged and tingling kept me good and fucking hard and bulging and pudging in my briefs. My captors made sure that my hole was rarely unoccupied. When they discovered that the vibrating butt-plug made me hard they milked me even more, driving me nearly out of my mind with it, forcing me to guzzle the aphrodisiac they had used to capture me. (More on that very soon.) During the night as I slept (if there were no customers that is) my captors collected vials of my jazz and piss, milking me and stroking me till I pissed a few times each night. Not a drop of my juices was wasted. And may God help me if I pissed without their permission, as I was told from the beginning of this nightmare. As I said, I didn't get much sleep at all.

Fuck, how could something this awful have happened to me, *me of all people???*

And after the last show of my sold-out concert tour, making it all the worse… I had been prepared for a final after the show party that night; instead I wound up being kidnapped. It had been an awesome tour, millions of happy and screaming fans in every city I played in. There were even unhappy fans that had clamored for tickets but were unable to get them due to shows being sold out so quickly.

I could remember as if it had just happened, it was all that shocking…

I had come off the stage amid the screams, cheers and clapping of the audience at the sports stadium we had just performed at. The crowd was cheering and hooting for yet another encore. The show, like all the shows before it had been sold out. Thousands of people screaming my name at the same time and cheering for me as I wound up the show with my last song for the evening. Dressed in tight fitting leather pants (which really showed off and accented my tight butt cheeks), a black button down silk shirt unbuttoned down to my belly button, (showing off my muscular chest, washboard abs and big nipples) and a pair of black slip-on Prada shoes I stood there sweating. I was smiling that killer smile of mine from ear to ear. I waved at the crowd of screaming fans, most of them young girls. Every time I took a deep breath my muscular chest heaved around my unbuttoned shirt, threatening to push it off me. That got even more screaming from the audience let me tell you. My band members gathered around me along with the dancers and back-up singers who had shared the stage with me all during the tour. We all bowed a couple of times before leaving the stage. The dancers left the stage first followed by most of my band members. As we had done in all the other shows my muscular guitarist and my equally muscular drummer squatted down, grabbed my legs and hips and got me hoisted and balanced up on their broad shoulders. The fans went even crazier as the two band members slowly carried me across and finally off the stage, me waving at the fans and smiling real big.

"Man, that was a great finale show," John the guitarist said as he and Dan the drummer carried me on their shoulders down the hallway and toward my private dressing room. "You really got this crowd going crazy."

"Thanks John, that's cool of you to say," I said, basking in the glory, always loving the good feeling I got at the end of a good show. "I just cannot believe that the tour is over."

"Yeah, I'll bet you're more than tired though," Dan said, one of his hands squeezing my black socked ankle as we neared my dressing room.

In front of my dressing room they put me down and I shook hands with both of them.

"I suppose I'll see you guys back at the hotel later on," I said, not knowing that I wouldn't be seeing them for quite some time. "I need to relax a while before getting changed. You're right Dan. I am very tired."

"Take your time man," John said. "Your driver will wait outside and the guys with your mineral water will be here in less than a few minutes."

"Thanks guys, I'll sure need that water after that show," I said, opening the door to my dressing room. "And guys, thanks for the lift from the stage to here."

We all laughed heartily and I closed the door behind me.

I was breathless, sweating and exhausted. I unbuttoned my shirt the rest of the way, un-tucked it from my pants, shucked it off and flopped down in the chair in front of my dressing table. My wearied reflection stared back at me. My brown wavy hair was mussed and soaked with sweat, as was my muscular and somewhat hairy chest. My leather pants stuck to my tree-trunk-like legs, the scent of leather emanating from there, filling the air around me. I leaned back in the chair, slid my shoes off my feet and closed my eyes. The scent of my sweaty and musty black socks emanated up at me as well. God, but I was one tired and sweaty stinky rock star. I had played twenty cities on this tour. It was twenty cities to promote my latest album and teasing the audience with a couple of songs from my upcoming album. I worked out before each show, ten miles of jogging and then two hours of heavy-duty weightlifting. Fuck, no wonder I was exhausted. Anyone who even thought it was so great and glamorous to be a rock star didn't know the half of it. But God man, the audience response made it all worth it...

A knocking at the door startled me from the light doze I had momentarily fallen into...

"Uh yeah?" I called out, sitting up straight in the chair, looking at the door to my dressing room.

"Mineral water Sir," I heard a male voice reply.

"Oh good," I said, stood up and padded on my socked feet to the door.

I opened the door and two rugged, very muscular looking guys walked into my dressing room, each of them lugging a medium-sized cardboard box filled with bottles of mineral water. The shorter of the two guys had a backpack slung on his back.

"Wow, I don't recall ordering this many bottles," I said with a grin, stupidly closing and locking the door behind the two men.

"Well, I'm sure that a performer of your caliber can do with extra water Sir," the bigger of the two guys said with a grin on his face as well.

It was at that moment that I realized that these two big guys were not the usual two who delivered my water while I was in this particular city.

"Say, uh, where are the other guys who usually deliver my water?" I asked, watching as the shorter of the two delivery guys took a bottle from his box and uncapped it for me.

"They got a little tied up on another delivery Sir," the bigger guy replied. "That's why we're sort of filling in, yes, we're filling in."

"Here you go Sir," the shorter guy said to me with a big smile, holding out the bottle he had just opened for me to take. "Down the hatch. The way you're sweating it sure looks like you can use it."

"Yeah, I sure can at that, thanks man, I probably smell like a locker room," I said, took the bottle from him and sipped it down gratefully.

As I drank the water down I realized just how very thirsty I really was. I sipped it down faster.

"There you go Sir, bet you're feeling better already," the bigger guy said, taking a bottle from his box and opening it.

When I had finished the first bottle of water he took the empty from me and handed me a second.

"Drink up Sir, it'll put hair on your chest," the bigger guy laughed, handing me the bottle.

"Thanks, I guess a guy can always use some more hair on his chest," I replied stupidly and scoffed down that bottle of water as well.

As I sipped down the water I noticed the two guys checking out my big chest, my fleshy pointy nipples and my Adam's apple as it bobbed up and down. It didn't bother me in the least, at least not at that moment it didn't bother me. I knew that I had gay fans. Being the star I was I had to accept fans of all kinds and of all persuasions. But truthfully, these two didn't appear to be your average gay guys. They just seemed to be really checking me out, drinking me in if you will, and sizing me up. It was when the second bottle was empty and I was being handed a third that my head started spinning and I felt a sudden tingling throughout my muscular body...but mostly in the area of my big rock star meat stick.

"Ohhh whoa, I must have guzzled that water too fast guys," I said and dropped the empty bottle on the floor. "M-my head seems to be spinning."

"Better get you seated then Sir," the bigger guy said, grabbing my upper arms and guiding me to my chair. "Otis, bring the rock star here another bottle of water."

"Uh, I-I don't think that's necessary bud," I said sheepishly. "I'm not all that thirsty anymore and to be real frank the need to piss is already starting to set in good and heavy."

"Just what I wanted to hear," the bigger guy said and put a third quart-sized bottle of mineral water to my now quivering lips.

The way my head was spinning I didn't resist and simply sipped down the water. My entire body was tingling at that point and I realized that I had popped a major-sized boner in my leather pants. It was just a tad more than evident let me tell you. I was woozy and yet somehow erotically charged up and horny all at the same time. The guy held the third bottle to my lips his other hand on the back of my sweat sopped neck as I gulped the fluid down. When I was done my vision blurred and I looked up to see the two men looming over me.

"Feeling okay Sir?" the shorter of the two guys asked me.

"Oh, he's feeling more than okay Otis," the bigger guy said with what looked like an evil grin. "This rock star is feeling awesome. Aren't you bud?"

"Wh-what's going on?" I asked, feeling totally disoriented and totally horny.

It was at that moment that I realized that there had been something other than just water in the bottles I had just guzzled. I gripped the arms of my chair and didn't fully realize that the bigger guy was feeding me a fourth bottle of water…while his buddy was working at getting my leather pants off me…SHIT!!!

I was too woozy to do anything to stop the guy from de-panting me. I simply sat there gripping the arms of the chair while being forced to guzzle and guzzle the mineral water…and whatever the fuck it was spiked with. When the fourth bottle was empty the two men again stood looming over me, looking at me lustfully. With my head lolling back I looked up at them.

"Y-you bastards," I whispered, sitting there in my white Calvin Klein sweat soacked briefs, a big tenting bulge in them and my black calf-length nylon smelly dress socks. "Wh-what's the point of this?"

"Man, we sure picked good this time Otis, better than good, we picked fucking fantastically awesome," the bigger of the two guys stated triumphantly.

"Told you so Cleeve," the shorter guy replied. "We'll not only have a great fucking time with this rock star hunk, but we'll make plenty of money at the same time."

"Fuck man, m-my bodyguards will make short work of the two of you," I panted and gripping the arms of the chair tighter I tried to stand up.

"Easy guy, easy," the guy named Cleeve said to me and reached down, grabbed a handful of my hair and yanked me back into the chair. "Now sit still. You've consumed a heavy dose of our secret drink mix. You're worked up hornier than a cat in heat on a hot summer night, but you're not in any condition to be making any stupid moves."

"HA, you mean like the sexy moves he makes when he's on stage Cleeve?" the guy named Otis laughed.

"AHHH, fuck, m-my dick feels like it's hard as steel man," I panted.

I watched through hazy vision as the big lug reached into his jeans pocket and brought out a clear tube-shaped vial, about seven inches long or so.

"Now Otis, if you wouldn't mind," Cleeve said. "I'd like to get the first of his creamy loads from him."

At the sound of those words I nearly blanched in the chair. I mean fuck I was totally heterosexual, despite the ugly rumors that had gone around. (Just because I had been secretly photographed while working out clad in just a Speedo with my trainer did not make me gay. Just because my trainer made me use him as a human barbell and had me lift him over my head a few times in succession did not make me gay. Just because I had popped a hard-on while working out with my trainer did not make me gay. JEEZ, the things people will believe just because of some pictures that had been taken.) Now, these guys being faggots really grated on me. Not that I had anything against gay men, I just didn't want to have sex with any of them. But then, in the condition they had me in there wasn't all that much I could do to stop them from doing what the fuck they wanted to me…and with me. Otis happily squatted in front of me, slid my under shorts down in front and my uncut boner popped up between my legs. It was huge, thick, hard and oozing and oozing what looked like massive droplets of crystal clear pre cum. My dick is a good eight to nine inches long, thick and beefy and veiny along the sides of my shaft. All three of us looked at it in wonderment, as my big meat seemed to be throbbing and pulsing with a life all its own, my slit opening and closing like a single eye.

"OHHH GOD," I garbled as Otis slicked up my entire shaft and crown with the heat-up lubricant. "F-fucking perverts."

The three of us watched as my dick seemed to grow harder still as Otis slathered it up and got it real slicked. The more he rubbed the lubricant on it the more it heated. Cleeve squatted down next to me, held the opened vial at my wide sexy slit and began stroking me with his other hand.

"G-God man, m-my bodyguards will get you for this," I mumbled helplessly, feeling the orgasm building in the base of my big meat stick. "God almighty, wh-what is that stuff you made me drink? And what is that shit you slathered my dick with?"

I gripped the arms of the chair tighter still and pressed my socked feet harder against the floor. Fuck man, but the guy was really, *really* jacking me the fuck off.

"Well, seeing as making conversation will pass the time till I get your juice I'll tell you," Cleeve said, stroking my foreskin erotically back and forth over my hardness. "The mineral water was laced with a potent aphrodisiac serum from the Orient, mixed with some potent vitamins and some extra minerals. A doctor friend of ours gave it to us, for a price of course. He tested it on a college jock while he had the kid strapped to a table and an electronic sucking device attached to his dick. The doctor fed the aphrodisiac to the kid intravenously. That jock spewed more loads than he was able to count and then some by the time the good doctor released him. According to the doctor one vial of the stuff mixed with some water is enough to make a guy able to shoot more loads than he can count. In your case we gave you more than a few vials of the stuff. You see, we need you to be potent for the next few days."

"Which means you'll be downing the stuff on a regular basis," Otis said and tweaked one of my nipples good and hard.

"N-next few days?" I stammered and watched; chills coursing through me as the big guy worked my dick faster, stroking me harder.

11

I had been right. I was horny and hard enough for at least three or four women. But that wasn't what these guys wanted. They simply wanted my jazz, and they planned to really milk it from me…constantly. I thought about whoever the poor college jock was that Cleeve had mentioned, him hooked up to a suction machine and my heart raced in fear.

"And as for the lubricant we slathered onto your massive meat stick here it's simply a lotion that heats up when it comes in contact with human skin," Cleeve went on, still stroking me, getting me closer and closer to a man's explosion. "And may I say that I am very impressed with the size and girth of your manhood, as our customers will also be I have no doubt."

"C-customers? J-just what the fuck do you guys plan on doing with me?" I gasped; the sound of my dick being stroked turning into a loud squishing at that point.

But then…

"OHHH Oh fuuuuuccccckkk, y-you perverts are goin' to get my nut," I suddenly garbled and my head lolled back further still.

"Just what we wanted," Otis said and gave one of my nipples another good tweak as I spewed what would be the first of many loads of rock star goop for the two men.

"OHHH GOD, fucking A," I bellowed as Cleeve held my meat stick tight and straight out, my jazz landing in globs in the vial he held over my spurting slit.

"Yeah, that's it you handsome fuck, fill this thing for me," Cleeve said demandingly, stroking me like crazy. "We'll get at least a thousand fucking dollars for each vial of your mess."

"OHHH sshhhittt, sleazy perverts you two are," I grunted angrily.

My cum being deposited into that vial sent a horrible feeling through me, for whatever the reason. When I was done shooting my load Cleeve capped the vial, handed it to Otis and took another vial from his pants pocket. I sat there gasping for breath, stinking of sweat, my slimy manhood semi hard and peeking out of my foreskin.

"Okay handsome guy, what I want you to do next is piss," Cleeve said, getting my piss slit situated in the tip of the new vial. (God, what a sight that was…) "Piss till the vial is filled. When the vial is filled stop pissing. If you need to piss some more I'll use another vial."

I looked at the guy incredulously. First he'd raped my cum out of me, and now he was after my piss. With my head spinning the way it was there wasn't much I could do to stop these two from doing what they wanted with me. Without a word I took a deep breath and pissed a long yellow urine sample into the vial. Cleeve had been right. It would take two vials to collect all my piss. What with the four large bottles of mineral water I had consumed it was no wonder.

"Good boy, you learn fast," Cleeve said, holding my shaft in his fingers as I filled the second vial with my piss. "And if you piss without having us fill one of these vials you will pay like you wouldn't believe."

Fuck, I did as they said because I wanted them gone. I had heard of fans doing crazy things and carrying out crazy stunts on their idols, but this was beyond ridiculous. I wanted them to get what the fuck they wanted and then leave. But God, hadn't they said something about wanting me potent for the next few days? And didn't they mention their *customers* enjoying the size of my manhood?

"Okay Otis, that is a good start," Cleeve said, holding up the three vials, one filled with my milky cum and the other two filled with my rancid piss.

He carefully slid the three vials into one of his jeans pockets.

"OHHH GOD, th-that shit you guys fed me sure packs a wallop," I said, my head still spinning, every part of me alive and tingling.

I gripped the arms of the chair tighter, my head lolling forward. My God, I wanted to cum again so badly, I was that horny. And I had just shot my load, go figure.

"OHHH fuckkk," I gasped, watching this time as the guy named Cleeve stroked me toward another gusher.

Once again he was squatting in front of me, an empty vial held under my slit. He had gripped my cock again so fast that at first I hadn't realized it. My head spun and I curled my toes back under my socks in the forced ecstasy I was enduring.

"Down the hatch Stud," Otis said, forcing a bottle of the aphrodisiac laced mineral water to my quivering lips. "We want to keep you good and fucking horny…"

With no choice in the matter I sipped down the water, every last goddamned drop of it. As I did the tingling sensations throughout my body intensified, especially in my big throbbing meat stick. I was harder than I had been when I'd shot the first load for Cleeve and his buddy Otis.

"Mmmm…" I crooned around the tip of the bottle, trying to let the two thugs know that I felt it, I was cumming again.

Otis took the bottle away from my mouth and the next thing I knew I was spurting another hearty mess of rock star soup into a vial for Cleeve.

"OHHH GOD, fucking sleazy perverts," I grunted, watching as my cum was collected in the vial.

When I was done I was told to piss again, thus filling yet another vial with my yellow juices. This time when I was done I sat there slumped in my chair, gasping like crazy for breath. I was still pretty worked up and as semi hard as I was I knew that my meat stick would soon be at full erection in no time. I was that horny.

"Okay Otis, we can stay here all night milking this rock star," Cleeve said. "But eventually people will be looking for him and knocking on his dressing room door here. Let's get him packaged and get the fuck out of here."

"Sure thing Cleeve," Otis said, taking the backpack off his back.

He opened the backpack and I gulped hard in terror when I saw the pile of rope he pulled from it.

A few minutes later I was standing and feeling totally helpless and more than stupid for having fallen into the mess I was now in. When I had seen that these two weren't the usual guys who delivered my water I should have realized something was wrong. God, but now it was too late. Fuckers had tied me up real good and tight and even gagged me, with a pair of my stinking jogging socks no less. My hands were tied tightly behind me at the wrists. My black socked feet were tied securely at the ankles and to keep my dick rigid and stiff they had meanly tied a length of rope around the base of my big Spanish nuts, leaving my Calvin Klein under shorts pulled down in front. I was hard as a fucking rock all over again, oozing pre cum, feeling totally humiliated, but this time I was what I suppose would be called fear-hard. Or perhaps it was a combination of fear and the aphrodisiac they had tricked me into drinking. Rope was wound tightly around my big biceps, over my chest and pinned my arms to my upper torso. When I saw Cleeve rummaging through the laundry bag that contained my dirty clothes I knew I was in for something real nasty. Grinning from ear to ear he held up a pair of my calf length thick white sweat socks.

"WH-what the fuck are you planning on doing with my socks fucker?" I asked stupidly.

The socks smelled beyond pungent with my foot stink, seeing as I had jogged better than ten miles in them with my sneakers along with my personal trainer that morning. Cleeve turned the foul smelling thick white socks inside out, tied the toe sections together into a tight ball and crammed the ball of them into my mouth. He then tied the slack of the socks behind my sweaty neck, effectively gagging me. Each time I swallowed I was treated to a mouth and throat-full of my own foot stink. My dick throbbed harder.

"There, that looks good," Cleeve said as he and Otis stood looking me over.

I scowled fiercely at them, my eyes ablaze with more than anger and hatred for the two men. The serum that they had made me drink was still causing me to feel somewhat dizzy, but not as much as earlier. As I stood there totally helpless the two men leaned down at my big chest. They each slurped one of my big pointy nipples into their mouths, going to sucking and slurping work on them.

"Hhhhrrrrmmmmfffff!!!" I gasped, as pearls of pre cum oozed from my slit.

Of all the fucked up things I thought miserably.

I wriggled erotically on my bound feet, trying my best not to lose my balance. Cleeve and Otis reached down and behind me, squeezed my melon shaped butt cheeks and slurped and sucked my nipples harder still, admittedly driving me batty. Damn, but for a guy I sure do have sensitive nips.

"Hhhhrrrrrmmmmffff!!!" I sputtered and swallowed hard, the awful taste of my sweat socks filling my mouth and sliding down my throat.

"Ha, now you know why we had to gag you Stud," Cleeve laughed and slurped my nipple quickly back into his mouth.

My eyes rolled in my head and when they stopped working my nipples (about fifteen minutes later) they were totally hard and more than erect, sticking out real provocatively on my chest.

"Perfect," Cleeve said, giving the tip of one of my now overly sore and erect nipples a squeeze and a twist. "Now Otis, if you would please do the honors."

"With pleasure," Otis said and again reached into his backpack or should I say his bag of tricks.

He brought out a pair of sharp-teethed alligator tit clamps, along with a heavy chain between them.

"RRRRMMMFFF!!" I wailed shaking my head "no" wildly as Otis squeezed the tit clamps open.

"HA, we should have blindfolded you asshole," Cleeve jeered at me. "But we need to get your titties up to twice their size. A lot of our customers just love sucking big rock star tits."

Standing there tied and sweating in one pair of socks and chewing on another pair I was helpless to do anything to stop Otis from clamping my poor nipples.

"HHHRRRMMMFFFF!!" I bellowed in the stinging pain when my nipples were clamped tight, the teeth of the things biting meanly into the tender flesh of them.

I threw my head back and forth, standing there still trying not to lose my balance.

"Goddamn it Otis, look at this," Cleeve said, hooking a big hand around my throbbing hardness. "Looks like this rock star is ready to be milked again."

I gulped a big breath through my nose at Cleeve's touch and grip on my hard dick. I was feeling real sensitized at that point let me tell you.

"Yeah sure Cleeve, but do you think we have the time?" Otis asked merrily.

"Sure do Otis, third time is the charm after all," Cleeve said, giving my dick a twist, getting a loud grunt out of me.

"But if you milk him while his tits are clamped the pain in them will become hundreds of times worse," Otis said jokingly.

I looked at him and scowled behind my sock gag.

"Yeah, and ain't that just too fucking bad?" Cleeve asked, taking an empty vial from his pocket and starting to stroke me yet again, sliding my foreskin back and forth over my throbbing crustiness.

"Hhhhrrrrmmmmmmfffff!!!" I sputtered as Cleeve worked me, holding the vial at my wide slit.

"Otis, would you care to sample his shit chute?" Cleeve asked his buddy.

"I thought you'd never ask," Otis replied and squatted behind me.

He yanked my under shorts down in back, spread my sexy ass cheeks apart and plunged his tongue into my sweat sopped and stinking hole.

"HHHRRRRMMMMFFF!!!" was all I could say and I nearly jumped out of my socks as the two men worked me front and back like some cheap whore.

Damn, the way I had sweated on stage not all that long ago my hole had to be rank and stinking like no one's business, and it should have been no one's business, yet Otis slurped and sucked at it like his life depended on it. Then, for the third time I felt my orgasm start to build in my rock hardness. My tied balls ached as the fucking guy stroked me and stroked me.

"Yeah, he's getting there already Otis," Cleeve said, leering at me as I scowled at him. "Eat his hole man, its making him sexy crazy."

Truer words were never spoken. The guy's tongue flicking around my pink shit smelling hole made me pull myself to my socked toes, gyrating myself stupidly. God, what a sight I must have made at that point. Then, breathless and swallowing my foot stink I felt it. I was about to shoot a third load.

"RRRRRRMMMMFFF!!!" I screamed in a mixture of ecstasy, fear and pain all at the same time.

Cleeve went on stroking me, catching my mess in the vial as I seemed to cum and cum. Damn, but that serum they'd made me drink really did the trick let me tell you.

"Oh man, look at this, another man-sized load of rock star goop," Cleeve said happily. "Damn, we can't leave those bottles of water and serum here Otis. I want to make him drink this shit every hour or so."

But Otis didn't respond. He was in too much elation eating and sucking madly at my hole. As I shot my load the pain in my clamped nipples intensified about two hundred percent, just as Otis had predicted.

"RRRMMMMFFF!!!" I wailed miserably.

Man, I would have paid anyone a hundred bucks to get those clamps off my poor nipples at that moment. When I was done shooting my creamy load Cleeve capped the vial and held another one at the tip of my semi hardness. He simply glared into my eyes. I took a deep breath and managed to piss, filling the vial for him.

"Good boy, good rock star," Cleeve said, sounding like a proud parent, sounding totally twisted. "Got anymore?"

I nodded "no." Finally, Otis stopped eating my hole and got to his feet, licking and smacking his lips together. He left my underpants pulled down in the back and I felt his saliva trickling out of my hole...

"MMMMMFFFF..." I moaned, feeling a slight draft waft up into my saliva soaked hole.

"Okay Otis, before we get this show on the road let's get his hole plugged up," Cleeve said. "I want this rock star to start getting used to the feeling of his shit chute being constantly filled up."

I looked at Cleeve with confusion in my eyes and watched as Otis again reached into his backpack. He brought out a fat long latex, pink colored butt-plug. He held it up for a few seconds for me to see, to mock me as well, and to really make me drink in the sight of the damned thing.

"RRRRMMMMFFFF!!!" I garbled and tried to take a step backward, almost toppling myself on my bound feet.

Otis flipped a switch on the base of the butt-plug and the thing came to purring and vibrating life. God, just the sound of the thing filled me with dread. They weren't really going to shove that thing up my ass were they? Were they???

"Spread his cheeks for me Cleeve, please," Otis said. "It's going to be a pleasure to slide this thing up inside this handsome rock star."

Fuck, they really were going to shove that thing up my ass. I trembled in my socks as the two men stepped behind me. Cleeve did the honors of grabbing two handfuls of my melon-shaped butt cheeks, kneading them as he did so and spread them apart, once again revealing my pink and stinking hole.

"Hhhhrrrmmmmfff!!!" I gasped, felt humiliation sear through me and then felt the vibrating device being slowly inserted into me, inch by goddamned inch. *"RRRRRRRMMMMFFFFF!!!!"*

I arched my back and my chest heaved forward. I balled my tied hands into fists as the invasive thing instantly drove me crazy. Goose bumps broke out all over me at the sensations of the vibrating butt-plug. It felt as if a swarm of bees was buzzing around in my stinking hole. When the thing was wedged deep inside me the two men stepped back in front of me. I stood there tied, gagged, and tit clamped, stinking and sweating. The sound of the vibrating butt-plug was music to my captor's ears. As a rock star it was not the kind of music I wanted to hear.

"Okay Otis, let's get this show on the road, no pun intended there seeing as he's a rock star," Cleeve said, looking lustfully and hungrily at me. "You carry the boxes of mineral water and I'll carry...*him*..."

"MMMFFFFFF!!!" I sputtered desperately, the realization kicking in good and fucking hard.

I *was* about to be kidnapped. And right out of my dressing room no less. I should have realized that when all this had started. And, I should have realized that fact when Cleeve had mentioned customers of theirs enjoying rock star's big tits. Speaking of my tits, the heavy chain on the clamps was pulling real hard on my poor nubs. God, if they didn't take the clamps off me soon my nipples would be swollen to more than twice their size. But I somehow got the feeling that that was what they wanted. I stole a quick look of dismay down at my poor nipples as Cleeve stepped over to me, a mean looking grin on his face. I looked at the man in horror, he who was about to literally carry me away. He hoisted me easily and effortlessly off the floor and up into his hugely muscular arms. Actually he lifted me in the fashion of a groom lifting his bride before carrying her over the threshold of their honeymoon suite.

"RRRMMMMFFF!!!" I wailed in the big guy's face, his puss inches from mine.

The base of the vibrating butt-plug stuck embarrassingly out of my hole as Cleeve held me aloft. Fucking guys had left my under shorts pulled down in the back. Grinning sadistically Cleeve pecked me on the cheek, giving my rancid socks gag a sniff.

"Whew, I'll bet those sweat socks of yours taste downright awful at this point huh Stud?" he asked me mockingly, holding me tightly and close against himself.

Otis slung his backpack onto his back, opened the door to my dressing room, hoisted the boxes of mineral water and led the way out to the hallway. As Cleeve carried me toward the door I suddenly felt very sorry for him and Otis. My bodyguards were *always* right outside my dressing room door *and always on the alert.* Man, did I feel sorry for these two jokers. My two bodyguards would make very short work of them. Of course I figured that I would have to endure the feeling of humiliation when my bodyguards saw me being carried tied up and gagged in just my under shorts and socks. But as my bodyguards they would not breathe a word of the incident to anyone. Fuck, they wouldn't want anyone else getting the idea of working me over in my dressing room and almost kidnapping me. No, they would simply rescue me, make short work of Cleeve and Otis and the occurrence would be put behind us. Actually, at that moment I didn't know why I was thinking that Cleeve and Otis would succeed in kidnapping me, knowing my bodyguards were very close by. I suppose being captured in the dressing room did sort of scare the fuck out of me, but once my bodyguards' saw what was happening this whole incident would be over. But the horror I had been feeling was suddenly increased about a thousand folds when I saw the sight before me in the deserted hallway. On the floor were my two brawny and muscular bodyguards. They were seated back to back and securely tied up and gagged. Actually, they were tied back to back to each other, both of them totally immobilized and totally unable to help me at all.

"MMMMMFFFFFFFF!!!" I garbled crazily, looking down at them as they looked up at me, looks of total helplessness in their eyes.

"Now remember boys, if you want to see this handsome rock star again soon you'll both keep your mouths shut about what you just saw here," Cleeve said, standing with me in his arms over my two bodyguards. "Just agree with what you'll see printed in the tabloids and the newspapers starting tomorrow. After a few days you'll all be back in business. Otis and I rarely hold onto a mark for more than twenty-four hours. But this rock star is something special after all, so I'm figuring on three to five days at the most with him."

The bodyguards nodded miserably and I fleetingly noticed how they seemed to be looking up lustfully at my tied, socked feet as they dangled over them. Cleeve smiled, pecked me on the cheek again, called me his million dollar rock star, and sauntered slowly down the hall with me.

"HHHRRRRRMMMFFFFF!!!" I bellowed, turning my head to look back one final time at the two men who were supposedly paid to prevent things like this from happening to me.

We exited the stadium through a back entrance, which led to a deserted alleyway. There were no cameras in that area of the stadium seeing as it was hardly ever frequented by anyone. As Cleeve carried me he seemed not even to be slightly winded when we got outside. I mean, I'm no lightweight not by a long shot. I work out everyday and weigh in at a good two hundred pounds of sheer muscle. At the back of the alley I saw a navy blue van, almost the size of a moving van. Otis was loading the boxes of mineral water into the back section of the vehicle as Cleeve carried me over to him.

"Go loosen the ropes on the bodyguards Otis," Cleeve said. "Just enough for them to work themselves free once we're gone, long gone."

That said Cleeve again pecked me on the cheek. This time I looked at him in disgust.

"Do you think we can be sure that those bodyguards of his won't say anything Cleeve?" Otis asked, giving one of my socked feet a squeeze.

"I'm more than positive of it," Cleeve replied. "This guy is their meal ticket. They won't risk anything happening to him. Now, do as I said and loosen the ropes on them. I'll get this handsome guy strapped up in the van."

"Sure thing Cleeve," Otis said and dashed back into the stadium.

It seemed to me that it was Cleeve who gave the orders in this outfit.

"Man oh man, we are going to make a fortune with you Stud," Cleeve said as we looked directly into each other's eyes as he carried me up and into the back of the van. The walls of the van were covered with thick rug, no doubt to soundproof it. I suddenly got the feeling that I wasn't the first poor slob to be abducted by these two psychos. I did think however that I was the first real celebrity they had abducted. In the center of the rug covered van was a long operating room sort of cushioned table, bolted to the floor. Straps were attached to the table from the top to the bottom of it. Cleeve set me down atop the table, stretching me out on my back.

"MMMMMRRRMMMFFF…" I sputtered up at him, drool running sloppily out of the sides of my gagged mouth.

My dick was fear hard and sticking up straight, oozing pre cum all over again. Without a word Cleeve quickly strapped me down to the table from my chest area to my feet. Looking straight up I saw that the van had a skylight window. Once I was strapped down tight Cleeve stepped to the middle of the table and took my balls in one hand. I squirmed at his touch.

"Okay bud, the ride from here to where we're taking you will take a few good hours," Cleeve said, giving my tied balls a fast squeeze. "Just relax and try to enjoy it."

"RRRRMMMMMFFF!!!" I railed at him.

Just as Cleeve was exiting the back of the van Otis returned sprinting as fast as his feet would take him.

"Let's get moving," Otis said. "The way I see it those bodyguards of his will be untied very soon."

Cleeve quickly slammed the van doors shut, plunging me into semi darkness, the only light coming from the skylight window above me. I heard the two men laughing as they stepped up into the front section of the vehicle. Somehow I knew that Cleeve was in the driver's seat. Actually, I now knew for sure that he was in the driver's seat for this entire fiasco... As the van pulled away my heart pounded in mortal fear...

As the van moved along I looked up at the skylight window and saw that it was gradually becoming darker and darker, fewer and fewer lampposts lit the road as we drove along. Watching the clouds go by I felt slightly dizzy and the tingling in my meat stick and balls were increasing with every passing second. My hardness throbbed like crazy and I have to admit that if my hands were free I would have jacked off like a mad man. God almighty and I had already shot three damned loads. In my mind I saw myself tied up, gagged with my sweat socks and helpless as the big guy named Cleeve hoisted me off the floor and into his hugely muscular arms. His biceps and triceps were of the astronomical size, not the kind of muscles a guy achieves at the gym, more like muscles one gets when working in construction or something like that. Not even steroids could give a man the size of muscles that Cleeve sported. The butt-plug buzzed crazily in my hole and the tit clamps chewed and gnawed on my poor nipples. In my mind again I saw Cleeve holding me close to himself and as he carried me he pecked me on the cheek. My hardness pounded like mad...

A good half-hour or so into the drive my dick was beyond rigid and stiff between my legs. My tied balls were aching anew and throbbing as well. My nipples stung like murder in the clamps and the vibrating butt-plug felt like it was literally cooking my hole. God, but I needed to shoot my load. My foreskin snaked back sexily over my hard manhood. That always drove me sexily crazy, not to mention different girls throughout my past. Pearls of pre cum and beads of piss formed at the tip of my wide dick slit. My God, but I was more than horny at that point. I was in a total lather...

Can you believe that shit? Kidnapped, and I was horny as a toad. Fuck, but that serum they'd tricked me into drinking sure did work, that was for sure.

About two hours or so later, by my best estimates the van pulled to a slow halt. I wondered if we'd arrived at the destination they had planned to bring me to. My meat stick stuck straight up, long, beefy and hard. I heard the two men disembark from the front of the van and the back doors were pulled open. Light from a lamppost that they'd stopped under and the moon shining in the skylight window were the only sources of light.

"Enjoying the ride asshole?" Cleeve asked me as he and Otis stepped up into the back of the van.

The sound of the butt-plug vibrating in my hole was the only sound in the deserted area where we were.

"RRRMMMMFFFF!!!" I railed crazily at them as they stepped to either side of the table I was strapped tight to.

Obviously we had stopped somewhere along a deserted road. Looking out of the opened doors of the van all I could see was woods on either side of the road. I wriggled my toes under my black socks.

"See Otis, I told you he would be ready to be milked again," Cleeve said, taking an empty vial from his pocket and hooking a hand around my throbbing hardness. "Fucking hard as a rock all over again."

"Hhhhrrrrrmmmfffff…" I sputtered in ecstasy as Cleeve started stroking my dick in and out of my foreskin, the vial held at my slit, ready to be filled with my sexy mess.

As Cleeve stroked me Otis took the socks gag out of my mouth.

"Huuuuuuuhhhnnnnn, bl-blasted kidnappers, gagging a guy with his smelly socks has to be the shittiest thing you can do to him," I said stupidly, breathless as I was stroked toward another gusher. "And stealing a rock star's jazz *has* to rank up there as just about as shitty as gagging him with his socks."

"Oh believe me you stud, there are worse things we're going to *and* have done to you than gagging you with your stinking sweat socks and collecting your jazz," Cleeve said as Otis opened the bottle of the aphrodisiac laced mineral water.

"Come on handsome guy, drink up," Otis said, lifting my head up off the table.

"*Oh no,*" I whimpered as he put the tip of the bottle to my lips.

With no choice other than to do as I was told I sipped down the water. Laying there stretched out on that table, tied up, strapped, I watched as Cleeve stroked me and stroked me while I was sipping the water at the same time. The aphrodisiac serum made the sensations in my dick, tied balls, clamped nipples and plugged hole all the more intense as the guys worked me. Aidios Mio, I thought in Spanish, Cleeve would need two vials for my mess this time. Otis stroked my hair as I sipped down the bottle of water.

"Okay Otis, he's getting there now," Cleeve said, holding my meat stick straight out, the vial under my gaping slit. "I can feel his python throbbing."

Otis stopped feeding me the water and then I felt it, deep in the base of my rock hardness and in my tied balls and in my clamped nipples I felt it. I was going to shoot my load like crazy.

"OHHH fuuuuuccckkk, ohhh GOD," I gasped and writhed madly in the tight bondage as Cleeve milked the bejesus out of me. "F-fucking guys, perverts, *k-kidnappers!!"*

The two men watched, in awe as my thick and creamy rock star jazz filled the vial.

"OHHH yeah, fucking A, blasted guys got me creaming like crazy," I garbled, arching my head back and clenching my hands into fists.

When I was done the pain in my clamped nipples and plugged hole was more than immense. I screamed bloody murder as Otis gave the chain attached to the tit clamps a mean tug.

"AYYYYYYYRRR FUCK man, my poor tits!!" I ranted.

"Yeah, ain't that a bitch," Cleeve said mockingly, capping the latest vial that was filled with my jazz.

He then took another empty vial from his pocket.

"Whenever a guy shoots his load while his tits are clamped the pain in the poor guy's nubs increases about a thousand and one percent," Cleeve added.

"Y-you sure can take that shit to the bank," I said through clenched teeth.

Otis fed me the rest of the water as Cleeve filled two more vials with my piss, holding my shaft between his fingers as he did so.

"Man oh fucking man, we are going to make a fortune marketing this rock star's juices," Cleeve said as Otis crammed the sweat socks gag back into my mouth and tied the slack of it behind my neck.

"RRRRMMMMMFFFF!!!" I garbled angrily, again swallowing my foot stink every time I gulped.

Laughing, the two men exited the back of the van and closed and locked the doors behind them. I again heard them get in the front section and again we were on our way…toward where I had no blasted idea…

From the time I was a teenager I knew that I wanted to be some sort of musical star. I had the voice it just needed to be properly trained. I had the moves I just needed to master the art of dance. Thank God my parent's saw fit to send me to dance school when I was young and I took music class in school every semester, even joining the glee club so I could work on my voice. When I was nineteen I attended a school of dance in lower Manhattan. I was one of the few guys in the class I had enrolled in and it was in that class that I first realized just how attracted to me a lot of women...and some men were. I quickly realized that I was probably the only straight guy in that particular dance class. While the instructor put us through the rigorous dance routines over and over, making us sweat like crazy I took note of how some of the other students were really looking me over. Not to sound vain or anything mind you but it was a fact after all. My fate was sealed. *I had to make it big and I had to make it big as rock star.* It was a Friday afternoon and a couple of the girls in the class had invited me out to dinner after our dance lessons. (Actually I got the feeling that they wanted to have a little more than dinner.) Needless to say we were always tired and hungry after a two-hour dance class so I gladly accepted their offer. I mean, who knew where dinner would lead to after all? I was in the men's locker room by myself getting changed. My locker was near the entrance of the locker room and I was bending down to get my sweaty underpants off when I heard the door pushed open.

"Are you coming or are you going to take the rest of the evening to get changed?" a sexy girl named Susan asked me, sticking her blond head in the ajar door.

"I-uh," I gulped, my ass facing her, my legs slightly spread and my big nuts dangling, sweaty and hairy between my parted thighs.

I could feel her eyes take in the sight of my exposed ass crack. It was all musty and grungy, but that didn't stop her from really taking a good hard look at it. I quickly stood up straight and faced her, my white under shorts in my hand, my big dick semi hard between my muscular legs. Standing there now in just a pair of white calf length silk ribbed dance socks I felt real sexy and vulnerable let me tell you. I hadn't been quick enough to cover my semi hardness, nor my big juicy balls. My foreskin halfway sheathed my big organ, making it look even sexier.

"I-uh, I'll be along shortly," I said, looking at Susan in embarrassment and accidentally dropped my briefs on the floor. *"Oh God..."*

Behind her the other girl who had invited me out to dinner, Maria, pushed her way into the locker room behind Susan. Standing in front of my locker my meat stick chose that moment to grow stiff and hard. I gulped hard and curled my toes back under my socks. The two girls seemed to literally drink in the sight of me standing there all sweaty, muscular and sexy in just my damned silk dance socks.

"Well now, this is kind of awkward," Susan laughed.

"Yeah, you could say that," I said throatily and without realizing I did it I jutted my chest out.

Needless to say I was feeling a little more than vulnerable at that point, which I suppose made me even harder. Beads of pre cum formed at the tip of my wide slit and the two girls looked at it breathlessly. They boldly stepped into the men's locker room, letting the door close behind them. We all smiled... They approached me slowly and I stood there as they ran their hands over my huge chest, through my longish (at the time) hair and stole squeezes and tugs on my big balls...my balls being their utmost target. I was breathless then as they squeezed my nipples a few times each and commented on how they grew harder each time that they tweaked them. They treated my nipples to more than a fair share of hard and tight squeezes. I didn't utter a word. I simply stood there totally breathless and stiff in the cock as the two girls felt me up all over. Before I even knew what was happening the two beautiful girls were squatting down at my sides and, *and* licking my sweaty balls like their lives depended upon it. I stood there propped against my locker enjoying every goddamned moment of it as they polished my big smelly testicles.

"I told you he had really big balls," Susan said to Maria in between licks. "I could tell from the bulge in his tights while we were dancing."

The sounds of licking and slurping filled the area and I didn't once think that anyone would catch us...

"Oh yeah, yeah, feels so good," I panted after a while. "Lick my nuts girls; eat 'em up real good."

They each pulled one of my big sweaty and hairy balls into their mouths, sucked and slurped at them and my head spun, more-so than when the dance instructor had made us spin in place over and over. I never knew that having my balls serviced in this way could feel so fucking awesome. Their soft lips were like velvet all over my balls and their tongues worked sheer magic on me.

"Oh yeah, looks like I'm the main course on tonight's dinner menu eh ladies?" I asked breathlessly.

They ran their hands over my thighs, down my legs and playfully snapped the elastic in my white silk socks as they really went to town on my balls, driving me crazy.

A few minutes later when I could not stand any longer they had me seated on the bench in front of my locker, facing forward. I leaned my upper body back as the two girls took turns sucking my big dick. Susan had a great time playing with my foreskin, saying that it was beyond sexy. When I shot my load it was Maria who had me in her mouth. Fucking beautiful and greedy girl gulped down every drop of me as I writhed in ecstasy on the bench.

"OHHH yeah, yeah, you two really made this a night to remember," I panted as my big meat stick slid out of Maria's mouth.

They each kissed me on the lips, cheeks, ears and earlobes about a thousand times each, squeezing the back of my neck and even giving my sensitive dick and balls a few squeezes each as well. That made me gasp real loudly.

"Okay handsome, we'll wait outside till you're finished getting changed," Susan said with a sly looking grin on her pretty face.

I sat there on the bench watching as the two girls sauntered toward the door to the locker room. I was also grinning from ear to ear and feeling real good. When I reached down to get my silk dance socks off I saw that they were no longer on my feet.

"Ha, ha, crazy horny bitches snagged my socks right off my feet," I laughed.

After dinner that night Susan and Maria came back to my apartment to spend a long sex-filled night with me...

Now, the memory of that night seemed a million years away as I lay helplessly in the back of Cleeve and Otis' van...

As we drove through the night toward their destination I thought about Susan and Maria snagging my dance socks off my feet that night in the locker room. Obviously they thought it was real cute and all in fun. I wondered if they still had my socks, maybe having kept one of them each. I also wondered how much money they could get for them now that I was more than world famous. Probably just as much as Cleeve and Otis planned to get hawking my cum and piss to anyone who was willing to pay top dollar for them... I lifted my head up off the table and looked down at my black socked feet. I wondered with a feeling of dismay how much my two captors would get for the socks I was presently wearing. With tears of rage and fear in my eyes I lay my head back down on the table...GOD, if Susan and Maria could see me now I thought miserably...

When the van rolled to a stop better than two hours or so later I thought we had reached our destination. That was not the case however, at least not yet. My dick was again rage hard between my legs, pointing straight at my face as the van stopped. I looked up at the skylight and the shining moon illuminated my hardness. I saw pre cum trickling from my slit. God, that aphrodisiac they had given me was still working its evil magic.

"Good evening Officer," I heard Cleeve say loudly. "They must be short handed out here if they have you guys working the toll booths."

"Yes, you could say that Sir," I heard a male voice reply.

Fuck, it was a cop that Cleeve was talking to.

"MMMMFFFF!!!" I sputtered insanely against my socks gag. "HHRRRRMMMFFFF!!!"

They had stopped to pay a toll and there was a cop out there working a tollbooth. A cop who had no idea whatsoever that these two thugs had the world's most famous rock star trapped in the back of their van. I struggled like a madman under the binding ropes and straps, sputtering and gasping against my gag.

"HHHRRRRRMMMMFFFF!!!" I sputtered, spittle flying out of the sides of my thoroughly gagged mouth, craning my neck around thinking that the cop would hear me if I did. "RRRRMMMFFFFF…"

"Well, you have a good night now Officer," I heard Cleeve saying.

"You too Sir, drive carefully," the cop replied and once again we were moving.

"RRRMMMMFFF!!!" I ranted, my dick twitching and flicking between my legs, the sound of the vibrating butt-plug mocking me.

Cleeve had made sure to let me know that he and Otis had just greeted a cop. The bastard wanted to make sure I knew that no one; *no one* was going to help me let alone rescue me.

"Damn Otis, that's the second time we saw Officer Aldana at that tollbooth," I heard Cleeve saying, lust in his voice. "We have to snag his ass for some fun at some point."

"I'm not so sure of that Cleeve," Otis responded. "He could identify the van and trace it to your house."

"Shit, I hadn't thought of that," Cleeve said stupidly or perhaps for my benefit, letting me know that they could pretty much do whatever the fuck they pleased.

It was another half-hour when we finally arrived at Cleeve's house. This time when the van rolled to a stop and I heard the two men disembarking I somehow knew that we had arrived at our destination. The back doors of the van were pulled open and the two men stepped inside, looking down at me totally lustfully.

"Damn, another boner," Cleeve said, hooking a hand around my hardness as Otis undid the straps holding me to the table.

"Mmmmfff…" I sputtered, wanting at that moment to be jacked off so bad that I could taste the need for it.

Actually what I was tasting was my damned rancid sweat socks…

"Yeah, waiting for it is worse than actually suffering the consequential pain in your tits and your plugged sexy hole huh Stud?" Cleeve asked me mockingly and let go of my hard manhood.

"Hhhhrrrrrrmmmfffff…" I wailed.

A few minutes later the straps were off me and the gag was out of my mouth. Still securely tied up I was helpless as Cleeve hoisted me easily off the table and into his huge muscular arms. Following Otis he carried me out of the van.

"Fucking bastard, put me down, fucking carrying me like I was a sack of laundry or something," I grumbled, but then at the sight of the massive house my words became stuck in my throat. *"H-holy shit, y-you guys own all this?"*

"I do," Cleeve said, looking at me out of the corner of his eye and giving me a sloppy wet kiss on the cheek. "And for the next few days I want to share all of it with you handsome."

"B-but who the hell are you that you can afford a house like this?" I asked as Cleeve carried me toward the mansion-like building. *"And did you say the next few days?"*

To that question I received no answer…

The sound of the buzzing vibrator/butt-plug in my hole filled the silence as Cleeve walked with me in his muscular arms and Otis led the way. The house was set all by itself on a long stretch of land. Well-tended hedges and large trees surrounded it and only the lamppost on the road and the moon in the sky made it visible. As I was carried helplessly closer to the house my heart thundered. Who the fucks were these guys and just what the hell had I fallen victim to??? They had stealthily captured me, made me scoff down some sort of twisted version of a Spanish fly, siphoned my cum and piss from me and from what I could tell they planned to sell my juices on the black market. GOD almighty was that how the man named Cleeve and his CO-hort Otis made their money, by selling famous guy's sperm and piss to the highest bidders? And what would those bidders do with it? As if I needed three guesses… The inside of the house was just as magnificent as the outside. It appeared that the place had more rooms than the Carrington mansion on the nineteen-eighties TV show Dynasty. Many rooms, but I would only get to see the inside of one during my time there with Cleeve and Otis and their customers… I looked around at the expensively furnished place as Cleeve then tossed me over his shoulders and lugged me up a flight of stairs to the second floor.

"Should have blindfolded you," Cleeve said irritably. "The way you're looking at my place I'm getting the feeling you'll want to make your place look like it."

My place, fuck, I wondered if I would see my place again anytime soon...

My dick pounded long and hard as Cleeve carried me toward the room where I would be kept for the next few days...

In the room Cleeve lay me down on the raised bed and the two men quickly got to work on me. They untied my hands but didn't give me a fighting chance at escape.

"HUUUUFFFFFF!!! B-bastards," I ranted through clenched teeth as they each yanked one of my wrists up against the sides of the bed board. "Fuckers, let go of me and then we'll see just how resourceful you two are then!"

"You're not going anywhere Stud, so you may as well quit your infernal struggling," Cleeve said as he and Otis got busy roping my wrists to the bed board. "No way you handsome fuck, you're not going anywhere.

I turned my head wildly from side to side, watching in tortured agony as they roped my wrists tightly to the bed board.

"Fucking kidnappers, untie me, I'm trained in one on one combat," I said stupidly.

"Yeah, a fat lot of good it did you huh Stud?" Cleeve asked me.

When they were done they untied my lower body leaving just my wrists tied up to the bed board. I sure made a kinky picture at that moment let me tell you, tied to the bed, my white under shorts bunched up under my crotch and my black socks down around my lower calves. I thrashed madly on the bed as the vibrating butt-plug and the tit clamps drove me nearly insane. Fuck, it all added up to the throbbing hard-on I was sporting between my muscular legs. With a leering grin on his face Cleeve produced an empty vial...

"Ready asshole?" he asked me.

"Fuck you man, I thought you said you didn't have any more empty vials," I responded angrily.

"I lied," Cleeve snickered. "And I wanted to make you wait to cum this time. As much as you hate the fact that you're being helplessly and unwillingly milked of your precious rock star juices you can't deny that you can't wait for me to start jacking you."

Cleeve settled on the bed next to me, took my hard-on in hand and began stroking me, holding the vial over my wide slit. I gasped and hawed in the forced ecstasy, watching as my droplets of pre cum dripped into the vial. There was something twisted yet sexy about that, seeing my most private juices slithering into a test-tube like device.

"Fuck man, you really are a sight you handsome fucking rock star,"

Otis said, leering at me from the foot of the bed. "I tell you Cleeve, *we have* to take our turns with this guy before the customers start rolling in here."

"I'm reading your mind Otis," Cleeve said, stroking me a tad faster. "Let me just get his nut again and then we'll get that butt-plug out of his hole and christen it the right way."

"You blasted perverts!!" I ranted more than angrily at that point. "I'm not a faggot!! Let me go already!!"

"And if your gay fans heard you say that Stud," Cleeve chuckled as he stroked me some more. "I doubt that would make for good press…"

I thrashed madly on the bed, struggling like crazy to get myself untied but it was no use man. These two had me and they had me good and cold…and they would have me some more at that.

"AYYYRRRRR GOD, I-I'm cumming you bastards, already I'm shooting my damned creamy load," I grunted, clenched my hands into fists and squeezed my eyes shut.

My juices spurted into the vial, filling it halfway.

"OHHH GOD, got me creaming like a damned bitch in heat," I seethed in ecstasy and anger all at the same time.

When I was done I screamed in a man's pain because the pain from the vibrating butt-plug and the tit clamps suddenly intensified about a thousand folds… As I screamed and ranted like crazy Cleeve filled two vials with my sour piss.

"Damn, watching this guy shoot his load over and over has me horned up like I can't fucking believe Otis," Cleeve said, capping the second vial of my piss.

I watched helplessly as Cleeve stood up and began stripping his clothes off, starting with the clonky work boots he had on.

"Otis, get his hole unplugged," Cleeve ordered. "I'm going in for a landing or a few."

"Sure thing Cleeve," Otis responded. "And you can best believe I'll be right behind you!"

"No, *no, oh no, not this you guys,*" I pleaded as Otis grabbed the base of the vibrating butt-plug and slowly pulled it from my hole, twisting it as he went. "AYYYRRRRRRRR, ea-easy with that thing fucker!"

As Otis pulled the butt-plug from my hole my damned dick betrayed me by getting hard all over again…

"Damn, looks like we'll have to milk him again soon," Otis laughed.

"Yeah, we'll jack him off after every time he gets fucked," Cleeve decided.

"And from the look of things that's going to be quite often," Otis said and relieved my hole of the butt-plug.

I farted involuntarily and Otis prodded my wet hole with a few of his fingers, just to grate on my nerves no doubt...

"AYYYRRRRRR GOD, g-get your damned fingers out of my hole Pervert," I seethed at Otis.

When I looked up again Cleeve was stripped, bare. My breath caught in my throat at the sight of his body. The guy was a muscle god if ever there was one, all six feet or more of him. He looked like a man of iron. My God, no wonder he had been able to lift and carry me with no problem whatsoever. If there was an ounce of fat on him anywhere I didn't see it. His dick was of the jumbo-size as well. It had to be at least nine or ten inches long and his balls looked like two plums dangling between his legs in his sac. It was thick and beefy along with being long. How the hell was he going to fit that monster-sized dick inside me? It was unthinkable. He was harder than what would usually be defined as hard as he approached me, then, squatting on the bed between my legs and grabbing my socked ankles real tight.

"Look at you Stud, all horny and ready, begging for me to plow your hole," Cleeve said, leering down at me, hoisting my ankles aloft, really exposing my wet asshole.

"Oh God no, no, please," I pleaded miserably as the guy started entering me inch by painful inch. "OHHHRRRRR *Good Gods almighty!!*"

I thought then and there that if this were what I would be subjected to for the next few days I would never get used to it, never learn to like it.

"OHHH you bastard," I grunted as Cleeve held my ankles tighter and higher and entered me more and more.

"Oh yeah, fucking A you handsome rock star," Cleeve said breathlessly. "Your goddamned hole is hugging my big meat stick."

"OHHH no, no, *it's too big man, take it out, oh please take it out,*" I garbled insanely.

"Take it out?" Cleeve laughed. "Stud, I'm not even halfway inside you yet."

To quiet me down Otis placed a bottle of the aphrodisiac laced mineral water by my quivering lips. With tears of pain and rage in my eyes I sipped down the water as Cleeve entered me some more, stretching my hole to epic proportions. Then, when the big guy was thrusting in and out of me like mad, really slamming and jack-hammering my shit chute the aphrodisiac took real effect. Unbelievable to me I was hard as fucking diamond as Cleeve de-virginized my poor hole. I farted a few times when he pulled out before ramming back into me harder and harder with each thrust. My head spun and my vision blurred. When I looked up again I saw that it was Otis who was fucking me now… God, I didn't even recall Cleeve having shot his load deep inside me…

That first night that Cleeve and Otis had me there they must have fucked me at least four or five times each. My hole felt scorched and awful and when Otis slid the vibrating butt-plug back up inside me I screamed and ranted bloody murder. Cleeve did the honors of milking me a few more times, getting his blasted vials filled with my cum and piss. He jokingly said that he planned to charge at least a thousand dollars or more for each vial of my cum, a hundred for my piss.

It was on the second day that they had me there that the guy with the cigar fetish had his way with me. Before his arrival Cleeve came into the room they kept me in and got me groomed and ready. He told me that they had a real special and very important customer coming to see me, but for reasons I could not know I was not to see him. That said Cleeve tied a red silk blindfold over my eyes, telling me that the customer had sent the blindfold specially.

"Fuck man, why are you covering my eyes?" I asked miserably. "This is really scary now."

"If you knew who the guy coming to see you is you wouldn't believe it Stud," Cleeve said and kissed my cheek.

I had gotten used to the guy doing that. I sort of got the feeling that he was erotically in love with me.

"Actually, the guy coming to see you can't believe that it's you he's going to fuck," Cleeve said, squirting some gel into my mussed hair and then combing and slicking it back. "Got to make you real pretty for him because he paid more than the usual price for you. He's been to your concerts and told us that this is going to be more than a dream come true for him."

When Cleeve was done combing my hair I could feel him looking me over as I lay there miserably on the bed. He pulled my socks up to my calves and yanked the butt-plug out of my hole. I managed not to fart that time but the draft that I felt every time the plug was taken out sent shivers through me.

"He'll be here very soon Stud," Cleeve said meanly, the sound of the vibrating butt-plug filling the sexually scented air. "Make sure you do whatever the fuck he says."

"Do I have much choice?" I asked sarcastically, shaking my bound wrists against the bed board.

I heard Cleeve leave the room, shutting the door behind him. I tried to breathe as calmly as possible. My dick was as usual rage hard between my legs. I had been made to drink the mineral water aphrodisiac just less than an hour ago.

About five minutes later the door opened again and I heard a soft spoken male voice saying thank you to Cleeve and Otis for this rare and special opportunity. Then the door closed. Even blindfolded I knew someone was in the room with me.

"My God, it's you, *it really is you that they have here,"* I heard the man saying, a slight Southern accent in his speech.

I smelled rich and fragrant cigar smoke.

"This is truly a dream come true," I heard the man say and my breath then came in short gasps.

Could it be who I thought it was??? Was it even remotely possible? No, it couldn't be, it just could not fucking be…but the cigar…and the accent…

"Did Cleeve and Otis tell you what I expect of you?" he asked me, running the tip of a finger over one of my very erect and very sore nipples.

"N-no, actually they didn't tell me anything other than to do whatever you wanted," I replied and received a blindfolded face full of cigar smoke.

"You are going to smoke cigars," he said to me and placed a lit stogy between my quivering lips. "One there in your sweet, sweet mouth and another you'll smoke through that special pussy hole of yours that I've been told about."

I nearly bit down on the cigar he'd placed in my mouth. Instead I inhaled it deeper than I had intended to.

"Now, I want you to lift your legs as high as possible," he said to me. "That way I can get this other cigar inside you."

I balled my hands into fists and did as he said, lifting my socked feet off the bed as high as possible.

"Will you be able to hold your feet up there or will I have to tie them above you to the bed board?" he asked me, squeezing one of my socked feet.

I nodded "yes", the thought of being in the position he described to be unthinkable.

"Okay then, but the first time you lower your feet they get tied to the bed board," he said and I felt the wet end of the cigar being inserted into my cum slopped hole. "Get your pussy lips wrapped around this thing."

I flexed what was left of my ass muscles and did as he said. He inserted the cigar further inside me. I puffed on the one in my mouth, feeling the ashes flicking over my neck and chest.

"When I take it out of your hole I'll smoke it with your raunchy ass taste on it," he said to me. "Then I'm going to plow you like a field."

I held back a gulp and felt his tongue slather over one of my socked feet. I heard him taking puffs on his cigar while I puffed one and another smoldered in my hole...

"I think that it's real kinky that Cleeve and Otis left these stinking socks on you for this escapade," he said to me and took the cigar out of my mouth.

"Th-they plan to hock them to the highest bidder," I said softly.

"So I was told," he said to me and I heard him puffing the cigar that had just been in my mouth. "I bid five thousand dollars for them."

This time I did gulp hard, and in disbelief. Anyone that would pay five thousand dollars for a pair of socks worn by a rock star had to be a fanatic of some kind.

"Mmmm, this cigar with your mouth taste on it is real sweet," he commented and trailed a finger over my blindfolded eyes.

"Pl-please help me man," I whispered. "Th-those guys kidnapped me."

"Yes I know," he said and I could feel him smiling meanly.

My legs felt totally awful in the position they were in. I wished like crazy that he would get the damned cigar out of my hole and do his thing already, much as I knew how it was going to smart when he got down to fucking me. Sweating like crazy I did my best to hold my legs up as he had ordered me.

"D-do you think they'll sell you my socks?" I asked, wanting to make conversation, wanting to avoid the inevitable when he would fuck my poor hole.

"Maybe, unless someone presents a higher bid," he said and gave one of my nipples a squeeze, smoking his cigar.

Then, I felt him tug on the cigar that was jammed in my hole.

"Loosen your pussy lips now," he said with authority.

I did as he said and heard the sound of contentment purr from him as he placed the cigar in his mouth. God, he was eating my damned ass raunch off the stogy.

"Ah yes, even better than my wife's pussy," he mused and I grimaced as he blew smoke in my blindfolded face.

For a few minutes he sat next to me in silence, squeezed my nipples, toyed with the knot in my blindfold and even forced me to take a few puffs on the ass tasting cigar. Given the position I was in I had no choice but to do whatever the fuck he wanted... Alas, he didn't give me permission to lower my legs and by then they were in more than immense pain...

"AYYYYRRRRR GOD," I found myself ranting in pain a little while later as the guy proceeded to mount me and began thrusting his hardness deep into my poor hole.

"Ah yeas, oh yes, as I said better than my wife's pussy," the cigar guy panted.

As he fucked me like a madman, my legs in the air, my feet resting on his shoulders the smell of expensive cigars and sex filled the air.

"OHHH G-GOD, man, y-you sure got a big meat pole," I squawked miserably and stupidly.

He kissed my blindfolded eyes his dick buried deep inside me. It seemed like most of the customers enjoyed doing that, really getting their dicks as deep as possible into my poor, poor hole...

"Oh yes, this is worth every dollar of what I spent on you, you gorgeous rock star," the guy gasped, thrusting in and out of me like his life depended on it. "Even down to the red silk blindfold."

He took my socked ankles in hands, held them aloft and plowed into me and plowed into me and plowed into me...

They released me in the morning of the fifth day...

I suppose I had slept that night because when I came to I found myself looking straight up at the skylight in the back of Cleeve and Otis' van.

"Wh-what happened?" I garbled, lifted my head up off the table and instantly fell back to sleep.

I don't know what it was that sent me back to dream-land but for a split second I saw Otis' face and a spray can pointed at my face...

When I slowly came around the next time I found myself sitting on the ground against a brick wall in the alley behind the stadium where I had played my last concert on my tour.

"OHHH f-fuck, wh-wha..." I groaned, pressing the palms of my hands against the ground.

I opened my eyes slowly and looked around.

"Oh fuck, bastards let me go and they got away too," I said miserably.

Looking down at myself I saw that I was most scantily clad in just my under shorts, the same ones I had on the day Cleeve and Otis had captured me. My feet were bare. I fleetingly wondered which customer had bid the highest and gotten my socks. I was sort of glad at that moment that they hadn't auctioned off my under shorts as well, otherwise I would have been completely naked there in that alley. Somehow I did not think that Cleeve and Otis would have provided me with any clothing. Slowly, I stood up. My hole felt as if there were still a dick or two jammed up there. Cum dripped from my rectal canal into the back of my under shorts. I needed to get to the dressing room in the stadium.

Hopefully I would find something there that I could wear.

Luck was on my side after all. Not only were the dressing room door unlocked but all my stuff was still in there. I supposed that no other performer had played the stadium since I had been there... Standing there shaking with the door now locked I shucked off my under shorts and found a note taped to the inside of them. I gulped hard and with my hand trembling I read the note...

"Dear Stud, thanks for being so giving of yourself the last few days. In time your hole will be as good as new. You will be happy to hear that your smelly black socks went for more than ten thousand dollars. The customer who purchased them says he plans to keep them forever. Perhaps you and he will want to work out a deal where you can buy the rancid stinkers back from him. HA! All counted you took better than forty big dicks up your sweet hole. You really are a piece of work and sure can take it. The aphrodisiac we administered to you is harmless and will wear off soon, if it hasn't already, seeing as we didn't give you any during your last day here with us. We left you right where we found you, at the stadium you last played. We managed to get the doors to the place open, insuring that you would gain entry and be able to get some clothes on before anyone saw you in your nakedness. The bids have already started coming in for your cum and piss that we collected from you. You will never see us again Stud, so please go through life assured that we won't kidnap you again...although we cannot say the same for other people who find you to be so tempting. We wish you the best in your music career. Laughingly, C&O.

I crumpled up the letter, tossed it to the floor and sat down in the chair in front of the mirror of the dressing room table. I yanked my big dick out of my under shorts and began stroking it, stroking it, stroking it...

The cum that dripped from my hole squished in my underpants, the sound driving me batty as I shot my load...

As things started to return to normal my bodyguards and I never discussed my capture. What we did discuss however was how many times they could each plow my new cunt hole each day... As I said earlier, I would never get used to being fucked on a regular basis. I suppose I was incorrect...

The End

PS: A year later I was on stage performing during my most recent concert tour. Looking down into the audience I could have sworn I saw a guy waving a zip lock plastic bag with what appeared to be a pair of black socks in it... I gulped hard but quickly got on with the performance...

WHAT HAVE I GOTTEN MYSELF INTO

by Anonymous Cop

The Cop

Patrolman Dennis Mulroney was justifiably nervous as he drove to the meeting spot. He was going all out for this and it could very well possibly get him into a lot of trouble, trouble that he would have a hard time getting out of, if indeed he could. But he had convinced himself that it would be all right and he knew deep inside that if he didn't do it this time he never would. He had had this desire, this urging, *this need* for bondage and domination and leather and rubber…and, oh shit, he thought…the entire S&M thing…seemingly forever. True he was a cop and cops allegedly were always in charge and in control, but Mulroney knew that this applied only while on duty and that off duty he was as susceptible as any man to the inner sexual drives and desires that haunted his mind. The internet had helped because there he came in contact with other guys, both dominants and submissives who thought as he did. He enjoyed chatting with them, but of course, all the time he kept his identity hidden. He enjoyed being submissive and got hard and horny having dominants insult and belittle him online. And best of all it was safe. Since Mulroney wasn't out of the closet he had to be careful not to reveal his identity and have it splashed all over the net, which could very well mean the end of his promising police career. The officer knew that many of the so-called dominants he chatted with were phony and pretenders but it didn't bother him too much because he felt that in a way he too was a phony. His name online was "bondrubsub" and although he never gave out his true name or address, he was honest in his description of himself: 5'10, 175 lbs, good shape, blue eyes, close cropped dark hair, 7 inch cut cock, low hanging hairy balls. And he was honest in what he was looking for: domination, humiliation, bondage, rubber, leather, boots, etc...but only online in cyber; no real time sessions. Before becoming a police officer Mulroney had had some sexual experiences with men, only vanilla exercises consisting primarily of cock sucking and body worshipping. He had never allowed anyone to actually penetrate his anus but in private he had poked his fingers in and around his hole and basically he enjoyed the sensation. He knew that someday he would succumb to a total man-to man sexual engagement, but that day would have to wait.

Then, in one of the online leather chat rooms he met a dominant who called himself "NChargeLthrMaster" and they hit it off immediately. It seemed a perfect match with the Master ordering around the submissive and the submissive willingly obeying. To the cop it was the perfect online fantasy and role-playing game. It progressed to the point where the Master was having his "slave", as he now called Mulroney; tie himself up under his direction; making the slave use ropes and duct tape and handcuffs. As Mulroney became quite adept at doing this the Master made it more difficult by having the slave put the handcuff keys in difficult places to get at...once the Master even had him freeze the keys in a gallon jug of water and Mulroney had to wait in tight bondage until the ice melted and he could get to them.

The next step occurred when the Master ordered the slave to buy a cam so that he could watch while the slave did as ordered. Officer Mulroney was hesitant at first because he didn't want his face seen and his identity revealed but he solved that problem by buying a couple of hoods, one leather and one rubber, and whenever the two were online together the slave would always be hooded. Actually, it had been the Master who had suggested this solution to the cop and it was just one of the many things that helped cement the cop's trust in the Master. NChargeLthrMaster had told Mulroney that he too was not out of the closet and that he had a great deal to lose if this aspect of his life came out. The cop believed him.

NChargeLthrMaster lived in a small town a couple of states away from Mulroney and he provided the cop with his phone number so that the two could talk more easily. Again the cop was initially hesitant but the Master recommended that the slave always do the phoning and to block his number so that it was never revealed. This way it made it appear as if Mulroney controlled their sessions and gave the cop the feeling of more security, and further deepened his trust of the man, and leading him deeper into a trap.

And so it went for weeks with the policeman performing more and more acts for the Master. Self bondage became more complex as the Master had the slave dress in rubber and/or leather gear when he tied himself up. Acts of humiliation, such as wearing latex jocks under his clothes or having to sit on the porcelain part of the toilet whenever he took a piss were actually turn-ons for the slave/cop.

Officer Mulroney had never been happier. He was getting the kinky attention that he wanted and craved and his jack-off sessions were fantastic. Then, one day while they were chatting online the Master suggested that they meet in person. Mulroney instinctively knew that he wanted to do that. He felt he knew and trusted Master enough and that he would be safe. It was decided that the cop would use four or five days of his leave time and drive to the Master's home. They would have days of "role play", mostly with the cop being tied up or when free of restraint being slave to the Master. It would all be just hot fun and games. So Mulroney agreed, even when the Master warned him that he would have to obey all his orders for the entire time they were together. Safe words and signals were exchanged for emergencies. The Master again warned the cop that he would be put into some humiliating and foolish positions but since the meeting area was a good five hundred miles from the cop's home he felt safe. He agreed and actually looked forward to it.

So here he was driving to that meeting, his rubber and leather gear packed and stowed in the trunk. He admittedly had some last minute qualms about what he was doing, but he dismissed them. Mulroney told himself that he totally trusted Master and that if he were to be dominated this was the man he wanted to do it. Who knew where this could lead, he thought, and if it didn't work out he could always just leave. The meeting spot was a fast food burger place on the outskirts of a small town. The directions were good and the cop didn't have any trouble finding it. Since he was early for the meeting he drove off to a more secluded area where he prepared himself for the first part of his upcoming ordeal. The orders from the Master had been that he was to be totally naked of regular clothes, but wearing a pair of chest high rubber waders and his elbow-length rubber gloves. To the cop this was a great beginning. He would be in a humiliating position but would also be in rubber. He undressed in his car, got the waders from the back seat, pulled them on, tightening them around the waist with a belt and slipped his wallet into the waterproof pocket inside the chest. He grinned to himself as he felt his cock grow thick inside the waders. Damn but he loved the feel and smell of rubber. He drove back to the fast food burger place and working up his courage entered the place. There were only a couple of other customers sitting in booths and although they stared at him no one actually said anything. It was a warm day and he reasoned, hopefully, that they thought he had been out fishing. His orders were to buy himself one of the large colas and sit in a booth until he was contacted by the Master. He took off his gloves to reach for his wallet when he ordered the cola and got a little red in the face from the look the young clerk behind the counter gave him. Well, he would never see that kid again so what difference did it make? He sat in a booth away from the counter and wondered, not for the first time, just what the hell he had gotten himself into.

The Master

I was standing in the trees on the far side of the restaurant when I saw the car drive up. There he was, my dumb fuck cop slave, in his rubber waders. I laughed to myself. This asshole was too much; he looked like a fucking moron in those waders. Ah, it was going to be fun breaking him down and turning him into a total obedient pig slave. If he only knew what plans I had in store for him. The shit-head had lied to me, telling me he was a construction worker, but once I got him to call I found out just who and what the fuck he really was...a pig cop. Thank God for my buddies in the telephone company who were able to trace his calls. Has he got a shock coming to him when he learns what's in store!

I watched him through the window as he ordered his cola and sat down at one of the booths. I waited a good fifteen to twenty minutes more, making him sweat and worry whether I was actually coming. I could see him fidgeting and looking around and I could see the other customers staring at him like he was a freak...fuck, he is a freak! I figured the time had come so I went around the back so he wouldn't see me approach and entered the place.

I walked to his booth, stood there in front of him and said, "Well slave, I see you made it and are obeying orders."

He stood up, "Yes SIR, here I am and looking forward to our time together."

I looked him over and had to admit that he looked even better in person than he did on the cam. I had never seen his face but I liked what I saw there... dark blue eyes, close cropped dark hair, a nose maybe a tad too big, but in a sense perfect for that face. I liked the way little drops of sweat were trickling down his chest.

"Go get me a large cola too, boy, and it looks as if you're almost finished with yours, so get yourself another too," I ordered.

"Oh, I'm fine," he answered. "Don't need anymore."

"Boy, I said to get yourself another one...large...and one for me. No

ice this time. Now do it!" I ordered again.

He stood there, a little confused at first, but accepted the order and turned to go.

"And boy," I added. *"Don't take your gloves off when you pay for them like you did last time."*

I could see the startled look on his face as it dawned on him that I had been watching him all this time, but he accepted it, and I think with a bit of admiration. Seeing him trying to get his wallet from inside his waders and then get some money out to pay for the two drinks was a show worth paying for. The thickness of the fingers on those rubber gloves made handling anything small a real challenge. Even the clerk was amused and had all he could do to keep from laughing. Finally my cop slave managed to pay for the drinks, got his change and brought them back to the booth. I was sitting there watching him and when he put the drinks down I ordered him to go back and get some straws. Of course his appearance had everyone in the place staring and some teenage girls who had just entered were giggling and whispering among themselves. The cop was obviously embarrassed but I could see that he was determined to go through with it all. He came back to the booth with the straws, handed me one and was about to sit.

"I didn't say you could sit down boy," I said.

He was momentarily stunned but stood right back up.

"Sorry SIR," he said.

"In fact boy, I think you should be kneeling," I said.

"What?" he asked.

"You heard me boy, kneel," I said again. *"We'll drink our colas and chat a while before heading out."*

This was something he hadn't expected and he looked around the restaurant truly embarrassed. He wanted to say something, but after a few seconds he got down on his knees. Oh yes, this pig was going to be easy to train. We stayed like that and I quietly praised him for following the orders so well-figured to give him a little praise to keep his morale up before I tore him down completely. He ate it up like it was worth a million bucks. What a dumb shit he was and to think he was a cop and carried a gun. Damn, they must be desperate for help in his city's police force. I told him that we weren't leaving the restaurant until he finished both his colas and with that he drank them down quickly. I had not even touched mine so I had him carry it out to his car. I told him that I had had a friend drop me off here so that we could leave in his car. I then told him that I would drive, ordering him to give me the keys. He started to take off the heavy, awkward rubber gloves to get to the keys in *his wader's pocket but one look from me and he knew that wasn't allowed. It was fun watching him grope around in his chest pocket and finally he managed to get the car keys out. He handed them to me. I had him continue to hold my drink while I drove off.*

"Well boy," I said. "You still happy you came here today?"

"Oh yeah," he answered. "I'm a little scared and anxious, but excited too."

"No regrets boy?" I asked him.

"None at all," he replied.

"Okay, but some things you have to learn right off," I said. "First is that I am in total charge here; I am the Master and you are the slave. So you will ALWAYS address me as either Master or SIR. Is that understood?"

"Yes Sir...Master," he said.

"Good boy, now when we were online or on the phone I had you practice cum control, holding you off from shooting your load for over a week sometimes," I said. "Do you remember?"

"Hell yes, it was agony for me," he replied.

"How the fuck did I tell you to address me boy?" I asked him sternly. "You will be punished for that."

"MASTER...SIR...MASTER...sorry, I forgot Master..." he quickly corrected himself.

"Better, but don't forget again," I said. "That holding off from shooting your load was for your own good boy. It was to teach you that you just can't do whatever you want whenever you want. I control your actions now boy...ALL your actions... You won't do anything on your own without my permission. Is that understood boy?"

"SIR, yes SIR, understood Master Sir," he replied heartily.

"Well, I'm going to teach you another form of control boy," I went on. "It's called toilet control. You are not allowed to piss or shit without my permission. Understand?"

I could see that this bothered him, but all he said was, "Yes Master."

"Good boy," I said. "Now I really don't feel like having that cola after all, so why don't you finish it off for me...now!"

I could see that he understood immediately what was happening and where this was going. He had already downed two large colas and now he was too drink one more. If he didn't already then he soon would have to take a monster-sized piss. He looked worried but damn the dumb fuck cop actually started sipping the drink.

"Drink it all down at once boy, better for you," I said to him.

He sighed but did as ordered.

"We're about forty-five minutes away from my place, boy, so sit back and enjoy the scenery," I said.

He almost immediately started to squirm and fidget in the seat and I could tell he was doing all he could to hold back his piss. We talked some more, me handing him some bull shit about how much fun we would have role playing etc. After about fifteen minutes he turned to me and said, "MASTER, may I please get out and piss MASTER? I have to go badly SIR."

He was sweating in his waders and rubber gloves and looked miserable.

"Boy, I told you that you have to learn self control," I replied, glancing at him as he sweated. "You can piss when we get to my place and not before."

He let out a quiet groan and grimaced, but accepted his fate. Laughing to myself I watched him sweat some more as I took the long route to my place.

It wasn't too much later when I heard him huff loudly and then I heard the first tinkle of a sound as he lost the battle of holding back his piss as it started flowing. It must have been a slow trickle at first because he grunted through clenched teeth, still trying to hold it back. But once he acknowledged to himself that he had lost it he just let it all come out. I could hear the sound of it splashing against the interior of his rubber waders. It was a sound that was actually music to my ears.

"Damn boy!" I shouted. "Don't you know how to obey an order? I told you not to piss until we got home but you deliberately disobeyed me. You'll be punished for this boy."

From the look on his face I had the feeling that my new slave was torn. He was relieved that he no longer had to suffer from trying to hold his piss back, but he was obviously concerned about what would happen to him as a punishment. Me? I was smiling inside. Yes, I was going to enjoy training this asshole.

The Cop

Officer Mulroney was pleasantly surprised at the sight of "Master", which was the only name he knew the man by. He more than lived up to the description he had provided of himself: close to six feet and two hundred pounds of muscle, in great shape with piercing dark eyes. He had a marine style haircut and a solid square chin. He was dressed in tight leather pants with biker boots outside the pants and a thick leather belt holding them on. He had on a tight fitting white tee which accentuated his muscular chest and arms. All in all much more than the cop had visualized and fantasized about. He was happy. The Master's orders about getting the colas and having to kneel beside the booth shook the cop a little but he reasoned that he would never see these people again so what did he care if they were staring at him. Besides, the humiliation of it all added to the excitement and inside the waders his cop cock was harder than ever.

In the car when the Master ordered him to down the cola the cop panicked a little. He knew that he would have to piss soon and that the Master was testing him to see if he could hold it in. He sighed and fought to do just that, losing that great hard-on in the process. The Master was chatting about what fun they were going to have together, with the bondage and the leather and the rubber etc, but the cop could not concentrate on what was being said. Thinking about not pissing made him want to piss all the more; his whole mind, body and soul were working on not having to piss. But he lost out and eventually he had no choice but to let it go. He could feel the hot piss streaming down his legs and settling in the foot of the boot. He was ashamed of himself but at the same time relieved that he no longer had to fight the urge to piss. The Master said he'd be punished for disobeying and that he would have to keep that piss in his waders for the rest of the day. The cop didn't really mind, now that the urge to release the piss was gone.

After about an hour they pulled up in front of a small, fairly secluded house on the outskirts of a town. The Master ordered the cop out. He then told the cop to get his luggage and to bring it in the house. Once inside, the luggage deposited in a bedroom, the cop was ordered to come to the Master who was sitting in a chair in the living room. The cop had to kneel before the Master and he groaned inwardly hearing the slosh of his piss in his waders. He also now felt that cool piss flow up his legs as he knelt. He automatically placed his hands behind his back and lowered his face to the floor as he knelt there. Once again the Master asked him if he was sure he wanted to go through with this and once again the cop answered that he did, that it was exciting to him and that he was willing to play the slave to the Master.

The Master then laid out the rules:

1. The cop was always to refer to the Master as just that, MASTER.

2. The cop could never refer to himself as "me", "I", or by his real

46

name. He would always call himself "it" or "this slave."

3. The cop was never to speak unless spoken to. If the cop had to say something he would first ask the Master for permission to speak. Otherwise his only words would be "Yes Master", "No Master", or "Thank you Master."

4. The cop was to instantly obey all orders from the Master, no questions asked.

5. The cop was not allowed on any of the furniture in the house unless specifically directed to do so by the Master.

6. The cop was to stay on its knees whenever in the house unless undertaking specific orders which required his standing.

7. The cop was to accept all bondage he would be put into and would not complain.

8. The cop, for the period of time he was with the Master, would be the total property of the Master who could do whatever he wanted with the cop.

The cop readily agreed to all of the above and in fact remained hard as a rock while kneeling in front of the Master as he received the rules. Damn, he thought, this is everything I've always fantasized about. And since it is only for a few days with no chance of being spotted by anyone who knew him, the cop could not have been happier.

The Master said they would get into the bondage in time but that first the slave...as he now called him...had chores to do. While still on his hands and knees the cop was led into the Master's kitchen where he saw a sink-load of dirty dishes. In fact dirty dishes and pans were piled high not only in the sink but on the shelf adjoining the sink. The cop was told that the Master didn't have a dishwasher and that the slave had to do all the dishes and clean the kitchen to the Master's satisfaction before he would get his bondage reward. The slave groaned at the thought of the task ahead of him but, still in the waders with a load of piss in them, he tackled the job.

The Master

Shit, this guy was too much. Even through the thick rubber of his waders I could spot his dick getting harder as I laid down the rules. What a fuck head! I'm glad I saved up all those dishes and pots and pans from the last week so that the slave has something to do before his real ordeal begins. I went through his luggage to inspect his rubber/leather gear and noted that he had some useful stuff. I bet this fucker looks great in skin tight rubber or leather. Mmmmmm...can't wait to see. I admit he is one great looking dude. I had fixed up the basement dungeon and would get him ready for his first major bondage session once he finished the kitchen. I got a laugh going in there and yelling at him for taking so long; it was fun to watch as he doubled his efforts. So far he was doing a good job, but hell, I wasn't going to let him know that. I didn't want to over-praise him. It might spoil the dumb shit, ha, ha!!!

I figured I would watch some porn movies while I waited and maybe snooze off while he worked. Damn, every man should have himself a slave.

....

Now, look at the dumb fuck crawling on his hands and knees and then kneeling there looking up at me. Shit, I love this.

"You finished slave?" I asked him.

"MASTER, yes Master," he responded.

"I'll inspect your work later and if you didn't do a good job you will pay heavily my little slave boy," I said threateningly. "Now follow me, there's something I want to show you."

I led him downstairs and into my dungeon room. Now it probably isn't the largest or best equipped dungeon in the world, but it is more than satisfactory for me. Plenty of equipment...a rack, a Saint Andrew's cross, an examination table, a cage, a dentist's chair, lots of manacles, handcuffs, collars in leather, iron, rubber and hoods in equal array. I let the slave sit up on its haunches and I could see from its expression that he was floored by the display.

"Okay boy, it's time you took off those waders and gloves," I said.

I watched as he willingly undid the belt around his waist and then unhooked the suspenders and removed the waders. All this he did still with his gloves on. The almost overwhelming odor of sweat, piss and rubber escaped from the waders and it was fun making the slave stick his head deep inside them and breathe deeply. The slave's body stunk and I thought about making

48

it take a shower but then rejected the idea. I kind of enjoyed the smell. I had it crawl to the spot where I had cuffs and chains hanging from embedded hooks in the ceiling. Before it crawled it had taken off its rubber gloves. I had it stand and raise it's arms, then cuffed it's wrists above it's head. Next, I had the slave spread its legs and cuffed its ankles to special fetters embedded in the cement of the floor. It was suspended from the ceiling with its feet planted firmly on the floor.

I stood back and looked at my victim and I was beyond impressed. He may have been a dumb fuck but he sure was one well built and good looking dumb fuck. Its muscular arms were pulled taut and tight, making the muscles of its abs and chest stand out even more. I walked around the slave and took in its great ass, bubble ass, oh man, what an ass, muscular ass, a perfect fucking ass. Yes, this cop slave was okay. I went to one of the shelves nearby and returned with a leather hood which I fitted on its head. Pulling the straps on top and on the side I worked it until it fit like a glove. It had nose and mouth openings but no eyes so at this point the slave was effectively blindfolded.

Then I began to rub my hands all over that body, feeling up every last goddamned inch. I was growing excited myself as I felt the slave tighten up as my fingers probed it's muscular arms, it's robust chest, it's tree-trunk like legs, it's massive ripped back, that wonderful, wonderful ass and finally it's cock and balls. And believe you me, that cock and balls of the slave's were wonders in and of themselves. Not the largest cock I had ever held, maybe around eight inches when hard, but oh so perfectly formed with a mushroom head that throbbed and pulsated with a life all it's own as I caressed it and a shaft in which the veins seemed almost designed by hand. They were so perfectly symmetrical. The gods had really smiled on this slave when they'd made him it seemed. The slave moaned and groaned in obvious pleasure as I fondled it.

Then, I could not stop myself, it was crying out to me it seemed so I knelt before my new slave and slowly, gently, but firmly began to lick it's wonderful cock. Being a Master I do not usually do this. But this cock was so perfectly and well proportioned that even I could not resist sampling it in this fashion. I licked the slave's hairy balls, subconsciously saying to myself that I would have to remove that hair eventually. I began on its cock head. The poor slave moaned and I could hear it's half whispered half spoken phrases like, "Yes," "Oh fuck", "Don't stop." Yes, my slave boy cop was enjoying this. But then so was I! I took that cop's tool into my mouth and worked it up and down in my throat. Although he was chained to the ceiling and floor, the slave began swaying and moving with me and it wasn't long before I felt the pre-cum and then almost immediately the full force of my boy's explosion of cum. Damn that *slave boy must have been saving it up for days because the flow didn't seem to want to stop. Just when I thought it was ending its body would tense up again and a whole new load would burst forth. It was a phenomenal experience and I swallowed it all.*

Finally, the slave seemed spent. Its body just sort of hung there inert. I moved away and took down one of my rawhide whips. I caressed the slave's delectable ass one more time and then let it have it. The first WHACK took it by total surprise and it cried out. "Shut up slave!" I yelled and proceeded to give those beautiful cheeks another twenty to thirty good lashings. I stopped when I noted that it was about to open up cracks of blood. The slave was whimpering and moaning when I stopped.

"Fucking pussy wimp," I said. "You want all the pleasure but can't take the pain. Well slave boy you are going to get the pain, lots of it, if you don't do what the fuck I tell you. Fuck I hate crybabies. Hell, I'll give you something to cry about."

I got a pair of tit clamps and snapped them onto its protruding nips. The slave cried out again in pain. Then I tied its balls together and attached a couple of small weights to them; larger weights would come later once I had broken it in more. I went to a cabinet and took out two items. One was a thick four inch butt plug which I lubed and then shoved unceremoniously up its ass. The slave cried out again so I took the second item, a black rubber ball gag and inserted it in its mouth, fastening it tightly.

"Okay wimp, we'll see how much pain you can take," I said. "You wanted this treatment asshole and now you've got it. I'm going upstairs to inspect the job you did on the kitchen and if I'm not happy with it, then you'll experience the sting of my whip again. So just make yourself comfortable here boy and I'll be back...eventually."

I heard one long sigh as I switched off the lights and left.

The Cop

The cop, now known as the slave, or known as it, hung there in the basement dungeon, his mind awhirl and full of mixed emotions. He had never felt such pain before, what with the ass whipping, the clips on his nips, the weight on his balls, and worse, the plug wedged up in his ass. He thought to himself, "Shit, what have I gotten myself into?" He had wanted to know what it would be like to be a slave, to be dominated by another man, to be tied up and mistreated but in his fantasies it had never hurt this much. And he had always produced major hard-ons and exquisite cum sessions when he would fantasize this. But this, this wracking pain, it was more than he had bargained for. Or was it, he wondered. Even now, strung up there in that basement he was beginning to feel stirrings as his cock once again began to tingle and his balls fill up with blood. He thought about how the Master had sucked him off and he knew that it had been one of the most fantastic moments of his life…such pleasure, such excitement, joy, happiness. Fuck yes; it was worth the suffering he was now going through.

"Is this what is meant by the pain and pleasure sensation?" he wondered to himself. "To get that high do I have to first be brought down low? Must the pleasure always be mixed in with the pain?" And he thought about the man he called Master and how just the sight of him stirred deep emotions. Damn but he was handsome, so impressive in those tight leather pats and motorcycle boots. The cop had wanted to get on his knees and tongue clean the Master's boots and then work his way up those leather pants to what he knew was a cock he could easily worship. He still wanted that and just thinking about it made his own cock harden and twinge with sexual anticipation. He wanted that man; he wanted so badly to please him and be with him. "I will do anything he says," the cop said to himself. "Anything…"

What he hadn't anticipated was the feeling of anxiety and even fear at being alone in the dungeon, not being able to move or even to see. How long had he been there; how much longer would he have to stay in the position he was presently in he wondered. Master was inspecting the kitchen. Damn, he hated cleaning because it seemed so beneath him. It was a lowly task meant for servants and hired help. "Wait a minute," he thought to itself. "I am a servant, in a sense it probably would be my duty to do all the cleaning, to wait on Master hand to foot, to do whatever is necessary to please him. Damn, I hope Master is pleased with the way the kitchen looks. And if he isn't it means more punishment…probably more whipping. No, damn, I don't want that. Shit no! From now on any chore Master gives me I'll do the best job possible… anything to avoid getting him angry and upset with me."

The plug in the slave's ass for some reason began to hurt more than it had. Was it because he was thinking about it? It was a plug after all, not one of those huge dildos he had spotted in a case in the dungeon. And why had Master inserted it in his ass? Not just for punishment, surely, but most likely to widen the slave's hole so that when Master fucked him… No, wait, the slave had not agreed to being fucked…no way. But it didn't appear now that it mattered what the slave agreed to. Master could and probably would do whatever he wanted. And, the more the slave thought about it, the more the slave was turned on by the thought.

"Oh shit, how much longer do I have to stay here like this in the dark?" the slave said to itself. Where is he??? What is he doing??? What is going to happen to me? Shit, what have I gotten myself into???"

The Master

Damn, my kitchen never looked better. This slave is going to make one fine house boy, that's for sure. But, shit, can't let him know that. Better let him think I'm not happy with the job he did, make him do it again. Ha, ha! Damn, but I love this! Okay, better get down there and let him down; don't want him spraining anything by being in that position too long.

I turned on the light and looked at this specimen strung up in my dungeon. Yes, he was something to see. Amazing, the son of a bitch was hard again. Damn, how could he have any cum left in him? This fuck head is enjoying this almost as much as I am.

I don't think he heard me come in and walk over to him...fucker seemed to be on another planet...so he was startled when my hands started caressing his ass, that sweet ass, that delectable ass, that muscular ass, OH GOD, that ass! "Ah, my little slave boy," I said. "Are you enjoying yourself?" Only a muffled "MMFFTT" came through the ball gag. I pulled off the tit clamps and he screamed as the blood rushed back to those tender nipples. He screamed and twisted even more when I unceremoniously yanked the butt-plug out of that wondrous ass but he only sighed when I removed the weights from his balls. I unlocked the fetters on his ankles and then his wrists and he immediately dropped to the floor. I'd like to think it was because he was obeying me and wanted to worship me but I suspected it had more to do with exhaustion. I left him there and got a thick metal collar from a shelf and snapped it around his neck. I locked it securely with a padlock. "That's your slave collar boy and you'll keep it on as long as you are with me," I ordered.

Of course the fucker couldn't see it, but his hand reached up automatically to feel the iron.

"MMMMPHHHPPP" he said, which I interpreted as "Thank you Master."

I then released him from the leather hood and his handsome face was covered in sweat, his hair matted down on his head.

"Did you enjoy that boy?" I asked him.

"Yes MASTER, thank you Master," my slave replied.

I walked him over to the barber chair I had set up which I oftentimes used as a throne, my feet extended out on foot level. I figured it was probably best to get him right into it. He was kneeling directly in front of my booted feet, his face practically on them.

"My boots are dirty boy, clean 'em," I commanded.

The fucker didn't hesitate; his tongue darted out of his mouth and he began cleaning the toe of my right foot.

"Don't forget the sole, boy, that's dirty too," I said.

He immediately switched to the bottom of the boot and started licking off the dirt and crud that had built up there. Damn, what a total pleasure it was watching this cop work so diligently at licking my boots, a joy for any Master to see. I talked to him as he cleaned the boots.

"Well boy, I inspected the kitchen and I am not pleased with the slip-shod job you did," I said. "You call yourself a slave but you sure as hell ain't too good at being one. You're gonna need lots of practice and training before I can say you're ready. When you finish my boots you can go back to the kitchen and do the job right this time."

I could sense him flinch and tense up as I criticized his work and his face got red with embarrassment, but he never stopped his licking.

"Good boy," I said softly.

I had him on the boots for almost an hour and I could see that it was beginning to wear on him and his tongue so I declared him finished for now. I then told him that one of his many duties as my slave would be to keep ALL my boots in top spit shined condition and if I found any that weren't he would be punished for it. What I didn't tell him then was that I had fourteen pairs of boots of all lengths and design.

I attached a leash to the collar and led the slave, still on his hands and knees, back upstairs. I brought him to the kitchen and made him start cleaning all over again, pointing out spots that I called "filthy", but were actually cleaner than they had ever been before. I worked him this way for an hour standing over him and yelling at him while he worked...the poor stupid son of a bitch was shook and humiliated but he worked all the harder. Finally I told him that although it still didn't meet my standards it would have to do this time as I had other tasks for him.

Since he stunk of sweat and dirt I decided it was time for him to shower, but of course I let him use only the cold, cold water. It was sheer agony for him but he came out of it clean, if not a little raw and red from the cold water. Back in the living room I cuffed his wrists behind his back and made him kneel in front of me while I sat comfortably in my leather recliner. This was to be the moment of truth as far as I was concerned and I would know whether this boy was a keeper or not. I sat up, spread my legs and ordered him to clean the dust from my leather pants. The way he attacked this chore was like he had been promised a million dollars to do it...his tongue went wild licking and cleaning the black leather that covered my legs. I could feel the pressure of that tongue through the leather and before long I was sporting one huge boner. When he reached my crotch it was obvious that I was harboring a mighty hard-on under the leather, but he didn't hesitate, in fact, just the opposite. He attacked that bulge like it was an ice cream cone on a hot summer day. He used not just his tongue but also his lips and his whole damned mouth. My order was quiet but forceful... "Unzip me boy!" I said. He did with very little trouble and following my next order he undid my belt and the top button of my leather jeans. The leather was now open and since I wasn't wearing briefs my hard as a rock cock popped out. I didn't need to give him an order, he just started licking it, first the head then the shaft, then back to the head and soon he was sucking the whole nine thick inches down. I watched him as he worked in wonderful rhythmic precision going up and down on my tool, his eyes closed and a look of heavenly contentment on his face. I held back as long as I possibly could but this guy was a natural cock sucker and soon pre cum preceded an explosion of Masterly cum beyond anything I have ever done before. I could not believe how fantastic it felt and load after load erupted into the slave's mouth...and he swallowed every drop of it, not taking his mouth from my cock until it no longer had anything to give and had settled into a more flaccid state. Even then he continued to lick it, cleaning my cock head and lapping at my balls.

"Enough slave boy," I said and he pulled his face back.

His eyes were sparking and he had a smile on him that showed me this was a slave who was content in his work. Little specks of my cum dotted the corners of his mouth. I tucked my cock and balls back into my leather pants, looked down at him and said, "Well boy, what do you say?"

"MASTER, thank you Master," he called out.

"You did just fine boy and I enjoyed that, but now I have some questions for you," I said. "Why did you lie to me?"

He looked up at me and that smile turned into a look of utter confusion.

"Master, what do you mean?" he asked. "I never lied to you."

"Asshole, I thought one of the rules was that you never refer to yourself as a person," I stated. "You are a fucking slave and an "it", a nothing...don't say I."

"MASTER, sorry MASTER, this slave is confused MASTER," the slave started again. "When did it lie to you Master?"

"You told me you worked in construction boy," I said. "You did not tell

me you were a pig cop. Why did you lead me to believe you worked building houses? You are a fucking cop, a pig, the lowest form of life on earth. You lied to me, but then again I guess all you pigs are nothing but stupid liars and cheats."

"NO MASTER, no, honest," he blubbered. "This slave did not mean to lie, it's just that when in those chat rooms it was better not to reveal who… (he almost said "I")…this slave actually was. When slave first talked with you MASTER it thought you were just another guy but once slave got to know you it never thought about correcting that story. MASTER, please forgive this stupid slave."

It was as I suspected but there was no way I was going to let him off easily.

"Well pig slave you have to be punished for lying, you know that don't you?" I asked him.

"Yes Master, pig slave deserves whatever punishment you give it Master," he replied.

The Slave/Cop

The cop was floored that Master had learned that he was indeed a cop and not just some construction worker. How had he found out? The cop was beginning to think that the man had special powers. Now what? Should the cop call the whole thing off, pack his gear and go home? Not too much chance of that happening he thought, seeing as he was naked and collared. So the cop just followed the Master back into the dungeon, ready to accept his punishment. He was led back to the spot where he had been previously shackled and was once again cuffed with his hands above him and his legs spread. The Master then started berating the slave for lying and letting him know that as far as the Master was concerned cops were the lowest form of existence. And since the slave was a cop he was beyond mere contempt. When the slave opened his mouth to protest and defend himself the Master shoved a ball-gag in and tightened it with straps behind the slave's neck, thus silencing him. Then, the Master took down a mean looking leather paddle and began to systematically once again paddle the slave's ass. The slave screamed through the gag and tried to use the safe words that he and the Master had agreed upon, but all the Master heard were grunts of "MMMMPPHHH" and so he kept at it. The slave screamed and pleaded to no avail as the paddling grew more and more intense and harder with each blow, and finally he seemed to collapse in his bondage. The Master stopped and approached the slave.

"Well my little slave boy…pig cop…did you enjoy that punishment?" the Master asked.

Of course the slave didn't answer, he just let his eyes drop to the floor, a beaten and exhausted man. The Master then pulled on a pair of tight fitting, soft rubber gloves and began to slowly, gently, lovingly caress the slave's body. The smooth, cool rubber felt heavenly to the slave and as the Master's hand glided over the slave's chest and arms he felt himself becoming aroused and his cock responding.

"Damn," the slave thought to himself. "Here it is again, pain and pleasure. Oh no, don't let me get hard. What have I gotten myself into? I have to get out of here."

But no matter how hard he tried to fight the sensation he could not stop his cock from expanding. The Master played gently with the slave's cock and balls and the slave could be heard making moans and sighs of pleasure from behind the ball-gag.

"Ah, my little pig slave enjoys having its balls played with," the Master commented mockingly. "Well, your Master enjoys playing with them slave boy, but there is too much hair. Master likes his slaves to be smooth, not hairy like some wild untamed animal. Yes, I'll have to do something about that."

The slave heard the words but the sensation of that cool rubber on his balls distracted him and he didn't really pay attention to what Master was saying. Then Master stopped, went away for a short time and returned with what were obviously shaving cream and razors.

"Oh my God," the slave then said to himself. "He's going to shave my crotch. Oh no, not that."

Once again behind his ball-gag the slave screamed but of course only "MMMPPPH" sounds were heard.

"I suppose you're telling me that you agree that hairy balls and ass don't look good on slaves," the Master said with a grin. "Well, don't worry my little pig slave, we'll soon fix that."

And he did. Painstakingly the Master clipped and then shaved the hair around the slave's crotch and then did the same around the slave's asshole and cheeks. The feeling of the razor as it glided over the slave's most private regions was maddening in a way.

"Ah, that's much better, but you know, now that your important parts are smooth, it makes the rest of your body look weird," the Master stated. "Maybe I'd better take care of that too now."

The slave knew there was nothing he could do to stop the Master so he didn't try to wiggle away or twist his body. He accepted it; he accepted it all;

he kept his eyes closed as he would feel the heated shaving cream on his legs, then his arms, his chest, his back, his entire body. It took over an hour but when Master was finished his slave was smooth all over.

"There now, you look so much better slave boy," the Master stated happily. "Smooth and oh so lovely to the touch all over. Well, no, not all over. You still have that hair on your head…hmmmmmm. I suppose that will have to go too."

Hearing this the slave panicked. He could not have his head shaved. How would he explain that to the guys on the force when he got back?

"Damn no…no Sir…don't do that," he screamed behind his ball-gag.

He also screamed out the safe word but nothing but unintelligible moans and groans were heard. When he saw the Master approaching him with an electric razor he tried to kick out and bust away from his iron bonds, but of course, once again to no avail.

"Ah boy, its good to see you so excited about this," the Master laughed. "I'm sure you'll like the results and it'll only take a few minutes if you would just relax."

And so it did. First the Master cut away as much of the hair on the slave's head as he could with the electric razor, then he used the heated shaving cream and straight razor and turned the slave's head into a shiny, gleaming hairless ball.

"Perfect my boy, you look great," the Master said. "I'll get my full length mirror so you can see for yourself."

The slave could not believe the figure reflected in the mirror before him-a totally hairless body…like Samson shorn of his manliness and strength. He was a defeated, beaten nothing, no longer a man.

The Master undid the bondage on the slave's arms and when they fell listlessly to his sides he cuffed the slave's wrists in back of him before undoing the shackles that held his ankles. Master led the slave, now docile and unresisting, to a waist-high bench and leaned the slave over it, stomach down on top. Master then strapped the slave's chest down on the bench with leather straps that were attached to the sides, effectively holding the slave down. The slave's legs were spread wide and his ankles strapped to the corners of the bench.

The Master talked to the slave, saying, "Boy, you are doing fine. You will make me a wonderful slave but you have to learn to relax and give in to what is happening. You belong to me now, we are joined…you as the slave and me as your MASTER."

The slave simply moaned through his gag. The Master then took some soothing salve from a drawer in the bench and started to work it slowly on the slave's still red and very sore ass cheeks. It felt so good having the Master work the salve on his ass, gently rubbing it in, cooling the fire on his ass. The slave sighed and then realized that his cock was once again filling up and getting hard. The slave, at that point, no longer questioned these sensations that raced through him; he knew there was nothing he could do to stop them. He knew they were a part of him, as he was a part of Master, as Master was a part of him. Then he felt Master working his fingers in his hole and felt the salve being slathered in him. All the while Master was talking softly and lovingly to his boy, calming him.

The Master couldn't help it, rubbing that perfect, now smooth body was getting to him and he felt his own cock hardening inside his leather pants. He dropped the pants, pulled a condom on his now pulsating hard cock and slowly and gently inserted it into the slave's hole. The slave jerked up when he first felt the cock sliding into him, but then he settled down and let the cock inch up further and further. The Master began to push in and pull out of the slave's cunt, slowly at first then faster and faster. Master was delighted to feel the slave react beneath him, moving his ass muscles in conjunction with his thrusts. The Master maintained his efforts for as long as he could but that muscular body beneath him was too much of a treasure and he soon found himself exploding with seemingly endless floods of his man juices.

When he had totally exhausted his supply he left his cock in the slave's hole and then just laid his body on top of the slave's. For some time the two lay there, breathing in sync, two hearts beating as one. Neither wanted to move; each totally satisfied with what had happened. Master reached his gloved hand down below the table and felt the slave's hard throbbing cock. Master gently began massaging the cock, working it gently but firmly. It didn't take long before the slave too exploded in a burst of cop cum which spurted all over the floor beneath them.

Master eventually undid the slave but made him kneel down and lick up all the cum that he had spilled on the floor. The slave did it gladly, with no hesitation. He then moved to Master's boots and began to lick them. Master thought that yes he was going to make a perfect slave for the future.

GELDING JONNO
(VARIATION ON A THEME)

by Nicholas Bowman

"You OK?" Master Mark asked.

Jonno Amber knew what to say and he said, "Yes, Sir. I am, Sir."

But Jonno wondered why event organizers will respect latecomers with ten or fifteen minutes' grace, but won't respect those who arrive on time by starting punctually. Now if the latecomers were whipped, there might be something to it. Not that that was likely with an audience made up of almost two dozen doms and tops, masters and sadists.

Six-foot and spider-limbed, Jonno sat all but completely naked on the edge of the side of a gynecological examining chair. He had been waxed but for his pubic patch the day before. The pubes had been shaved off with a straight razor an hour earlier. He would have liked to shave his head of dark brown hair off as well, but he did have to look normal when he turned up at work Monday. He would have enough problems explaining the collar, which was now permanent.

He shivered as much from fear as from the cold. The thin skin of his sac was tight against his walnut-sized balls, but his seven-and-a-half inch uncut cock loomed large against his rangy, but ripped one hundred and fifty pound body. With a thirty-nine inch chest and a twenty-nine inch waist, there wasn't much, but what there was, was solid muscle.

Master Mark steadied Jonno with a firm hand on the shoulder. "You sure, boy?"

Jonno knew what to say and he said, "Yes, Sir. I am, Sir."

But he was both scared and turned on. Not that he could turn back at this point. This wasn't a scene with a safe word, which could be stopped if it got too heavy. He knew exactly what was going to happen. He had even volunteered for it. This was a scene that was going to go through to the end. No backing out. No second thoughts allowed.

Master Mark nodded and joined the other doms in the room.

Master Mark was about Jonno's height, but looked bigger because of a forty-three inch chest and a fall to the waist that topped one foot. He had a black moustache, hairy pecs, and a treasure trail that started at his breast bone and went straight down the centerline of his six-pack abs. He wore camo trousers, worn leather work boots and gloves, and dog tags that were actually his. A red handkerchief was tied over the top of his head.

Jonno supposed he could follow the master, but crossed his ankles and kept his left hand holding his right wrist behind him as if he were bound instead. He doubted moving around would loosen the dildo plugging his butt. It was a cast of his own cock. In a manner of speaking, he was fucking himself. But then again, by some standards, when he signed the consent form, he had fucked himself.

The room was large – a basement in a suburban house north of Los Angeles. The chair – and Jonno – was at one end of the room. Next to the chair was a rolling cart, the top of which was covered. Two semi-circles of folding chairs faced Jonno, the inner arc with eleven seats, the outer twelve, staggered so that everyone would be able to see the demo clearly.

At the other end of the room, a bar had been set up. Drinks – beer only, Jonno noted – were served by the only other bottom on the premises. The bar bottom wore a leather kilt with an Eisenhower jacket and a full set of well-defined swimmer's muscles.

The guests were all doms, milling about, talking and drinking. Leather chaps and vests mingled with blue jeans and white Tees. Everyone had boots, no one had hats. At least half of them had used Jonno as a cum dump the night before. The bartender would probably be the cum dump at the after party at 9:30. Jonno wondered if the bartender knew what the night's agenda was.

The din of the conversation almost covered the mix of Strauss, Sibelius, and Shostakovich that emanated from hidden speakers. The cold air held the scent of soap and fresh air with base notes of musk and vanilla. The ambient lighting was low, but there were spots in place to light the chair once things got going, which was supposed to be seven sharp. But even if it started half an hour late, Jonno doubted his technical manhood would last much past 8:30.

Suddenly he just wanted it over with.

But the doms continued to mingle. Jonno felt restless and wanted to leave. Then Master Mark came back.

"Traffic jam," Master Mark said. "The idiot didn't call until he could guess when he could get past it."

Jonno didn't point out that the idiot in question wasn't the dom leading the demo.

Master Mark reached down, picked up Jonno's cock, and ran a finger along the underside. Master Mark felt the cock expand in his hand.

"Ready for the show, boy." It wasn't a question.

Jonno knew what to say and he said, "Yes, Sir. I am, Sir."

"Good boy. Let's get you strapped down before the doctor gets here. Maybe take care of that dick of yours."

"Yes, Sir."

Jonno slid back onto the seat as he turned, swinging his right leg high enough to clear the kneepad on the bar of the stirrup and landing smoothly into the heel cup. He slipped his left foot into the other stirrup. Jonno let his arms fall to the sides of the examining chair.

Master Mark pulled a thick leather strap across Jonno's chest, across the rib cage right below the pecs. It felt snug, but not tight. Master Mark leaned forward, pinched and twisted Jonno's nipples. Jonno moaned in surprise and appreciation. The master grinned and then strapped Jonno's right wrist in a fleece-lined handcuff. The left wrist was cuffed next.

Master Mark stood between Jonno's legs and quickly strapped each thigh in place. Again the fit was snug, not tight. He looked at the bottom. Jonno was restrained, his body against the slanted back of the chair, arms held down and out of the way, legs spread wide leaving the cock and balls exposed, balls whose exact size and placement were all too easy to see beneath the thin skin of the sac. The master reached forward, took the dangling nuts in his hand, rolled them so that the cords crossed, and then squeezed. Hard.

Jonno jerked from the pain. "Thank you, Sir," he gasped.

Master Mark released the balls. He smirked, shook his head, and fastened Jonno's ankles to the stirrups. He then circled around to the back of the chair. He strapped Jonno's upper arms to the sides of the chair. Master Mark rested a hand on Jonno's shoulder and squeezed gently. Jonno nodded with a smile. The master pulled out a gag. Jonno opened his mouth and let Master Mark gag him.

Jonno forced himself to pace his breathing. Slow and even would control his fear and his anticipation. He looked around. The doms were taking their seats, though the three in the center of the front row were empty. He craned his neck. The bar had closed and the bartender was now naked.

Two of the doms marched the bar bottom to the chair in the center of the front row. One pushed the bottom onto the seat while the other pulled out six ropes, each about four feet long. The bottom's wrists were quickly tied behind his back with one rope, while a second tied them to the chair. Two more ropes were used to tie his ankles to the sides of the chair, keeping his feet off the floor. The last two tied his torso and his thighs to the chair. Then he too was gagged.

However he did have a clear view of Jonno's cock and balls, ringside, front and center. The two doms sat to either side of the bottom. They sniggered. The bottom kept his expression neutral, but expectant. Jonno wondered again if the bottom had any idea of what was going to happen.

The latecomer slipped in. Jonno recognized him. As a dom, he was as known to expand a sub's limits as he was to violate them.

The dom looked around and saw the bound bartender.

"Oh, does that mean they're going to do two tonight?" he asked as he took a seat in the second row.

Some of the other doms smiled or laughed. The bound bottom's eyes widened and he looked to the doms on either side of him for a clue if not an answer.

"You'll find out soon enough, boy," one said.

The bottom looked scared. Jonno wondered if he were even into Beavis and Butthead ball-busting, let alone CBT.

Master Mark cleared his throat. Jonno turned to look. The doctor came into the room.

The doctor was average height and kept his weight proportional: he clearly wasn't competing as a body builder. Neatly trimmed grey hair framed a square face. Wire rim glasses shielded brown eyes. Instead of black leather, the doctor favored green scrubs. It lent him an odd air of casual authority.

"Thank you all for coming," the doctor said. "And I appreciate your patience. It will be rewarded. This is going to be a demo of what some of us consider to be the ultimate scene: castration. Tonight we're going to cut off Jonno's nuts. Snuff his manhood. Deprive him of his masculinity. Alleged masculinity. After all, what does a bottom need balls for anyway?"

The audience laughed. The bartender looked fearful and tried to pull out of the ropes. His cock smalled and his sac shriveled around his balls. Jonno wondered who wanted to make the boy sweat. Master Mark began to massage Jonno's shoulders. Jonno squirmed around the dildo, letting his body enjoy the sensations of movement. His cock grew full.

The doctor continued the introduction. "As an interest, castration appeals to about one out of every six men involved in s/m. Analyzing the statistical runs Larry Townsend published in the second Leatherman's Handbook it would appear that tops are more interested in castration than bottoms by a ratio of about four to three."

When Jonno first heard that statistic he couldn't resist cracking wise and ask whether that was pushy bottoms or normal bottoms. It didn't reflect what most subs who hung out in such places as Eunuch.org's chat room experienced.

"Depending upon your definitions of fetish and fantasies, interest peaks either in the twenties or thirties. Jonno, for example, is thirty-nine."

Jonno wondered if the sporadic applause was for his stiffening cock or his age. Master Mark continued kneading, working his way down Jonno's pecs. Wiggling around the dildo felt good. It felt real good.

"We are, of course, talking about actual castration," the doctor explained. "But Townsend liked to point out that symbolic castration is part of regular s/m practice. Many subs enjoy the emasculation of being raped or being forced to wear women's clothes or undergarments. Master Mark likes to put sanitary napkins up his subs' holes. For others it's shaving the pubes or the whole body. Only men have hair on their balls. No hair, no manhood."

He paused and looked at Jonno's smooth and hairless body. He watched Master Mark play with Jonno's nipples for a moment before continuing.

"Rawhide around the balls, stretchers, and even banders all separate the balls from the body to greater or lesser extents. And of course any form of CBT carries the threat of permanent testicular damage if things go wrong. Long term, though not technically permanent, practices include various chastity devices."

One master had kept Jonno in one. Once the novelty wore off, he was only aware of who put it and why. And of course there was the routine degradation of having to squat to piss.

"Another approach is to make the sub cum before the scene. And then there's my favorite, infibulation."

Master Mark chuckled as he teased the insides of Jonno's thighs. Jonno realized the dildo had developed a life of its own inside his body. He would probably shoot his load before the doctor finished his introduction and the scene began. Even with the distraction of the bartender struggling against his bonds.

"Why of course is an interesting question. There is of course the narrative, the story we tell about selves to justify what we did and to explain what we do." The doctor smiled. "Told as some sort of quest, it gives shape and purpose to otherwise random events. Castration here can address such problems as being circumcised or having a cock greater than six inches. Oversized balls also hit that list."

Master Mark grabbed hold of Jonno's cock and began to work both the shaft and the foreskin. Jonno managed to groan audibly despite the gag.

"Some narratives go for behaviors: breach of the master/slave contract; infidelity; failure to follow orders; to make an unruly slave more cooperative; as an example to other subs, slaves, or bottoms; to satisfy the whim or curiosity of a top or dom; or to acquire a trophy or addition to a collection."

The doctor watched the squirming bartender for a moment, then looked at Master Mark and nodded. Did he know Jonno's narrative was that he needed to be castrated to be more docile, more useful and productive? Just like many male animals on a ranch like the one he worked on during college?

The doctor went on. "More serious surveys reveal interest in castration comes from a handful of reasons. The first involves the libido: don't like being gay; have an overactive sex-drive; or fear might commit offensive sexual acts. The second involves submission: sexual, to a master or owner or to a partner with a lower sex drive; or religious, for purification of some sort. The third is punishment for a real or imagined crime. The fourth is body image, either body integrity disorder or transformation to a eunuch. Two things occur with surprising frequency in the background of our interest: a history of child abuse and a history of working on a farm castrating livestock."

Master Mark pulled and squeezed Jonno's cock. The load shot out fast and thick. He collapsed against the chair. If he had to cum, he'd rather have an electro ejaculation probe up his hole than be milked. Especially if he were banded. Not that that was going to be option much longer.

"Quite a geyser. But if it's your last load, it had better be a good one," the doctor noted. "There are several methods of castration available. Banders like the elastrator or crushers like the burdizzo are the most common. Banding can lead to infection or gangrene. Burdizzos don't work more often than not. If you like to play with bands, keep it down to under 15 minutes."

The doctor looked away from the audience and back at Jonno. "Chemical castration is an option, though most popular for male to female transsexuals and sex offenders. The results are more or less reversible. Jonno was a chemmie for about a year, so you can draw your own conclusions about that."

The audience laughed. The bartender just stared and listened. Jonno wondered what he was going through right now.

"The best method is surgical, whether the male is human or animal," the doctor said. "It's even used on the better farms and ranches as Jonno would tell you if he could. Tonight we're going to demonstrate a testicular castration, leaving the penis and scrotum intact, though the scrotum may be removed later. This involves a midline or bilateral scrotal incision, the legation of the spermatic cords, and finally the removal of the testes."

The bartender began to panic. The two doms tried to steady him.

"For those concerned about such things, this is a consensual castration." The doctor looked straight at the bartender. "Though that's not always the case."

The bartender's eyes widened in fear and surprise.

Master Mark's eye roll told Jonno he wasn't the only one who was tired of the mind games being played on the bartender. Jonno decided that it was the dom who came late who must be behind playing the bartender. Otherwise, why wait for him?

The doctor turned, looked at Jonno, and smiled. Jonno felt cold goose bumps crawl and tighten across the skin of his abdomen. He took a deep breath and let it out slowly. This was it. Neutered to become a better workhorse. His owner had realized that Jonno was an animal trapped in a human body.

Jonno looked at Master Mark, who nodded and uncovered the rolling cart. On top was a range of medical implements, from needles to scalpels, from sutures to ampoules, from antiseptics to latex gloves.

Master Mark took a towel off the cart and splashed some antiseptic on it. The pungent odor filled the air. The master wiped Jonno's cum clean from his body, the chemical tingling lightly on his skin. After discarding the towel, Master Mark poured some of the solution on a cotton swab and cleaned under Jonno's foreskin and around the cock head.

After discarding the swab, both the doctor and Master Mark used the clear solution to scrub their hands. Then the two men pulled on sterile latex gloves.

"First," the doctor announced, "we have to restrain the penis. Usually it's just taped to the abdomen, but that's not that interesting."

The doctor turned his attention to Jonno. He picked Jonno's cock up and stretched the foreskin out. Master Mark handed the doctor a hollow medical needle. The doctor pushed the needle through the foreskin, piercing both sides, the needle crossing right in front of the pee hole. As Jonno exhaled to ride the pain, the needle was followed by a hollow metal twelve gauge tube. The standard needle method of American piercers produced a classic Roman infibulation.

The doctor checked to see that the piercing was right. Then the two tops changed their latex gloves for new ones.

Master Mark poured some antiseptic on another towel and quickly cleaned Jonno's nipples. He tossed the towel onto the other one. Then he pinched Jonno's left nipple, and twisted, kneading it into a rigid nub.

The doctor nodded and picked up another hollow needle. Jonno gasped as the needle and a second hollow tube pierced his nipple. A minute later, and another change of gloves, his right nipple was pierced as well.

Jonno leaned forward, looking down his chest to his cock. Three horizontal tubes now penetrated his body and his being. He watched as the two doms changed gloves. Then, the doctor pulled a length of fishing line from the top of the tray as Master Mark picked up a fishing weight.

The doctor threaded the fishing line through the tube through Jonno's foreskin. He pulled the ends so that they were of equal length. He pushed the ends of the line through the outside of the tubes through Jonno's nipples. The doctor pulled the ends together, centering them over Jonno's breastbone. He quickly tied a knot. Master Mark handed the weight to the doctor who fastened it to the knot. He let the weight fall onto Jonno's chest.

"You're cut, boy," Jonno heard one of the doms say to the bartender. "Maybe we'll do you with fish hooks to connect the line."

Jonno's eyes met the doctor's and then Master Mark's. For a moment, he thought the three of them were going to laugh.

Instead, the doctor said firmly, "The penis is now restrained."

Jonno craned his head to look. The weight pulled the line taut and his cock flat against his belly. It formed an upside down triangle, an arrowhead pointing down to where his balls dangled, exposed and unprotected, between his splayed and sinewy 22-inch thighs. His breathing felt deeper and heavier, but it wasn't from the weight resting on his chest. He looked at the doctor.

"Next," the doctor said, "The area will be numbed with a local."

After Master Mark and he changed gloves, the master prepared the injection as the doctor continued, "In this case two milliliters of buffered Lidocaine will be used as a line block along the scrotal raphe."

Master Mark handed the needle to the doctor.

With his left hand, the doctor pinched Jonno's sac between the balls, working a flap of skin loose between his thumb and forefinger. Once he had enough skin to work with, the doctor jabbed the needle into the skin, and injected the anesthesia.

Jonno heard the sound of several pairs of knee caps clashed together.

"What do you think of that?" one dom asked the bartender. "Ready to be taken to the vet, pup?"

Actually, Jonno liked that the doctor was a veterinarian. Nevertheless, Jonno would have rather been rounded up with the horses or sheep or pigs on a farm and done along with the livestock. Of course, there would be no line block if he were on the lineup for the castration chute.

The doctor pulled the needle out, discarded it as he turned to the audience, and cleared his throat. "It will take a couple of minutes for the Lidocaine to take effect. With human males, the area is draped, but Jonno here is more a manimal, so it's not an issue."

Jonno snorted through his gag. The audience probably thought it was to illustrate the doctor's point. While he was less than a real man, though still more than a true animal – hence manimal – the lack of draping was because being completely shaved down it wasn't an issue. Especially if the doctor wanted to make sure everyone could see as much as possible. And the continual glove changing dramatically reduced the risk of cross contamination.

Meanwhile, he felt the numbing creep around his sac, seeping into his balls, slowly, steadily draining any feeling of his sexual being from him. He was losing the physical sensations of his manhood before he lost his physical manhood. He steadied himself with slow, even breaths.

Jonno watched as the doctor stuck another needle into his sac and moved it around. He felt nothing. He realized he felt as numb as his balls.

"Next is a scrotal incision, which in this case will be about an inch along the raphe," the doctor said.

The doctor and Master Mark changed gloves again. Jonno saw, but did not feel, the doctor take the balls into his hand and cut into the sac. The doctor discarded the scalpel. He then probed the inside of the sac while squeezing the neck. The left ball popped through the incision.

The doctor let it dangle there for a moment so that the audience could get a good look. The doctor pulled the testes free. Jonno was surprised that he felt the tug right up into his abdomen.

Master Mark handed the doctor a clamp. The doctor clamped Jonno's spermatic cord. Master Mark then handed the doctor a needle and suture.

"For gluttons of detail, I'm using a two-zero Dexon absorbable suture. To prevent bleeding, the cord will be ligated twice."

The doctor quickly stitched the cords shut.

The doctor exchanged the needle for an emasculator. Jonno smiled behind his gag. Just like the animal he was.

Master Mark held out a small bowl.

The doctor cut the cord with the emasculator, and placed it into the bowl.

With one ball gone, Jonno was now a ridgling, just like some of the sheep at the ranch.

The doctor checked the cord for bleeding. He released the cord and it jerked back into the sac.

The doctor quickly moved to Jonno's remaining ball. He pulled it out; clamped and stitched the cords; cut off the ball; and released the cords back into Jonno's body.

Master Mark held the bowl with Jonno's balls out for everyone to see.

"And that's it. He's neutered. Didn't deserve balls and there's no reason for him to have them." The doctor smiled at the audience.

Beneath his own feelings of fear and shame, Jonno was aware that most of the doms were looking at the bowl with his balls. The bartender on the other hand couldn't seem to tear his eyes away from Jonno's empty sac. Jonno wondered what the boy was thinking. Did he really think the doctor would castrate two men in one night?

"Master Mark will now let each of you take a look while I finish off with the gelding here."

The doctor turned his attention to Jonno's sac. He sewed up the subcutaneous tissue and skin with the Dexon.

Master Mark brought the bowl to each dom in turn to let him see what had been Jonno's balls. Most murmured softly or looked silently. The doms flanking the bartender were happy to taunt the bound boy.

"Those could be yours," said one.

"You know you deserve it," said the other.

The bartender just whimpered.

Jonno wondered what was going to happen to his balls. Were they going to be a souvenir? Prairie oysters? Or tossed out with the trash? Not that he had any more choice in the matter than in being castrated in the first place. The hands at the ranch had introduced him to the logic of castration in general and the likelihood of his more than twenty years ago.

As Master Mark finished showing the bowl of balls around, the doctor removed the fishing line and the tubes in Jonno's nipples. He left the one through the foreskin. He cleared his throat for attention as he changed gloves again.

"Strangely enough, we're not quite done yet," the doctor said dryly.

The audience turned its attention away from the bowl of balls and back to the demonstration itself.

Master Mark returned to his station, put the bowl down, and changed gloves.

The doctor quickly changed the hollow tube for a ten gauge ampallang and screwed the knobs on either side of the metal shaft tight. The infibulation was now a permanent pierce, trapping Jonno's cock in the sheath of its foreskin. He wouldn't be able to get hard. But then again, without balls, he had a limp dick anyway.

Master Mark and the doctor peeled off their gloves.

The master released Jonno from the chair starting with the straps and cuffs around his upper arms and ankles.

The doctor addressed the audience. "For many this is the ultimate, though whether it's the ultimate submission or humiliation or both would be hard to say. It is safe to say that Jonno can no longer pretend to be a man. His public gelding means we all know who and what he really is."

Master Mark freed Jonno's thighs and wrists. Jonno slowly moved and stretched his limbs.

The doctor smiled. "Meanwhile, Master Mark and I have to clean up here. There are refreshments at the bar, but you'll have to serve yourself. The bartender will be providing other services. And if he doesn't, he knows what will happen."

The audience laughed, and began to move around, mostly toward the bar. Master Mark released the chest strap and helped Jonno sit up. The two doms on either side of the bartender carefully began to adjust the position in which he was held in bondage.

Master Mark got a carton of orange juice from the cart. He opened the carton and handed it to Jonno. He put an arm around him and held him close while Jonno drank the juice.

Master Mark leaned forward and spoke softly into Jonno's ear. "Ready for the next phase of your life, boy?"

Jonno knew what to say and he said, "Yes, Sir. I am, Sir."

Author's Note

Fans of Larry Townsend will recognize what passages from his works in general and from the two Leatherman's Handbooks in particular inspired this homage. The anecdote in The Sublime to the Ultimate chapter in the first handbook turned me on when I first read it as a teenager. I'm not sure I was actually old enough to buy the book, but I was old enough to enjoy its more select passages. Certainly his theory about the underlying castration complex influenced not only my play and fantasies, but also some of my mainstream work.

Of course there is nothing novel about someone getting castrated at an event. LaFarge used much the same idea in PBO and its sequel which was published in Drummer years ago. And it's the premise for hundreds of stories archived on the Eunuch.org website. Some of the statistics referred to in the story that did not come from the second handbook were gleaned from various posts on the Eunuch site. As far as the actual piercing and surgical procedures described, I tried to stick closely to what professionals in the fields would do.

Do as You're Told Rookie

by Tony Hedges

Ridgemount was a small town some miles away from the big city of San Francisco, a small town where crime was low and people felt safe. It was a town where people went about their daily business with a smile on their face, occasionally stopping to talk to their fellow neighbors and residents in the street, a warm handshake, a peck on the cheek, a happy good to see you hug, yeah, ordinary people caring about each other. They took great lengths to welcome newcomers into the fold as well. This story details what happened to the newly employed rookie police officer Chris Manning.

Chris was freshly out of the police academy and had been assigned to Ridgemount on a temporary term of duty. He would be patrolling the streets on a Harley Davidson bike. The rookie had been born to sit on two wheels. His youth had been spent in and out of juvenile for stealing bikes, robbing convenience stores, petty thievery and stuff, and he was going nowhere fast. He knew it was only a matter of time before his crimes would be anything other than petty anymore. A chance encounter with a California highway patrol cop, while under the influence changed that. The two men, both were missing something in their lives, the cop without a son, the youth with no father, and a common bond, the love of bikes and the road.

As Chris made his way into the kitchen Mark was sitting at the kitchen counter sipping his coffee.

"Well, well, Sleeping Beauty has awoken," Mark said sarcastically, looking at the younger officer in his pajamas and bare feet.

Chris rubbed his thick fingers through his short cropped hair, said

"Good morning to you too Sir," gave out a yawn and poured black coffee. With his cup in hand he made his way to the bathroom.

"Don't be in there all day, I need a piss before going on patrol," Mark called out.

Chris closed the bathroom door behind him, ignoring his housemate's comment.

Mark finished his coffee, dumped the cup in the sink and made his way out to the hallway. He checked the radio set on the kitchen counter. It was their link to the cop station in town. The officer picked up the radio and called in.

"Hey Alma, just checking in, how's it going?" Mark asked.

"The chief is out, Andy and Rick are out on traffic duty, Phil's writing up and you should be making your way in," the radio operator replied. "Your roomie should be riding the highways and byways of this lovely little town."

Mark grinned at Alma's little dig at small town life.

"Will do ma'am, over and out," Mark said, giving a mock salute to the radio set and placing the microphone back on the counter.

Sitting neatly in a row in the hallway stood the two cop's footwear, Chris' motorbike black Dehner boots polished to a pristine shine and Mark's Magnum boots were scuff-free and well buffed up. Even if their home skills left much to be desired their footwear and uniforms were treated with due care and respect. Mark picked up his Magnums and took them into the kitchen. He sat down and pulled them on over his thick white boot socks. He gave a yank several times as he tightened up the laces on them, finishing with a tight knot at the top. He then stood up and beat his feet on the tiled floor to ensure that his boots were properly fit, tight and snug.

Chris came out of the bathroom, towel wrapped around his torso. His muscular body was evidence of hard workouts on a daily basis. Under the towel he sported a slight boner this morning.

"Go have your piss Trooper," Chris said with a grin.

Mark took himself into the bathroom and closed the door.

Chris made his way into his bedroom, pulled open the wardrobe to reveal all manner of sweatshirts, jumpers, tee shirts, jeans and dress trousers. But hanging on its own to one side was his uniform, freshly clean and pressed. Chris let his towel round his torso drop, revealing an athletic well-toned body. He pulled a pair of white briefs from a pile and slid them on. He then pulled a white short sleeved vest from the closet and slipped it over his head. Checking himself in the mirror he then took his dark blue officer's shirt out of the dry cleaning cellophane wrapping and drew it to his nostrils. It smelled clean and fresh. Last time he had worn it, it had smelled all funky and moist. He had been involved in a drug bust and had had to chase down one of the assailants. He had run for blocks upon blocks in the heat and humidity, thus making his shirt a smelly and sweaty mess. But now it was all clean again and like him, ready for duty. He slipped the shirt on and buttoned it up, leaving his white vest exposed. Chris then went to his dressing table and picked up his badge and nametag. He clipped both onto his shirt and checked in the mirror to be sure they were straight. He then pulled his uniform trousers from the closet and took them out of the dry cleaning cellophane as well. He sat on the edge of the bed and slowly slipped them on, ensuring the creases were kept straight. He stood up and completed pulling them up and fastening them around his waist. Chris then buckled them into position with a belt. Next, he made his way into the lounge. Lying on the sideboard was his duty belt, black and highly polished. Chris checked it; all equipment was in its proper place, pepper spray, cuffs, gun holster, etc. The young officer then wrapped the duty belt around his waist and buckled it tightly in place. He turned on his socked feet and made his way to the hallway. He eyed his polished boots, remembering also that day when he'd had to chase the assailant and how scuffed they'd become. Now they were polished to a high shine. Chris picked up his boots and made his way with them to the kitchen table. He sat down, allowed his fingertips to feel and check the shine on each boot and decided they were perfect. He pulled his right leg up and slipped the boot on, pulling it firmly to ensure that it would fit and feel snug. He did the same with his left leg, encasing his foot and calf in it. He then stood up and stamped his feet on the tiled floor. The boots were on for the day. Chris made his way over to the sideboard in the lounge and took a small key from the shelf and unlocked one of the drawers. Inside was his gun. He took it out and held it up, opened the chamber and spied the bullets. It was full. He then pushed the chamber back and slipped the gun into his holster. One last check in the mirror to inspect his appearance and he turned on his booted soles to make his way through the kitchen to the side door that led out to the garage port. On his way out he grabbed his helmet from the kitchen counter.

"Hey Trooper boy, see you tonight," Chris called out and without waiting for a reply he wandered out to the garage port.

Mark finished pissing in the toilet. He allowed the last droplets to drip from the tip of his big dick, gave it a good shake and then zipped himself up. He heard Chris shout out about seeing him tonight. He didn't have a chance to reply because the next thing he heard was Chris starting up his Harley and revving the engine, putting it in gear and roaring off down the dirt road. Mark checked himself in the mirror, checked the windows and doors were securely locked, locked the side door and got in his patrol car. He leaned over, grabbed his peaked cap from the back seat, placed it on his head and adjusted it while looking in the rearview mirror to be sure it sat straight and proper. With that done he switched on the car's ignition, put the car in gear and took to the dirt road, ready for another day in beautiful, peaceful Ridgemount, yeah right...

Officer Mark Tyler had been with the police force for well over five years. He came to Ridgemount a little over three years ago on his own. He had transferred from the big city to Ridgemount with nothing more than a couple of suitcases and a few bad memories. He was no longer tied to a desk job in the station. He took to small town life almost immediately, and the captain took to him straightaway. It didn't take long for Mark to prove himself in the few criminal incidents that happened in the town. It was Mark who was there in the front line sorting it out, and through hard work and determination he was now out on his own, with his own cruiser and a lot of respect.

Motorcycle Officer Chris Manning had been patrolling the roads outside of Ridgemount. Except for a couple of speeding tickets there was nothing major happening on the roads. The morning was quickly fading away and it was now afternoon. This was where he could let the Harley out on full throttle, but Chris would find at certain times of the day, specific roads to be quiet and without anyone to see him. He allowed himself the luxury of letting the Harley go full speed down the empty road. There was nothing else quite like that feeling of the revving engine of the Harley between his legs as he sped down the dirt road.

Mark Tyler had been cruising the streets of the town, except for a barking dog and an illegally parked van there was nothing for the officer to do except cruise around the town and make the occasional radio call into the station.

"Alma today is not a day to arrest anyone," he said over the mic to the base.

"Honey, in Ridgemount, there isn't anyone to arrest, everyone is a law abiding citizen," she said sarcastically.

"Yeah, you're right there," Mark replied. "Tell me Alma, tell me that I've only another five hours before shift is over and I can say adios to you guys till Monday."

"Unless there is a riot at the local store honey pie you've got to use up that quality time with whatever and whoever," Alma said.

"Well, I'll get whatever later in the bar, but the whoever I'm not rightly sure about," Mark chuckled.

"Listen Officer Tyler, just patrol the streets," came the blunt reply.

"Yes ma'am," Mark said and placed the mic back in its holder on the dashboard.

"Hurry up the day," he whispered to himself.

Chris looked at his watch mid afternoon. It sure was a slow day. He parked in a picnic area and was leaning against his Harley, his long legs crossed, watching the occasional car go by. He radioed into the station.

"This is Officer Manning reporting in," Chris said.

"Hi Chris, tell me you caught some bad guys today," came Alma's mocking plea.

"Sorry Alma, cells going to be empty tonight," came the bored reply.

"Why don't you call your house mate, he's just as bored as you," Alma said. "Over and out."

Chris' radio fell into silence. He gave himself a brief moment to decide on his next course of action. He clicked the mic back into action.

"Calling Officer Tyler, calling Officer Tyler, give us a shout," Chris said.

There was the sound of static and then nothing for a moment.

"Yeah, what do you want?" came the voice of Mark Tyler.

"Hey buddy, how's the patrolling coming along?" asked Chris in a cheery sounding voice.

"Listen Rookie, just remember since you're finishing early you can stop off at the hardware store and get that washing line for the backyard," Mark said sternly. "I'm fed up not having anyway to hang my wash outdoors."

"Yeah, yeah, I haven't forgotten, keep your hair on," Chris said and gazed down at his black boots, checking the condition of them.

They were still pristine, still highly polished, no scuff marks.

"And remember I'm out tonight with the guys from work to chill out," Mark went on. "You can play with your play station."

Chris' attention came back to the call at hand. He hadn't been paying that much attention, but buying the clothesline stuck in his brain. At least that was one thing he would remember.

The day seemed to drag, but they normally did when nothing was happening and for both officers it was a case of just making their presence noticed. And that was done just by cruising around Ridgemount making sure they were noticed.

Chris looked at his watch and realized that he had about forty-five minutes left on his shift. He would drive into town to pick up the washing line. By then he would radio in and sign off for the weekend, bring the bike back to the house, chill with a few beers and get out the play station…yeah, right…

Chris then speeded back into town and pulled into High Street. First stop, the hardware store. The rookie officer pulled up outside, kicked out the kickstand on his Harley and let it rest. He unbuckled his helmet, pulled it off and dismounting from the Harley made his way into the store. He asked George, the owner of the store where he would find the washing line. George directed the rookie down one of the aisles. After a few minutes Chris had purchased a few meters of white nylon cord, perfect for hanging out the washing. The rookie got back on his Harley and revved it into gear. He sped out toward the town limits.

Chris made his way up the dirt road to the small house. He slowed down as he drew nearer and parked in the garage port. The rookie dismounted and unbuckled his helmet. He pulled it from his head allowing the late afternoon cool breeze to blow across his buzz-cut. He took a deep breath and stepped up on to the front porch making his way to the front door. He pulled out his keys and opened the front door. It was a routine, or in the beginning when he'd moved in, it was Mark's orders. He was to place his helmet on the side. He would then unbuckle his gun holster and pull out his gun. He would place the gun in the drawer of the dresser till the next time it was needed, in this case Monday morning. The rookie then made his way into the kitchen. He placed the coil of washing line on the side, picked up the mic from the radio and called into Alma at headquarters.

"Alma, just calling in to say goodbye till Monday," Chris said happily. "Have a lovely weekend and enjoy your evening with my housemate. I'll be thinking of you, signing off."

"Yeah, well make sure you come into the office first thing bright and early, and I mean bright and early," came the sarcastic reply.

Then the radio went dead. The weekend had begun. All Chris needed now was for Mark to return, get changed and leave for the evening, leaving him to his own pleasures.

The rookie went to the refrigerator and grabbed a beer for himself. It was then he felt the sudden rush of air hit the back of his neck. He turned around and immediately gazed down at the kitchen floor. He noticed small pieces of broken glass beneath the side kitchen door. He stepped over, the sound of the glass crackling and crunching under his boots. Kneeling down Chris touched the broken shards of glass. He looked up at the side door and saw that a small pane of glass had been knocked in. The rookie began to quickly put two and two together, but suddenly the sound of a gun being cocked made him turn around. Chris found himself gazing into the barrel of his own gun. He gulped hard in sheer terror.

"Best stand up Rookie," came a man's voice.

Chris instinctively raised his hands above his head as he slowly stood up to confront two men. One of them was pointing the gun directly at him; the other was standing a few feet behind and was holding what looked like a baseball bat. They both looked as though they hadn't shaved in a few days and they were dressed in baggy jeans and grey sweatshirts with trainers that had seen better days, all torn and dirty.

"Into the other room Rookie," the guy with Chris' gun said and waved him into the dining area.

In the room was a wooden dining table surrounded by matching wooden high-back chairs.

"Pull yourself out a chair and take a seat Rookie," the guy with Chris' gun ordered.

Chris, with no choice in the matter did as he was instructed. He wasn't sure how to evaluate this situation. He would have to play it by the book and hope that Mark would come back soon. Chris sat down on the chair, his arms now raised again.

"Hey Ricardo, bring that rope in," ordered the intruder. "We're going to tie this rookie up.

At least now Chris knew the name of one of the intruders.

"Now Rookie, I'll tell you like it is," the intruder said, waving Chris' gun from side to side. "Do as we say and we won't hurt you. Try anything and you won't see the cop shop Monday morning."

They had obviously overheard Chris' message to Alma.

Ricardo came into the room. In one hand he was carrying the bat and in the other the coil of nylon washing line. Chris had to wonder at the irony of this, that he was going to be tied up with the washing line that he had bought. It was as if he had purchased his own bondage equipment.

Chris then felt his arms being grabbed and pulled roughly behind the back of the chair. He felt his wrists being crossed one over the other and the rope being wrapped tightly around them. Ricardo grinned as he worked the nylon cord around the rookie's wrists, taking pleasure in tugging frequently, ensuring that the rookie would not get free. Once he was sure he had tied the rookie's wrists securely he used the excess rope and began to wrap it around Chris' lean muscular torso, tugging occasionally to ensure that the rookie was securely tied to the chair. Again, once Ricardo was satisfied with his handiwork he drew the excess rope and coiled it around the wooden strut that held the chair legs together. He drew it through to the front legs of the chair and maneuvered himself in front of the chair. He knelt down, grabbed Chris' booted feet and began to use excess rope to tie the rookie's feet together. Ricardo wrapped the cord tightly around the shining black Dehner boots. The captive rookie could only watch as Ricardo finished his rope work, ending with a tight knot that held not only Chris' booted feet together but also held them securely to the front strut support of the wooden chair.

"Hey Rookie, you feel comfortable now?" came the chuckling comment.

Chris clenched his teeth as acute pain began to take hold in his wrists and chest as the rope dug into his flesh. He tried to twist and turn his wrists but all this achieved was the cord digging into his flesh.

"Holding a police officer against his will isn't exactly the smartest move you know," said the captive rookie through his clenched teeth.

"Hey Marco, this guy thinks we're not smart," Ricardo said.

Finally, Chris now had the other intruder's name. Now, with both names he could at least try and reason with them as his police training had taught him. But more than anything he needed to know where the hell Mark was.

Mark quickly took his hand off the steering wheel and looked at his watch. His shift had finished. He radioed in to the station.

"Hi Alma, just checking in for the last time, nothing to report," Mark said. "See you at Mickey's later on, aim for about seven thirty PM."

"Okay, I've got Andy and Rick coming along as well," Alma replied. "Phil has still got paperwork to complete. Chief is holding the fort this evening. See you tonight. Remember to get the beers lined up."

"Not if you're there first," Mark laughed.

"Yeah, yeah, whoever gets there first gets the first round, don't be late Trooper," came the order over the radio.

"Yes ma'am," was Mark's reply.

He placed the mic back on the dashboard and put his foot down on the accelerator. Home was a mere twenty minutes away.

Chris had now been tied up for about forty minutes. With the intruders still present and searching around the house any attempt to try and free himself was impossible. He had thought about trying to shout, but out here in the middle of nowhere who would hear? And what consequences would befall him if he did? A gunshot perhaps? Or a baseball bat to the head? He had tried to shift his weight on the chair as best he could but the ropes held firm and he was unable to alleviate the soreness that was beginning to start in his wrists and the tightness around his chest. He was finding it difficult to breathe. He was lucky he was wearing his boots. At least the tightness of the rope was cutting into the leather of the boots and not his skin. But they had been tied securely and trying to attempt any movement just resulted in the sound of his boots rubbing together.

Ricardo and Marco had been sitting in the kitchen, drinking the beer from the refrigerator. Occasionally one of them would go into the dining room and check on their prisoner, checking the ropes that bound his wrists and tugged at the ropes that held him to the chair.

"Hey Rookie, what's the C stand for on your badge?" Ricardo asked as he had been checking Chris' bonds and had come across Chris' name badge on the uniform.

"It's Chris," came the defeated rookie's voice.

"Well, pleased to meet you Chris," Ricardo said and mockingly extended his hand. "Oh, I forgot, you're all tied up."

The breath from Ricardo's mouth was not exactly pleasant. It was a mixture of beer and what smelt like chili lingering from hours ago. Chris turned his head away from the offending odor. It was not the thing Ricardo wanted to see.

"Hey Rookie, too good for us are you?" Ricardo asked snidely. "You think because you wear that smart looking uniform that you can push us around like low lives? It's a bit different now that *you're* all tied up huh?"

Ricardo began deliberately blowing his rancid breath into Chris' face. Chris tried to turn away but his captor grabbed him by the neck and held firm while he deliberately continued to breathe his foul scented breath into the young cop's face.

Chris' training had taught him that if he was ever captured and found himself in a predicament such as the one he was now in he was not to antagonize his captor or captors. He was taught to just try and pacify them in the hope that somewhere along the line they might let their defenses down and a conversation could start. He had to get to know his captor, and find out anything that he could use to in some way diffuse the situation and hopefully get free. But Chris' thoughts were cut short at the sound of a car approaching. Suddenly, everyone was on the alert.

Ricardo quickly drew his attention away from Chris' face and gazed at his partner Marco. The two men looked at each other intently as they heard the distant sound of a car drawing into the gravel side road leading to the house. Chris gazed up at the wall clock. It had to be Mark returning from his shift. A sense of relief swept over the rookie only to be almost taken over by a sense of awful foreboding. Here he was bound hand and foot to a chair, two guys that were either high on something or were just eager for some brutal action and nothing he could do so far to alleviate this situation. What would happen when Mark walked into the house? Chris' thoughts of his housemate being knocked out kicked to the ground or worse coursed through his tortured mind and he tugged at his bonds in a futile attempt to break free. A pointless exercise as all it achieved was acute pain in his wrists and ankles.

The sound of the car drawing nearer and nearer grew louder. Mark drove slowly up the gravel road. He was now finished and the sense of euphoria enveloped him. Now it was time to chill out, or so he thought. He viewed the house coming up ahead of him and made a glance at his housemate's motorcycle leaning on its prop and underneath the garage canopy. He drew the patrol car up alongside the bike.

Ricardo shot a glance at Chris. The thug immediately knew that the bound officer would make an attempt to shout out a warning. He quickly pulled a bandanna out of his back pocket and raced to the tied up cop. Chris' captor screwed the bandanna into a ball and pushed it against the rookie's partially closed mouth. Chris tried to resist the force against his mouth by trying to close it firmly shut, but Ricardo was wise to the rookie's move and squeezed Chris' nostrils tightly together, thus preventing Chris from being able to take in any air. If he didn't open his mouth soon he would be rendered unconscious or worse, he would suffocate. The bound officer looked into the eyes of someone demented, possibly someone on the brink of utter insanity, someone who would not care if a young rookie cop suffered. Actually, Chris had the feeling that Ricardo was enjoying making him suffer. Chris' thoughts raced through his head. It was a no go situation. He gave in and opened his mouth. The rolled up bandanna was roughly pushed into his craw. Ricardo meanly used his middle fingers to push the cloth into the rookie's mouth deeply down. Chris could feel himself gagging on the dry dirty cloth. Ricardo was no idiot. He knew that the rookie would eventually use his tongue to push the bandanna out of his mouth. The thug could not take the chance that the tied up rookie would shout a warning out, so he quickly produced another bandanna from his other pocket. He wrapped it hastily around the rookie's mouth and knotted it tightly behind his neck, thus now preventing Chris from spitting out the rolled up gag. Ricardo gazed at Marco who was showing signs of panic.

"Get behind the sofa," came the command from Ricardo.

Marco obeyed immediately and took his hiding position as instructed. Despite being in this dangerous predicament as he was, Chris' police training told him now who was the leader and who was the follower in this dangerous twosome. Ricardo retrieved the rookie's gun from the table and quickly and quietly walked up the hallway to the front door. He took his position behind it, ready for the visitor to walk in. Chris moaned miserably behind his gag.

Mark switched off the ignition and unbuckled himself from his seatbelt. He pulled off his cap and placed it on the backseat. The officer climbed out of the patrol car and securely locked it. He made his way to the front of the house, digging into his pockets to find the keys to the front door. He pulled them out. Mark was never sure with Chris whether the door was left open on the latch or been locked. He was never sure with that rookie.

The occupants of the house listened intently as they heard Mark's footsteps hit the wooden floorboards of the front porch, him coming closer to the front door. Droplets of sweat began to develop on Chris' forehead. The poor rookie thought that there had to be a way of warning Mark.

The sound of the footsteps stopped and the sound of the front door handle being turned took its place. The door hadn't been locked. Mark opened the door and sauntered in.

"Hi Rookie, where are you hiding?" was his only question.

Chris whimpered miserably at the sound of Mark's affectionate nickname for him. It was only a matter of seconds. The butt of a gun swung from behind and took the police officer unawares. It hit him squarely on the back of the head. Mark's muscular six foot frame crashed to the hallway floor. The cop was down for the count...

Mark lay sprawled out motionless on the hallway floor. Ricardo stepped from behind the front door. He gently closed it and viewed his new victim. Marco shot a glance from behind the sofa and grinned when he saw before him what had happened.

"Hey Kiddo, we've got ourselves another police officer," came a voice of triumph from Ricardo. "Help me get him inside."

Marco moved himself from behind the sofa and made his way up the hallway.

Chris gazed at the scene before him. He bit down into the bandanna gag and tried a futile attempt at struggling against his bonds in frustration yet again. But all it accomplished was more pain in his wrists and ankles.

"MMMMFFFFFF..." came the verbal protest from the bound rookie.

"Hey Rookie, looks like we got a friend of yours to join you," said the sneering Marco.

Ricardo knelt down and grabbed the unconscious cop's feet while Marco grabbed the uniformed officer's arms. Both captors pulled him up and moved him into the living room.

"What'll we do with this one?" Marco asked as both he and Ricardo struggled with the muscular cop.

"Best tie him up as well," was Ricardo's solution.

Mark's limp body finally found itself in the middle of the living room. Both captors unceremoniously let the body fall to the floor. Straightaway Ricardo went for the officer's gun holster and yanked out the weapon. There were no chances to be taken here.

"Get him over on his stomach," ordered Ricardo.

Marco gave a look of indignation. He was becoming a bit wary of taking orders. Chris viewed this reaction and knew that this could be a way of gaining the trust and confidence of one of the captors. Now, if only he had some way of communicating without the damn gag in his mouth, there could be chance of escape.

"MMMMMMFFFFF..." came the muffled sound out of Chris' gagged mouth, him trying to gain Marco's attention.

Marco shot a glance at the tied up rookie. Chris needed somehow to get Marco to remove the bandanna gag from his aching mouth. Chris tried to use his eyes to convey a sense of urgency, but Ricardo quickly intervened.

"Get the cop on his stomach and then grab some rope from the kitchen table," Ricardo said.

Marco knelt over the unconscious cop and rolled him over onto his stomach. He stood up and viewed Chris' face. He then walked into the kitchen to get the rope. Meanwhile Ricardo got to work on securing the officer's wrists. He snatched the handcuffs from Mark's belt and grabbed the cop's arms. He yanked them behind his back. The cuffs were quickly wrapped around the cop's wrists and clamped tightly in place. Next was needed the rope to tie the cop's ankles together. Marco appeared with the coil of rope in his hand.

"Give me that," barked Ricardo as he snatched the coil of rope.

He then knelt down and grabbed Mark's feet. The thug began coiling the rope around the cop's ankles, tugging at every opportunity to ensure that the cop's feet were tightly tied. Finally, when the rope was nearly finished Ricardo tied it off with a tight knot. He took a breath and stood up from the subdued cop, satisfied that the officer was now indeed his prisoner.

"Looks like we got ourselves a party tonight," Ricardo chuckled then looked at Marco.

"Now, get me a beer."

Yet another order. How many more of those would it take before Marco started to resent being pushed around? Chris' eyes viewed the reaction of the guy named Marco, working out his body language. There had to be a chance that Marco would turn on Ricardo at some point, but when? That was the weakness Chris wanted to exploit. With that, there was a chance for both him and Mark to get free.

"Why don't you get it?" was Marco's retort.

"Well, I've been busy tying up a bit of a problem, as if you hadn't noticed," came a mocking imitation of Marco's voice.

Anyone who's ever been knocked out with the butt of a gun can tell you that you dream some great dreams, but at some point you start to stir and come back to reality. And that reality is of a very sore head, your wrists cuffed behind your back (with your own handcuffs at that) and your feet securely tied with rope (rope that you asked your housemate to purchase on his way home, total irony).

"Oooooo…fuck, what the…" came the quiet murmurs from the waking cop.

Mark instinctively tried to focus his eyes and the first thing that came into vision was a pair of shining Dehner motorcycle black boots and what looked like white rope wrapped tightly around them. Mark had to blink a few times to adjust his focus on the boots. It was moments later when he confirmed that indeed it was a pair of boots bound together. He drew his gaze up from the boots, further, to view the bound and gagged Chris. Mark's reaction was one of confusion and then total fear as he tried to comprehend what was going on. He rose a bit from his position and it was then that his brain kicked into gear. Something wasn't right and suddenly he felt that he might be in a very dangerous situation. The cop's instincts told him he had to move, but carefully. It was then that Mark suddenly realized that he himself was in a similar situation of restraint. He tried to move his arms but they were pinned back behind him. The reasons for this came apparent to the police officer, the feel of the cold steel tight around each wrist told him he was securely handcuffed. His ankles didn't fare any better. Trying to move his feet did nothing but cause the leather of his highly polished police issued magnum boots to squeak. However, one saving grace, the leather of his boots was preventing the tightness of the rope to bight into his skin. Mark let out of sign of defeat and resigned to the fact that he was like his buddy, well and truly tied up, fuck, one up for the bad guys.

Chris viewed his housemate struggling against his bonds and let out a muffled warning through the tight gag. He shook his head slightly and widened his eyes to warn Mark that they had intruders in the house. Mark slowly lifted his head and turned it away from Chris to look the other way. Standing with his back to him, no more than a few feet away was Ricardo waiting impatiently for his beer. Mark spied the gun in the hand of the intruder, damn, two up for the bad guys. Marco came out of the kitchen. He was clutching two cans of beer. He held one out for Ricardo and it was quickly snatched out of his hand.

"Who's the other can for?" questioned Ricardo.

Marco viewed the second can in his hand and said, "It's for me, I thought we were going to party." Ricardo shook his head.

"No, no, my dear friend," Ricardo said and gave a nod at the bound officers. "I'm going to party with these fine young policemen. "You are going to keep watch."

"But why?" came the sheepish question from Marco.

"Because my little friend, that's the way it's going to be," Ricardo said and took a swig from the can in defiance. "You keep watch while I get our police officers ready for some fun."

Chris gave a look of concern to Mark. This was not looking good. Mark tried to move himself to alleviate the stiffness that was beginning to take hold in his bound limbs. Ricardo's attention shifted away from his partner in crime to the laying officer.

"And I think I'll start with him," Ricardo chuckled.

From the position he was laying in on the floor, stomach down, Mark could only partially see what was happening. He raised his head slightly to see Ricardo slam both the gun and the can of beer on the table. Ricardo leaned over the laying officer. Large hands grabbed at Mark's arms and pulled at him. Mark felt himself being jerked up from his laying position. Pain shot through his arms as he was pulled back.

"AAAHHH...YOU'RE BREAKING MY ARMS..." came the outburst from Mark as Ricardo pulled on the officer's limbs.

"I'll break your head if you don't do as I say!" Ricardo whispered threateningly in the suffering officer's ear. "Or do you want me to hurt your buddy there?"

Mark's muscular frame with his bound wrists and ankles didn't help him in any way to try and stand. Balance for him was not easy and Ricardo's patience was running thin. He eventually had to suffice with Mark ending up in a kneeling position.

"You're not doing yourselves any favors, keeping us like this; it's only a matt..." Mark began but his words were quickly cut off with a slap to the side of his head with Ricardo's hand.

"The only fucking favor I've got is you two, a gun, a beer and this prick!!" Ricardo thundered and his hand flew a gesture at Marco, indicating he was no more than a prick.

Marco lowered his head as though in shame or perhaps in defeat.

Chris could only watch the scenario being played out in front of him. It wasn't looking good. He could see that Mark was not faring well with the physical abuse he was getting from Ricardo. Not only that, but Ricardo's verbal bashing at Marco was showing signs of resentment brewing. Chris though, had not been idle; he had been trying to get free. Sadly, he had not fared well. He had tried to get hold of the knot that bound his wrists together, using his fingertips to somehow pick at it and maybe eventually loosen it. With that accomplished he would only need both Ricardo and Marco to leave the room for a few minutes. Chris could then tackle his bound torso and ankles free and raise the alarm by using either the phone or radio in the kitchen. But he had been tied too well and all his struggling resulted in was acute pain as the nylon cord bit into his flesh.

"Look, you have got to understand that keeping us hostage isn't doing you any good," Mark tried to reason with Ricardo. "Turn yourself in now…"

"Listen Officer, I've had about enough of your shit," Ricardo said and grabbed Mark's head and pulled it back.

Instinctively Mark opened his mouth to cry out in pain but the tight grip was greeted with a cascade of flowing beer. Ricardo cried out a mocking laugh and cackled in the officer's face, "Get that down Mr. Police Officer, we're going to get you in the mood." The beer kept flowing from the can and Mark tried to move his head but Ricardo had it in a vise-like grip. The beer continued to pour down the helpless officer's throat. Mark was choking on the continuing flow of alcohol but then it stopped, his head suddenly released.

"Hey Mr. Police Officer, lets get your buddy a beer," Ricardo said and now directed his attention on the chair bound rookie. "Marco, get a few more beers for the police officers."

All this time Marco had been watching from the kitchen door. He was watching his pal take control of the situation, watching him play out a cruel game on the unsuspecting officers, him wondering where it was going to lead. When would he and Ricardo start moving on again? He turned and did as instructed and pulled out more beer from the refrigerator.

Ricardo had moved away from Mark, leaving the officer bound hand and foot, kneeling, and beer dripping out of his mouth. Now, Ricardo was standing next to the bound and gagged rookie.

"You can't have a beer with that in your mouth," Ricardo said and began to tug at the bandanna that held Chris' gag firmly in place.

It took only moments to realize that he needed to untie the knot from behind Chris' neck to release the gag. The smell of stale booze and sweat from Chris' captor was overbearing and the urge to actually gag was imminent. Suddenly, the pressure of the tightly bound bandanna from across his mouth came free and Chris' immediate reaction was to spit out the gag. With his mouth now free the rookie took a combination of coughs and deep breaths.

"Fucking cunt," was the words that came next out of Chris' mouth.

Again however, Ricardo was ready to administer his own kind of answer. He pushed his forearm against the rookie's throat.

"Now I can carry on pressing hard against your windpipe, and maybe you'll pass out, or it could be worse," Ricardo said with a sneer. "Up to you Rookie, what's it to be?"

Ricardo slowly released his arm, pulling it away from Chris' throat to allow him to speak.

"Okay, okay, whatever," came the tired sounding words from Chris' mouth.

"Good, good Chris, now lets drink a few beers," Ricardo said and Marco came into the room with a four-pack in his hands.

Ricardo pulled one can away, pulled the ring and the foaming beer sprayed out.

"Fucking party, party," cried Ricardo. "Hey Chris, lets drink."

The open can of beer was pressed hard against the rookie's lips. Chris tried to keep his mouth closed, but a sudden punch to his chest caused him to try to shout out in agony. The sudden flow of cold beer into the rookie's mouth and throat prevented that.

"How long was this going to last?" questioned Marco to himself.

Marco drew a swig from his can of beer and watched Ricardo as he continued to pour beer down the rookie's throat. Chris tried to struggle, twisting his head, trying to avoid the spilling beer, but Ricardo wasn't having any of that. He resorted to rough tactics. He bent over and grasped Chris' balls in his hand and with a leering smile gave a slight squeeze.

"Hey Chris, good beer isn't it?" asked the sinister voice. "Hey Chris, answer me, good beer isn't it?"

Chris didn't need to be warned what would happen if he didn't chug down the beer. The bound rookie had no choice, he had to submit. He allowed the beer to carry on its deluge down his throat. This had the desired effect for Ricardo whose sweaty hand caressed Chris' balls, and just occasionally gave a slight tug and squeeze...just to show who was in control.

Mark could only watch as Chris had the indignity of his manhood being held in the hand of some deadbeat hell bent on perverse and twisted fun. How much beer was it going to be before the tied up rookie was intoxicated? Mark was beginning to have his own problems though, seeing as his knees were starting to throb with pain. He clenched his teeth, trying hard to suppress the feelings, but with his hands cuffed and his feet tied tightly together there was no way to try and adjust his posture and relieve at least some of the agonizing pain.

"You've got to let me up," finally pleaded the kneeling cop.

Both Marco and Ricardo suddenly drew their attention to Mark. Ricardo pulled away the spilling beer and Chris was able to catch a few gulps of air. The clenched hand around his balls was pulled away and for a few moments there was relief.

Mark turned his attention to Ricardo who was now slowly walking over to him. Ricardo's eyes were open wide with what could only be described as madness. The can of beer that he was holding suddenly went hurling across the room, spraying the last remnants of beer against the wall.

"You want to fucking get up?" Ricardo asked.

"I'm hurting in the legs, you've got me tied up and I can't do anything," Mark gasped. "Just let me up."

A booted foot came crashing against Mark's shoulder and he fell sideways onto the other shoulder.

"AAAAGGGHH!!!" screamed Mark.

Almost immediately the sole of a boot was pressed down hard against his cheek.

"So Mr. Officer is hurting," was the sarcastic rant from Ricardo.

The boot pressed harder.

"Fuuuuccckinggg bastar…" Mark began but his words were cut short as Ricardo's boot pressed down, stopping the bound cop from making any coherent words.

"Leave him alone!" came Chris' voice.

"Fucking hell, they all want to talk now," Ricardo laughed and the boot suddenly left Mark's cheek.

Ricardo marched over to Chris. The balled up bandanna that had silenced the rookie earlier was pushed savagely back into Chris' mouth and the other bandanna was securely tied in place. Chris was now no nearer to escape than he was before.

"RRRRMMMFFF…" Chris whimpered miserably at being gagged yet again.

Mark lay on the floor, immobile, fearing what was next to happen. His forehead was beginning to form beads of sweat. Suddenly he heard footsteps entering the kitchen, drawers being opened and closed, cutlery being pushed around.

"Just what I need," came Ricardo's elated voice.

Mark heard the footsteps come back into the room, and then he felt his head being pulled by his hair. He was going to instinctively shout out in painful protest but a cloth was then pushed hard into his mouth. Ricardo's finger pushed the cloth further into the cop's mouth, till only the white color of the cloth was visible between Mark's teeth. Ricardo produced another cloth and it too was wrapped around Mark's head, pulled tight and securely tied behind his big neck.

"FUCKING COPS, I've had about enough, I want to have some fun and all you can do is whine and moan," Ricardo ranted. "Well let's see this cop start dancing. Marco my buddy lets get the music going."

Both convicts spied the CD player stacked on a unit at the far end of the room. Marco walked over to the CD player and began fingering the control console, presumably looking for the "ON" button.

"Marco, get that music playing, we're going to watch our officers dance," Ricardo ordered and both Chris and Mark glanced at each other.

What was happening?

The CD player hummed into action. Marco pressed the "PLAY" button and the music and lyrics of rock band played out from the speakers, not loud enough to get Ricardo's head starting to sway to the music.

"Hey man, you got good vibes," Ricardo said and beamed a smile.

Mark and Chris continued to exchange glances, still worrying what the convicts, in particular Ricardo, had in store for them. Chris glanced at the wall clock. It was approaching seven thirty PM. He had been bound for ages now it seemed his hands now hopelessly numb from the ropes bighting into his wrists. His ankles had not fared any better, even his boots now could not prevent the tightness of the ropes cutting off blood circulation to his feet. His mouth again stuffed fully with a bandanna, tied tightly in place, thankfully for small mercies the beer spilled down his throat helped to quench the rookie's dryness of his mouth.

Mark was now standing upright, though like Chris the effects of his bindings were taking their toll and had to also concentrate on his balance. The CD player went silent for a moment as it changed tracks and a love ballad came on.

"You like to dance Officer?" Ricardo questioned the bound officer as he stepped up to him, them now facing each other.

The barrel of the gun was raised and put against Mark's chin before it was allowed to caress the facial features of the gagged officer. Mark tried to keep his cool, but he felt the droplets of sweat from his forehead trickle down. Ricardo watched as the gag gave the slight motion of the cop's erratic breathing in and out and in and out. The gun was moved slowly away and was put on the table, Ricardo still staring at the cop. Suddenly Mark felt an arm wrapped firmly around his shoulder. Ricardo moved the cop forward and Mark was forced to take small hops to be sure he would not fall over. Ricardo's left hand clasped Mark's scrotum and gave a gentle squeeze. Mark bit into the cloth gag to alleviate the pain that was coming from his squeezed and violated balls.

"Let's dance," Ricardo gently whispered in Mark's ear.

Ricardo began to gently sway the bound and gagged officer to the subtle music. Mark suddenly had to hobble to get in step with his captor. Wearing heavy boots that were bound together was not having the desired effect and it was becoming increasingly difficult to stand let alone keep up his hobbling.

Chris gazed at the scene before him, a police officer bound and gagged and being held by his balls by what could be a convicted psycho trying to dance to a love ballad, surreal or what? The bound rookie tried another attempt at the rope that bound his wrists, slowly twisting and tugging but it came to nothing. He allowed himself the luxury of a defeated sounding sigh through his gagged mouth. Marco throughout had been watching the scene unfold as well. He was not sure what Ricardo's motives were. They were only going to have broken in, steal some clothes and food and anything else they would need to get them safely across the border. But now, with two police officers being held hostage things were not exactly going their way. This had not been part of the plan when they had broken into the house. He shifted his weight from one foot to the other, becoming agitated that time was pressing on. They needed to get going, and soon. Ricardo was high no doubt about that. But he still had the presence of mind to know what he was doing. Too long locked away in a prison, manhandled by inmates and uniformed wardens alike, made to beg, assaulted verbally and mentally, sexually too. Ricardo had become bitter and twisted. The sight of a uniform had become something to despise and to take out his anger and rage on, but immediately. When Ricardo had realized that they had broken into a police officer's house it became evident to Marco what his new plans would be. And then, the sight of the handsome rookie confirmed and cemented those plans into place. Ricardo had learned that the best way was to torment his victims slowly and allow himself the pleasure of seeing them suffer, them not knowing their fate.

Mark was finding it increasingly difficult to maintain his balance despite Ricardo holding him upright. Mark's muscular weight was pressing down on his feet.

"MMMMMMPPPPP...NO," was the officer's muffled plea.

Ricardo released his grip on Mark and pulled himself away to stare at the trapped cop. The convict watched in fascination as the cloth strip that covered the officer's mouth again moved back and forth from labored breathing. He loved the way the cop was suffering in front of him. Beads of sweat were now slowly dripping into Mark's eyes and making them sting. The officer was constantly blinking, trying to alleviate the pain. Ricardo though was relishing every moment of this.

"Hey Officer, before this day is out you'll be dancing to another tune and that is a fucking promise," Ricardo said and pushed the bound up cop away from him.

With no balance Mark fell backward, crashing down to the floor. He lay still. The music CD suddenly finished. There was a moment of silence.

"MMMMMMMPHHH...FUC...KIN...!!!" came the gagged sounds from Chris.

He tugged and turned against the ropes binding him to the chair, putting all his strength and might into it, trying to escape and help his buddy. A swift hard slap against his face suddenly put a stop to his efforts. Again Ricardo's sweaty hand crashed hard against the rookie's handsome face. He grabbed and squeezed Chris' cheeks tightly, the convict's eyes blind and ablaze with rage.

"Lets see what you can do Officer Chris," Ricardo seethed and the rookie's eyes widened with not only pain from the slaps and subsequent grabbing of his cheeks, but the thought that this vile shit was now going to play with *him*...

Chris watched as Ricardo released his grip on his cheeks. The thug pushed Chris' face away and gave the rookie a glare. For some reason he trailed a fingertip along Chris' forehead.

"You're such a pretty rookie boy," Ricardo sniggered. "Do you know if you were in your pretty cop uniform in the pen with me I would make sure that you were mine."

Chris watched in horror as Ricardo picked up the gun from the table.

"Marco my dear, dear friend," Ricardo said. "Let's untie our rookie and have some fun with him."

Marco pushed himself from his leaning position and walked over to the tied up rookie. He stepped carefully over the body of the half conscious Mark, him still lying on his back, the wind knocked out of him, his face looking up toward the ceiling. It seemed as if Mark was trying to comprehend what was happening, but something in the back of his mind was gnawing away, something that was not altogether clear, something that was not a long ago memory. If only...

Marco stepped behind the chair that Chris was tightly bound to and began to play with the knots that held the rookie upright. He picked at the knot. Chris allowed himself a deep breath through his nostrils as the rope wrapped around his torso began to slacken. The rookie could feel his chest relax as the tight rope began to loosen. Marco then pulled the rope away and Chris was able to move slightly away from the back of the chair which had been pushing relentlessly into the back of his shoulder blades for hours. Marco moved around and began to tackle the rookie's bound feet. Marco's fingernails began to pick at the tight knot that held Chris' feet together. It took time but the ropes soon began to loosen. Marco was then unwinding the rope from around the rookie's ankles. Chris was finally able to slowly pull his booted feet apart. He let out a sigh behind his gag. Marco pulled the rope away from Chris' black shining boots. Now all that held the rookie prisoner was his bound wrists still behind the back of the chair.

"Okay Rookie, now get up slowly," Ricardo said and held the gun out toward Chris' muscular frame.

Marco stood up and moved away, coiling the rope that had held the rookie prisoner. Chris eased himself up slowly, trying to maintain his balance. He was okay. It seemed that the effects of the beer hadn't really done him in. He slowly maneuvered his arms over the back of the chair, standing himself upright, almost at attention, his legs slightly apart. His captors drank in the sight of him in that position with gusto. The rookie was movie star handsome in their eyes. It would not be long before full blood circulation would be back in the rookie's limbs. Chris flexed his fingers, trying in some way to get at the knot that bound his wrists together. But the ropes were knotted in a way that it would remain away from his prying fingers.

"How good a dancer are you Chris?" Ricardo asked.

The rookie's eyes widened. So he was going to have him dancing as well.

"MMMMMPPPHHH," came the muffled sound from Chris' gagged mouth.

"Hey Rookie, don't be shy, at least your feet aren't tied up like your buddy over there," Ricardo said and swung the gun in the direction of Mark, still lying on his back.

"Marco, play that love song again, let Chris have a little dance," Ricardo ordered.

Ricardo walked forward and stood in front of the rookie. He pressed the barrel of the gun into Chris' chest. Chris stood straight, a look of fear in his eyes, breathing heavily through his nostrils.

"You're going to dance Rookie, understood?" Ricardo asked.

Chris gazed into the convict's bloodshot eyes and acknowledged the threat with a slight nod. Marco fingered the CD player, trying to find the button that would play the love ballad again. Marco figured it out and pressed the required button. The love ballad played again.

Ricardo put the gun into his back jeans pocket and extended his arms out. He gently grabbed Chris' sides and began to sway to the music. He started to force Chris to move along with him. The rookie had no option but to move to the rhythm of the music. He was in his younger years a pretty good dancer and now Ricardo had found someone that at least seemed to have some rhythm.

Chris played along and allowed Ricardo to lead him in this insanely merry fiasco, but being allowed to move and sway allowed the rookie's feet and upper body that had been tightly tied for some time to begin to have the blood circulating. Even in his tightly clad boots Chris could feel sensation returning.

"Pretty good dancer for a pig," Ricardo commented as he moved Chris into the center of the room.

"MMMMPPPHHH..." Chris replied behind his gag.

The rookie continued to become more active in his dance moves and Ricardo gave him a smile of satisfaction. Chris' leather boots creaked as he began to become more agile in his footwork. Ricardo looked down and gave an admiring glance at the shiny glint they had.

Mark had had time to recover himself after being pushed down. He used the time to relax his body and try to gather his thoughts. There was still something that was not coming through to him. The music in the background wasn't helping as were the quick glances at Ricardo and Chris dancing together. Then it happened and it was coming together...

The phone rang...

"Hi, sorry we can't take the call. We're either on patrol in which case you can reach us on the radio, or out of the house. Please leave a message and we'll get back to you."

Even with the CD music on the answering machine phone message could not be ignored. It had become disruptive and a sudden point of focus for everyone in the room. There was a short audio tone from the machine, a beeping sound to be exact. Someone was about to speak.

"Hey buddy, where are you with the beers? We've been standing at the bar for the past God knows how long," the voice on the answering machine said. "Get your ass here now or else."

The connection went dead. It had been Alma from the station.

Mark closed his eyes and suddenly it came to him. He was meant to be at the bar with her and the other officers. He opened his eyes, realizing now that this could be the way of getting free. Alma wasn't one for being stood up by any of the officers. She would ring again, and again, and again.

Ricardo pulled away from Chris and immediately pulled out the gun, sticking the barrel into the rookie's chest.

"Get yourself down on the floor Chris," Ricardo instructed.

With no choice in the matter Chris kneeled down and then slowly laid himself down on his stomach. He was now next to Mark. He turned his head, as did Mark and they both locked eyes.

Marco switched the CD player off and gazed at Ricardo.

"We need to get away, we fucking need to get out of here!" came the panicked voice of Marco.

Ricardo turned on his heels and faced his friend.

"Listen, don't fuck with me, I got to think, I got to this…" Ricardo began but suddenly stopped himself, staring into empty space.

"Ricardo?" Marco asked, looking at his partner in crime.

Ricardo stood motionless. Marco suddenly realized what was happening. He had seen this happen before. It had happened in the cell he had shared with Ricardo.

Ricardo was formulating a plan, strangely enough, another form of escape, only it wasn't from metal bars, but from a brick house outside of a small town.

The two bound and gagged officers lay still on the floor. The only sound from them was their faint and labored breathing. What would happen to them? Time would tell.

"Look around the house, get some of their clothes and shoes," Ricardo said. "We're going to have to get out of these stinking clothes, change ourselves."

Chris suddenly felt a kick on the sole of his right boot. He looked up.

"Come on Rookie, get up, we're going to see what we can find so we can get out of here," Ricardo ordered.

Chris struggled to turn himself around and raise himself, but with his hands still tied behind him he could only sit up. The soles of his boots could not get a grip on the floor to allow him to get up and stand. Ricardo knelt down and grabbed the rookie from under the arms and hauled him up.

"Do as you're told Rookie and your buddy there will stay alive," Ricardo said and both captor and captive gazed down at Mark.

Chris reluctantly nodded. Sounds of drawers being opened and closed came from the officer's bedrooms. Marco was frantically searching for clothes and shoes, anything to change into, anything that could disguise their appearance.

Ricardo stood in front of Chris. They both looked into each other's eyes, both captor and captive registered fear.

"Going to get us some wheels pretty rookie cop," Ricardo said. "And you and your tied up buddy are going for a ride."

Chris' screwed his face in puzzlement. Where were the wheels coming from?

The phone rang again.

"Hi, sorry we can't take the call. We're either on patrol in which case you can reach us on the radio, or out of the house. Please leave a message and we'll get back to you."

Ricardo grabbed Chris by the arm and frog marched him out into the kitchen. He took the rookie out through the side door to the carport where Mark's patrol car stood. Mark watched helplessly as the rookie was taken. Alma's voice again rang out a message. Ricardo and Marco were too busy to listen this time for they knew that time was now precious and escape was essential.

"Where's the keys?" Ricardo asked, squeezing Chris' arm tightly, waiting for an answer.

"MMMMMM…Don'tmmmmmm have mmmm…" was the rookie's muffled reply.

The barrel of the gun was suddenly pushed into the centre of Chris' forehead. The rookie squeezed his eyes shut, waiting for the sound of the trigger being pressed and then oblivion. It seemed a lifetime for Chris, but in reality only a few seconds went by. A moment of weakness and tears welled up in the trapped rookie's eyes.

"NOOOOOO…mmmmmmppphhh…" Chris pleaded behind his gag, his eyes still closed.

The feel of the cold metal against his sweating forehead was awful. Chris began to recount his past memories, surely this happens when you're about to die he thought.

Mark lay still on his back. He stared blankly up at the ceiling. Even Marco's rummaging through the rooms didn't deter him. He was transfixed. His only thought was the hope that Alma would make the decision to come out to the house to see what was keeping him detained. He allowed himself the pleasure of moving his limbs as much as his restraints would allow. What did the future hold for him and his partner he wondered? What indeed? And then the sound, the awful sound of a gunshot ringing out from the carport. Mark closed his eyes. It was now only a matter of time…

It was silent. The last dim sounds of the gunshot faded. Mark still had his eyes shut. Maybe when he opened them it would be nothing more than a dream, all of this would have been nothing more than a dream. Things would, when he came through the door to the house be normal again. Chris would be sitting there all hunky in his briefs, the rookie's hands wrapped around a cold beer, watching TV. They would give each other the briefest account of the day's events. Mark would then change out of his uniform and take himself in the patrol to see Alma and the other officers at the bar in Ridgemount, all of it simply routine. But that wasn't today. As Mark opened his eyes he knew that it wasn't a dream.

Marco stood in the hallway. He was holding two large sports bags, no doubt the bags contained clothing and shoes from the officer's bedrooms. He stood motionless after the gunshot went off. He then dropped the bags and ran out toward the carport. Mark was on his own. A time to be decisive, he had to get free. He didn't know what had happened to Chris, but the gunshot had made the decision for Mark that he was not going to be the next in line for a bullet. He needed to get up and try to reach either the radio or the phone to summon help. It would be the phone he quickly thought. At least he would be able to just need to press the last number to get through to Alma. The gag posed a problem though but first things first. As he pulled himself up to a sitting upright position he pulled his bound feet up to him. His knees pressed up against his chest, an almighty push would be required. With that he would be upright and then be able to try to make his way on bound booted feet to the phone.

Marco stood in the doorway from the kitchen to the carport. He quickly surveyed the area. No sign of the rookie Chris.

"Ricardo, where the fuck is the rookie?" Marco asked as Ricardo came back in.

Ricardo gave Marco a blank look and said, "Get everything! We're going!"

"What about the cop inside?" Marco asked.

"He's coming along," Ricardo replied.

It took Mark a couple of attempts to build up momentum to push himself up but he had the good fortune to go to the gym regularly. Doing squats and exercises had now paid off. He was now on his feet and slowly pulling himself up to a stance of attention. He bit into the gag as he straightened himself. Time was everything. He looked over at the phone. He had to make it across without making any noise. Mark estimated that about three big jumps would suffice. He would then turn himself around, lean down and with some accurate positioning he would push the last number redial. That would be it. A muffled cry for help down the phone to Alma and hopefully the cavalry would come running to the rescue. It was that plain and simple.

Marco thrust the cases to Ricardo who swung around with them and threw them into the back seat of the patrol car.

"Get the cop," Ricardo ordered.

Marco's fear of being caught superseded his annoyance of being ordered around. He turned on his dirty trainers and went back into the house.

Mark bent slowly down by the knees to make his first jump. He gazed at his bound feet and then looked up to try to calculate where he would land. He had to be precise. Again he checked himself and took the jump. He landed, his knees bent. He gave himself seconds to adjust his balance but he had done it. Mark allowed himself a brief pause before attempting his next jump. This was going t o be alright. Again he bent his knees, ready to jump. He jumped, but further than expected. Mark closed his eyes in triumph. Now he only needed to take a few hobbled steps to be near the phone. Despite the tight bindings around his ankles Mark knew that if he took it slowly and carefully he could maneuver his feet a few centimeters in front, just enough to put him in front of the phone. He pushed his right foot against the rope and moved it forward. Mark heard the sound of his right boot squeeze against his left boot. The cop took a deep breath through his nostrils. He stood still for a moment then pushed his left booted foot forward again. The sound of boot against boot could be heard, not far now.

Mark wasn't sure what happened. But suddenly he was lying on the floor. He was now looking at a pair of well worn dirty trainers. He carried his gaze up till he could see the face of Marco. Mark took a deep breath of defeat. Marco had walked in on Mark's attempts to reach the phone and swiftly made it clear that the cop was not going to get it by a violent push in the small of the officer's back.

Marco knelt down and cupped the cop's face in his big broad hand.

"Don't try anything stupid Officer," Marco said softly. "He's done something to your partner and knowing Ricardo it isn't nice. Don't let him do something nasty to you too."

Mark suddenly realized the impact of what Marco was saying. Indeed, something had happened to Chris. Mark was now on his own.

"Come on, on your feet," Marco said and Mark felt himself being pulled up.

All his efforts of getting away were now all but gone. He was a cop at the mercy of two convicts, one at least who had no feeling for human life, the other, well, who knew?

Mark stood upright. Marco knelt down and began to pick at the tight knot that bound the officer's ankles together. Soon Mark could feel his ankles slowly come apart. The cop felt relief as he could feel sensation almost immediately fill his feet.

"MMMMFFFF…thmmmanks…" came the distorted sound of gratitude behind the gag.

"Take me to the car keys," Marco commanded.

Mark gazed down at his right side pocket.

"Okay," Marco said and delved his hand into the officer's trousers.

The thug pulled out two sets of keys. Marco could differentiate between both; one was for the patrol car, the other for the handcuffs that bound Mark's wrists.

"Outside cop, we're going for a ride," Marco said and holding the Mark by his arm walked the officer out of the house to the carport.

Ricardo stood at the side of the patrol car, holding the handgun firmly in his hand. Sunlight had now gone and in its place the purple glow of evening. This would be perfect cover to get away.

"Okay Officer, play this right and you won't end up like your pal," Ricardo said in a threatening tone.

Mark took a gaze as best he could around the carport. Chris was not to be seen.

"Get the cop in the driver seat, I've got something planned," Ricardo said to Marco.

Marco roughly moved Mark to the driver's side and opened the door.

"Now listen carefully Officer, do as you're told, okay?" Ricardo asked and then nodded at Marco. "Now, we're going to take that gag out and un-cuff you. We're going to put you in the driver's seat, cuff you to the steering wheel and you're going to drive out of here to somewhere else. Now, you try anything stupid and I'll make sure that the gun that will be pointing in your back from where I'll be sitting behind you will go off. You'll be gone and no one will know where you or your rookie buddy has gone. Understand?"

Mark nodded. Marco grabbed the cloth that held the gag in place and began to untie it. Mark felt the tightness around his cheeks ease and within moments he was able to spit out the gag.

"Release his hands," Ricardo said and Marco did as instructed.

More than anything now was to get away Mark thought. But how long would it be before someone would be coming looking for the officers? Mark felt the cuffs being released from his wrists. Once free he brought his hands in front of him to rub the blood circulation back into them.

"Okay, now get in," Ricardo ordered, swinging the gun in the direction of the driver's door.

Marco opened the door and the subdued police officer stepped in.

"Marco, cuff him to the steering wheel, he's going to be our chauffeur," Ricardo said.

Mark sat in the driver's seat and found his left wrist quickly handcuffed to the steering wheel. Ricardo leaned over and pulled the driver's seatbelt across Mark's chest and clamped it in. Ricardo then quickly yanked on the belt buckle, pulling up the excess, almost tying Mark to the driver's seat.

"Just want to make sure you're comfortable," was Ricardo's sarcastic comment.

"What have you done with Chris?" were Mark's first coherent words.

"Don't worry about him, worry about yourself," Ricardo retorted nastily.

Mark could hear Marco get in the back seat of the patrol car. Ricardo opened the back door and stepped in, gun still at the ready. Once both of the cop's captors had adjusted themselves in the back seat of the car Marco handed the ignition key to the secured police officer.

"Now remember Mr. Police Officer, there is a gun pointing at the back of your seat," Ricardo stated. "Do anything stupid and it's a bullet in you. Now start up and let's go."

Mark stuck the key in the ignition and turned it. The car engine purred into action.

"Where are we going?" questioned Mark.

Ricardo leaned over and whispered in the cop's ear, "To hell Mr. Police Officer, we're going to hell." As he whispered in the cop's ear Ricardo's tongue slithered over his lobe.

Mark pushed the patrol car into gear and moved off, leaving whatever hope and rescue…and an officer somewhere behind…

It was about ten PM and an area outside Ridge mount had been cordoned off with police vehicles and roadblocks. The non-appearance of a cop who was as regular as clockwork in keeping any appointment or meeting was met with caution. But receiving no reply from the phone or the patrol car radio, well, it just gave in to Officer Alma Hacker's female intuition.

"Okay, let me get this clear in my head," Officer Matthews asked Alma. "You and Officer Mark Tyler were due to meet after his shift in Annie's bar?"

Officer Matthews had been called from the next district police station. Alma, short and well rounded stood in the center of a living room.

"Always routine, whenever our shifts finished with the other guys we would get together and chill," Alma replied softly.

She was bighting her lower lip.

"And the rookie that lived here, what about him?" questioned Officer Matthews.

Alma took another gaze around the room. For all the activity that had happened a few hours ago it was relatively tidy. Save for a few items and bits of cut rope everything seemed only slightly disheveled. A pair of officers was examining the broken glass from the kitchen floor. Alma felt something was wrong, very wrong. She would have at least had Chris answer her to tell her that Mark was on his way, but to hear nothing from both of them was unheard of. She shook her head at Officer Matthew's question. She could not tell him a thing.

"Looks like the bedrooms have been ransacked," came an officer's comment from his search throughout the house. "Clothes and shoes missing..."

"I'm not one to make wild guesses Alma, but there is something not adding up," Officer Matthews said. "Two officers missing, house ransacked, missing clothes, broken glass on the inside of the kitchen, and no patrol car."

"I think we've got ourselves a hostage situation," said a voice from the doorway of the house.

Silhouetted against the porch light was a figure that all the officers drew their attention to. They narrowed their eyes to make out who it was. The figure slowly walked into the light of the house.

Standing there was a man of about five feet ten. He was dressed smartly in an all black tailored suit, the usual uniform of the FBI. He stood in black shoes that were cleaned to a high shine, his legs slightly apart.

"Agent Adam Brooks," he said.

The FBI agent pulled aside his suit jacket to show his ID which was inside the jacket pocket. Both Matthews and Alma immediately noticed the gun holster strapped tightly to his firm chest. He put his ID back inside his jacket and extended his hand. Matthews shook it as Alma gazed at the handsome agent of the law. He was no more than thirty, built like an athletic runner, maybe a swimmer, hell, maybe both. He beamed a smile to Alma and gave her a courteous nod.

"I'm afraid we've got a situation here that isn't exactly pleasant," he said, showing concern to his audience of police and forensics officers.

"What do you mean a hostage situation?" was the question that hung in the air.

The FBI agent looked around and pointed at a chair. The forensics officer nodded. The agent dragged the chair up and sat down. His firm thighs stretched out over the seat of the chair. He was almost too large for it, his big feet tucked under the seat.

"It looks like we had two prisoners escape from Wainwright Penn during the early hours of this morning," the FBI agent stated.

There was a sudden silence over the crime scene as "Wainwright" was mentioned. It was a place for the criminally insane at one point not so long ago, but apparently had been re-graded to mentally unstable, not much difference really.

"I'd be surprised if we don't find some bodies in the next few hours," Adam Brooks said in a solemn sounding tone of voice.

"What the fuck is going on? Who are these two guys that got out of a maximum security prison?" Alma asked.

Brooks took a glance at the female officer and from his training in profiles he instantly knew that this woman was keenly interested in the welfare of her missing work colleagues.

"I think you'd better come outside Sir, we found something," said a forensics officer.

Agent Brooks pulled his muscular frame up from the chair and made his way out toward the carport. Two forensics officers stood in a huddle, both of them looking down at the concrete floor.

"Hey guys, what have we got?" Brooks asked and both agents turned to the suited FBI man.

"Looks like we got some blood, almost certainly human," came the blunt reply.

It was night and the occupants of a certain patrol car were driving slowly through the dark country lanes of Ridgemount County. The uniformed officer was handcuffed to the steering wheel. He was driving under the anguish that a gun was pointing into his back from one of his backseat occupants, his seatbelt strapped tightly across his torso in a manner that prevented sudden movement. Mark viewed the open expanses of the country through the windshield, wishing he could escape, but he was trapped.

"Fuck Ricardo, where are we going?" Marco asked, sounding excitable.

"As far away as possible," Ricardo replied.

Both escapees stared out into blackness with only the headlights of the patrol car illuminating the way ahead.

"Hey Mark, you got a map?" Ricardo asked the cop snidely.

Mark looked up into his rearview mirror and saw his two captors. Marco was leaning back into the seat while Ricardo was sitting forward, his head leaning against Marco's headrest. The occasional feel of the gun barrel sticking into his back reminded the cop that he was still very much their captive. If he only knew what had happened to Chris.

"There's one in the glove compartment," Mark replied.

"Okay Mark, why don't you get it out?" Ricardo snickered.

"Ah, a bit difficult with my left hand cuffed to the steering wheel and my right not being able to reach over that far," Mark replied smugly.

Mark immediately felt his left ear grabbed and then it was being twisted.

"AAAAHHH…FUCK!!" Mark screamed in a man's pain as his captor continued quickly twisting his ear.

"Now listen carefully Mark, listen very carefully, if you want to keep your ear, understand?" Ricardo seethed. "Now, pull over…"

Mark gave a nod and almost immediately Ricardo released the officer's ear. The patrol car slowed down and Mark pulled into a small clearing. Trees surrounded the car from view of the main road. They were hidden.

"Keys," ordered Ricardo and Mark yanked the keys from the ignition.

He handed them over to the back of the car. Ricardo grabbed them. A hand appeared between the front seats and released the seatbelt from around the captured police officer's torso.

"Okay, let's have ourselves a rest," Ricardo stated. "Hey Mark, want to piss?"

"I need to stretch my legs, and yes, I need to piss," Mark said in a totally demoralized sounding voice.

Mark leaned over and rested his head on the steering wheel. It was a matter of seconds when suddenly tears welled up in his eyes. He began to sob. He could not take this anymore. He had had enough of the punishment, the torments, the abuse, physically and mentally. He was tired and hungry; he was a cop who had been beaten down by a couple of no good scum. How could this be? How could this have happened? As he then wiped away the slow trickle of tears down his cheeks it came to him, it was Chris. He wasn't so much concerned for himself, but for the young rookie who he didn't have much to say to, day in, day out, for the past God knew how long they had been sharing the house for. Now, in the midst of it all Mark had reached some kind of turning point.

There was silence from the passengers in the back of the patrol car.

"Hey, are you crying?" Marco asked the cop.

Mark didn't answer. He watched through watery eyes as the teardrops slapped onto his boots.

"Hey Mr. Police Officer are you crying?" Ricardo asked this time of the emotionally exhausted cop.

Mark raised his head from the steering wheel and gazed into the rearview mirror.

"Fucking hell guys, you've got me, please tell me what you've done to Chris," Mark tearfully inquired.

"Ha, ha, the hard cop *is* crying," laughed Ricardo. "So, do you want that piss?"

Mark gave a feeble nod.

"Okay Mark, lets get you out and into the trees," Ricardo said.

The two thugs got out of the back seat of the patrol car, Ricardo pointing the gun at Mark as he opened the driver's door.

"Marco, hold this while I unlock the cuffs," Ricardo said and handed the gun to Marco.

He then rummaged through his jeans pocket for the keys to the handcuffs.

Ricardo found the key and unlocked the cuff from the steering wheel.

"Okay Mark out you go and put your hands out in front of you," Ricardo ordered.

Mark pulled his feet out and let them touch the grass. He then pulled himself into the cool night air. He held his arms out as instructed and Ricardo quickly clamped the empty half of the handcuffs onto his right wrist. Mark's wrists were now bound in front of him.

"That's a good boy, now Marco is going to take you over to those trees so that you can shit and piss," Ricardo said, squeezing the officer's upper arm as he spoke to him. "And when you've done all that we might allow you to have a rest. Can't have a big hunky police officer crying all night can we?"

Mark simply looked forlornly at his captor and Ricardo let go of the officer's arm.

Ricardo gave a nod of his head instructing Marco to take Mark out into the forest of trees.

Despite it being night time a full moon was giving out plenty of illumination. Ricardo opened his left hand to reveal the keys to the patrol car.

He walked back to the trunk and traced his fingers along the side of the car. Then he stroked the trunk, moved his hands down to the lock and his forefinger suddenly picked at a hole, a hole produced by a gunshot. Ricardo inserted the key into the lock and turned. The trunk opened and the moonlight hit the figure of a rookie laying in a fetal position, hands tied behind his back, his mouth tightly gagged. Ricardo leaned over and checked the side of the rookie's head. A bruise was swelling up

"I'm sorry, I didn't want to hurt you that badly," Ricardo whispered.

Ricardo's fingers followed down from the rookie's head, over the muscular torso and to the black boots. The thug caressed the boots and then slowly leaned over and kissed them.

"You're going to be mine forever," Ricardo whispered again.

He placed his hand on the chest of the rookie and gave himself a satisfying smile as the muscular chest motioned up and down.

Chris was still alive…

Agent Brooks knelt down and gazed at the droplets of blood on the concrete floor of the carport.

"Well guys, any ideas?" he questioned the forensics officers.

"Well first checks tells us its human, and that's about it," one of the officers replied. "Can't do much more till we're back at the lab."

"Well, before going back to the lab can you think of some kind of scenario?" Brooks asked.

"Well, it's the only blood splat we can find," the forensics officer said. "I'm thinking not a fatal wound, a cut maybe, maybe someone hit with a blunt object."

Agent Brooks pulled himself up and laid his hands on his hips. He bit his bottom lip and then he spoke.

"I can only surmise that we had a break in here, the broken glass in the kitchen shows that," the agent said. "The rooms look like they've been ransacked. There's been activity in the lounge. The chair looks like its been used for something. Beer stains on the carpet, maybe the thieves were surprised by the officers. However, they somehow got the better of the officers, overpowered them, thus they could not get to a phone. They took the officers hostage and now they're somewhere out in the countryside, riding in a stolen patrol car and at least one of the officers is injured."

Everyone had been now staring at the suited agent and listening intently to his quick analysis. A few of the uniformed officers present gave a nod of their heads. What he said made sense and anyway what would the local officers know? Nothing like this had ever happened to the town of Ridgemount.

"The problem now is which way they've gone and what's their next move?" Agent Brooks went on in his inquisitive sounding voice. "We need to get back to the station. I want to see some maps."

Mark was stumbling through the undergrowth, his hands still cuffed in front of him. He tried to keep his balance as he was at the same time trying to avoid tripping and falling on tree roots and rocks. Marco was right up behind him, gun in hand, giving the captive officer the occasional push to make sure he was going in the right direction.

"Keep going Mark," Marco said sedately.

Mark detected something in the voice. Was this the first time Marco had called him by his name? And why so distant from the patrol car? What did the guy have in mind? They continued to make their way through the undergrowth.

Suddenly, Mark felt Marco's hand grab his shoulder. The officer stopped dead in his tracks. It could now be over, a bullet in the back, dead on the ground, not found for ages, if at all, or, they could just dig a shallow grave and leave him for the worms.

"Okay Mark, just over there," Marco said and Mark felt himself being guided to a small tree. "Okay, you can take your piss. Do you need to shit as well?"

"No, I just need to take a leak," Mark replied without turning around and looking at Marco.

"Good, then I won't have to take the cuffs off you," Marco snickered. "Hope you didn't think I would wipe your ass for you if you had to shit."

Mark breathed deeply and walked over to the side of the tree. He began to unzip his uniform trousers. Out in the woods all that could be heard were crickets chirping to their heart's content.

Mark pulled his cock out and immediately the warm stream of cop piss splashed onto the side of the tree. Droplets of it hit his boots and a small cloud of vapor rose from the ground. The scent of his cop piss was somehow intoxicating. Mark felt relief as the contents from the beers from earlier on in the house emptied from him.

It could not have been more than a minute or so later when Mark shook the last droplets of piss from the tip of his cock when he suddenly felt an arm wrapping itself around his waist. The feel of heavy breathing was on the nape of his neck but the barrel of a gun was in the small of his back.

"Do you care about him?" Marco whispered in the cop's ear, his lips grazing the officer's earlobe as he whispered.

It took Mark a few seconds to comprehend what was happening. He took a breath.

"Well, do you care about him?" came the inquisitive voice again, directly into the back of Mark's ear this time.

"Who?" came a shaken voice from the officer.

"Your handsome rookie buddy," Marco said insistently.

There was a pause. Mark felt a sudden air of unease as the thug held him tighter around the waist.

"I...I just want to know what's happened to him," Mark said, standing straight, gazing out into the moonlit woods.

He started to slowly pack his cock away in his uniform trousers when the arm extracted itself from around his waist. The hand slowly made its way to Mark's exposed cock. He felt it suddenly being softly held.

"What, what are you doing?" Mark asked, sounding startled.

He tried to turn but Marco had now moved directly to the cop's side, the gun barrel now digging into the side of the uniformed officer.

"Why did you cry?" Marco whispered directly into the cop's ear.

The thug's fingers of his left hand began to slowly caress the officer's cock, stroking it, lightly touching the foreskin, teasing the foreskin by rolling it back and forth a few times, rolling his dirty fingers around the shaft, trying to entice it to become hard.

Mark took a moment to pause.

"Well?" Marco asked.

"I...don't...really know," Mark replied breathlessly, having his cock played with causing that.

Marco detected apprehension in the cop's voice. He continued to caress the officer's limp cock and began to slowly and gently rub his clasped hand up and down the smooth skin.

Mark closed his eyes tight. This wasn't happening, not this as well. After so much happening at the house, the disappearance of Chris, the uncertainty of all that was going to happen, it couldn't get any worse. But now this thug was playing his cock like it was a musical instrument.

Mark could feel Marco's eyes staring at him intently.

"Please...don't do this," Mark protested feebly.

"Hey it's either this or a bullet," Marco threatened, but in an instant Marco suddenly changed his tone when he checked Mark's face.

It was a face mixed with emotions, fear, rage, humiliation and anger.

"Why don't you let yourself relax?" Marco asked calmly. "It'll be easier."

Ricardo had pulled the map out from the glove compartment and he was viewing it inside the patrol car. It took a few minutes to work out which way the map went, but still, the markings made no sense. Marco had been in the military. He would know.

"Where the fuck are they?" Ricardo said to himself.

Ridgemount Police Station was solid to capacity with uniformed cops and suited and booted agents. This was one hell of a night to have been taken hostage. Agent Adam Brooks had commandeered an office and had instructed the local officers to get him maps of the county. Within half an hour the walls of the office were covered in ordinance survey maps of various sizes. Brook's shoes echoed on the hard floor of the office as he wandered from one map to another. Standing around him were five uniformed officers, hands on their hips or arms folded, some of them with coffee cups in their hands. They were all waiting for Adam's next incisive comment.

"Can we be absolutely sure that all ways out of the town have been covered and cordoned off?" asked the FBI agent.

An officer stepped forward and gazed up at the map.

"We can say that between the time we got the call from Alma and the setting up of the roadblocks was no more than forty-five minutes," said the officer. "I doubt very much that they wanted to be spotted in something like a stolen police car for too long."

"You're quite right Officer, driving around in a stolen patrol car would stick out like a sore thumb," Agent Brooks replied. "Now, the only thing is that they've either stopped somewhere or have changed vehicles. Have we had any reports of stolen vehicles in the past hour or so?"

Everyone in the office gave a shake of their head.

"Okay, so somewhere in this county there are two escapees, two cop hostages, and a stolen patrol car," Brooks said, tapped his chin with his forefinger and walked close to the map.

"What would I be doing now if I was on the run?" he said to himself.

Mark stood almost at attention with his legs slightly apart in the woods, his wrists clamped tightly in metal handcuffs in front of him. One of his captors, a guy named Marco stood beside him, his face dangerously close to the cuffed officer's ear, gently breathing his beer odor across the captured cop's nostrils. Marco's left hand was wrapped around the cop's cock, slowly working his hand up and down to make the limp cock engorge with blood, and of course the ever-present gun was pressed firmly into the officer's side.

"Please…don't…" the cop pleaded.

Mark was running a rapid river of emotions within himself. There could not be a more logical explanation, taken out into the woods, his manhood abused, and then to have his life ended with a bullet in his back, the coward's way, then buried in a shallow grave, maybe never to be found. The cop closed his eyes and his bottom lip quivered.

"Please, just do what you have to do," Mark said in a trembling sounding voice.

Marco was achieving nothing with the cop's dick in his hand. There was no blood-rush to the limp cock. It was not going to happen, at least not now. He stopped and spoke into the cop's ear.

"Do you know what I want to do with you?" Marco asked the captive cop.

"Whatever it is, just do it quick," the cop replied, sounding defeated now.

Marco gave himself a puzzled look and then suddenly realized that the cop was waiting for him to shoot him dead.

"You think I'm going to put a bullet in you? Boy oh boy cop, have you got it wrong!" Marco said and took a small step back from his uniformed hostage.

He gazed at the once proud officer and allowed himself to take in the fine muscular frame of the cop. Marco's eyes traced his form from his piss stained boots to the tight black belt around his waist holding an empty holster and nothing more. His uniform shirt no longer ironed looking with crisp seams was now a disheveled mess. The cop's eyes were red from his tearful outburst and yet in the moonlight, yes, in the moonlight, he stood like a man.

"You think I want to put you out of your misery, fuck Mark!" Marco exclaimed. "I can't believe that! I just wanted to have some fun with you first, and then I'll think about shooting you."

Mark turned slowly and looked at his captor.

"Yeah, you'll stay alive if you do as I say," Marco said and gazed down at Mark's opened zipper with his cop cock still hanging out limp. Marco gave a knowing wink at the handcuffed and helpless officer.

Mark quickly pulled his cock back into his uniform trousers and drew the zipper up, almost in defiance.

"We've got time," Marco said, sounding unconcerned.

The sound of undergrowth being broken underfoot could suddenly be heard. A hand was just as suddenly clamped tight across Mark's mouth.

"MMMMMFFFF..." was the sound of the hand-gagged officer's only verbal outburst, before the gun barrel was pushed deep into his side as a warning to shut it.

Out of the shadows came the figure of Ricardo.

"Fucking hell Marco!" Ricardo shouted. "You were just supposed to make sure he had a piss and a crap if he needed it."

Marco stared at Ricardo and then at his prisoner.

"Yeah, he's done," Marco replied.

"Get him in the car, we need to check out some things," Ricardo ordered.

Agent Adam Brooks had been somewhat of a golden boy at the FBI training college. He was quick to be identified by the hierarchy as a "potentially gifted and knowledgeable agent." He was soon top of his league in practically all of his classes. He would be studying while other FBI trainees played. It became apparent that he would need to have essential hands-on experience and was given special dispensation to go out on the field with experienced agents. This was what he had been waiting for and soon he was finding himself propelled into the high profile cases of FBI investigations.

Brooks had taken a room at the local motel. Within the room the agent paced up and down in his clean ankle length boots, shirt sleeves rolled up, and hands on his hips. He couldn't sleep, not that he had any call for it. This situation was feeding his brain and keeping him active. Sheets of various size notepapers littered every piece of furniture. Occasionally he would stop, pick up a note and view it intently. He would then place the note back down. In all the cases he had worked on there had been motive, reason, yet there was nothing in either escapee's profiles that justified this. They were just not fitting any pattern. They were on the run and not heading anywhere.

Ricardo, Marco and Mark returned to the patrol car. Using the limited overhead light in the car Ricardo opened the map and placed it over the steering wheel. Mark sat in the driver's seat while Ricardo sat next to him in the passenger's side.

"Now Mark, before we get some shuteye I want you to tell me what these places are," Ricardo said as his dirty forefinger picked three places on the map that he couldn't understand what the symbols were.

Even Marco was at a loss to know what they were and decided to stand outside, leaning against the car, wondering about the earlier events.

Mark looked at the symbols.

"That's a disused quarry, that's a disused motel, and that was the old drive-in," Mark responded.

"Well thank you for that Mr. Policeman, now we can get some shuteye," Ricardo said. "Hey Marco! Take our officer outside and tie him to a tree. And make sure to take his boots off him till morning. We don't want him running off into the woods."

Marco pulled Mark out from the driver's seat and took a glance around at the sea of trees. He spied one that would serve his purpose.

"Come on Cop, lets get you all comfortable for the night," Marco said and pulled the cuffed officer by his arm and trampled the undergrowth.

He walked the trapped officer toward a slender tree, still with the gun in his side.

Mark felt the cuffs being unlocked from his swollen wrists and Marco allowed the cop the quick pleasure of rubbing his hands to try to regain some feeling back into them. Sadly it was too little too late.

"Sit down with your back to the tree," ordered Marco.

Mark turned around to see a small mound of earth stacked up across the tree. He dutifully did as he was told and sat down on the mound.

"Arms around the tree," came the second order from Marco.

Mark obeyed and drew his arms behind him and around the trunk of the tree. The sound of the cuffs being clamped around his wrists was becoming all too familiar to the captured cop. He tried to settle himself as best he could. He drew his head back to rest it against the trunk of the tree and took a long lengthy intake of cool night air into his lungs. Could he now rest he wondered.

Marco came around from the back of the tree, tucking the gun into the belt of his trousers.

"Give us your feet," Marco demanded.

Mark stretched his legs out in front of himself and Marco knelt down and grabbed them hard at the ankles. With both hands Marco pulled the cop's feet straight out. He pushed them firmly on the ground and allowed himself the pleasure of looking at the length of Mark's muscular legs encased in his uniform trousers. Marcos' gaze slowly also took in through the moonlight rays the shine of his captive's boots. Slowly, Marco pulled up the right trouser leg to reveal the length of the boot. It stopped short of the cop's knee. Marco's fingers touched the tip of the boot, stroked it, he felt the different textures between the smooth sleek surface and the slight stickiness from the beer laden piss dribbles that had dripped down from Mark's cock earlier on. Marcos' fingers continued upwards touching the high sheen finish. He caressed either side of the boot. He felt panels of nylon fabric that were there to give the cop movement to his ankle and also to keep it warm and dry. The fingers continued their search slowly to the front of the boot. The nylon fabric made way for the tough leather surrounding the bootlaces that crisscrossed the boot through eyelets, ensuring that it was tightly bound to Mark's foot and leg. A tightly doubled bow at the top of the boot ensured that the ends of the laces were bound securely together.

Mark watched with intensity as his captor massaged his right boot, almost in a reverential manner. The cop watched as the fingers stroked the different materials that made up the construction of the boot. Marco allowed his forefinger to slowly trail down the front of the boot, touching the crossover laces as he did so. The thug eventually arrived where he'd started, at the tip of the boot. Marco allowed himself to hunker down on one knee to get a closer look at the boot. He examined it with the light that was available. He had pulled up the cop's right leg and clasped the heel of the boot in his right hand. With his left hand he removed a small cloth from his back pocket. Marco gently applied the cloth to the boot, tackling the piss stains that were obscuring the full sheen of the black boot. At first he was slow and gentle, holding the heel of the boot with almost divine respect. But soon he was realizing that the stains were not going to be that easily removed. A shot of spit from Marcos' mouth was quickly released onto the cloth and soon he was rubbing into the supple leather with more vigor. Slowly but surely the caked on piss stains were rid of and Marco held the boot away. He admired his handiwork on bringing back the full sheen to the cop's right boot.

"I'll do your left one soon enough Mark," Marco said.

The convict placed the booted foot down on the grass floor. He then drew up Mark's left booted foot and closely examined the stains that hindered the perfection that Marco found so fascinating in the boots that Mark wore.

Again Marco feverishly did as he did before with the right boot. He used the cloth to wipe away the offending piss stains and brought the left boot to the same sheen as the right one. Once done he lay the left booted foot next to the right for a comparison. Both of the cop's boots now gleamed from the intense cleaning.

"I think they're pretty clean now Mark, what do you think?" Marco asked, sounding satisfied.

Mark took a look at his boots and despite the rigors of the day's events gazed at the work his captor had done. Indeed his Magnum boots did look appealingly well buffed up. Mark tapped them together, the boots making a clunking sound.

"They look pretty good Marco," the cop replied.

Mark drew his gaze away from his cleaned up boots and made eye to eye contact with Marco. They both stared at each other for a few seconds. White vapor poured out of both men's mouths in almost precise rhythm. The air was getting colder. Even the sound of the crickets seemed to evaporate. There was a sudden and intense searching for some kind of expression from either man. Mark didn't know what he was feeling. The action with Marco handling his boots stirred something inside, something he hadn't experienced in some time. Neither man made a move, least of all Mark being cuffed to a tree. Marco then drew his gaze away.

"Sorry...I'm going to have to take them off you," the thug said.

Marco reached down and again picked up the right booted foot. He rested it on his knee. Again he drew up the trouser leg to the top of the boot and began to pull at the double bow. He picked at it with his dirty fingernails to loosen it, to begin the task at tugging each part of the lace through its intricate weaving from one side of the boot to the other, to allow him to finally remove the boot from the captive cop's foot. Marco dug his finger underneath the tight bindings and tugged hard.

It was a sudden movement and Marco was unprepared for it. The booted foot was suddenly pulled away from him and his fingers. What happened next was an act of uncertainty from the handcuffed cop. Marco drew himself closer to the captive to retrieve the booted foot, but his action was interrupted when the shining boot came slowly forward to make contact with his groin.

Marco was taken aback by the sudden movement of Mark's right foot. Mark pushed himself back against the trunk of the tree as he slowly pressed his Magnum booted foot into his captor's groin. Marco drew the cold night air into his lungs as he felt the booted foot begin to slowly push against his cock and ball sac. Marco grabbed the boot heel and adjusted it slightly so that the rubber sole would dig into his groin. Mark watched with wide eyes as his right foot took on a life of its own. His blood suddenly accelerated in his body. He could feel his face becoming warm, making him feel euphoric. What was going on? Mark, the clean cut smartly turned out cop, that law abiding citizens looked up to in the town of Ridgemount was slowly feeling symptoms, symptoms not experienced in some time.

"Hold my boot firm, bastard," was the sudden outburst from the cuffed cop.

Marco was suddenly firing questions in his head. What was happening? It wasn't so long ago this cop wasn't having any shit done to him, and now? Fuck, does all it take is the cleaning of a pair of cop boots? Wasn't so long ago he had yet what could have been something of a rejection from this cop, but now?

Marco gave a puzzled look at his captive. Mark's face was slowly blushing with the surge of blood. He tried to shift his position against the tree. He was trying to adjust himself. He needed Marco to come forward to allow his boot to press deeper into his captor's groin.

"Move forward," whispered the cop.

Again Marco looked into the cop's reddening face. For whatever the reason there was that moment both men found common bond. Marco moved forward, allowing the cuffed cop to bend his right knee, slightly giving leverage to allow the clean boot to push deeper into Marco's groin. Mark dug the heel of his left Magnum boot into the soft soil to give himself stability.

Macro could feel the firm tread from the sole of the officer's boot rub against his thin prison issued trousers. Mark was slowly rubbing it up and down, trying to instill a rhythm. Marco was still cradling the boot and allowed the motion to take over. He then loosened his grip on the boot heel. Both men were now trying in some way to work in synch with each other. The vapor from their breath was becoming long and regular and lingered almost indefinitely in the night air. No words were needed at that moment.

Mark viewed his actions as his boot rubbed into a regular motion. Marco continued to stare into the cop's face. The friction of the clean boot was beginning to take its effect. Marco was feeling his cock engorge with blood.

"Oh yes Officer, that's it, rub that cop boot in hard," Marco whispered to his cuffed prisoner.

Mark dutifully obliged.

The magnum boot weaved itself up and down the growing shaft of Marco's cock. Through the thin material of the trousers Mark witnessed the growing length and now he himself was no stranger to this almost sensual scene as his arousal take on a more physical form. Mark felt his cock stiffen. He could feel it trying to become erect, but his tight uniform trousers and the way he had been positioned against the tree trunk had offered little for a man's desire to express his inner deepest darkest desire.

Mark needed room for his erection to maneuver.

"Take my cock out," the cop pleaded quietly.

Marco did as he was told and released the boot from his groin. He rested the right booted foot on the soft soil and crawled over to the bound cop.

"Fuck, my cock is going to burst to hurting if I can't get it out," Mark said next in rushed words.

Marco gazed down at the cop's duty belt and frantically began to tackle the buckle that tightly bound the officer's trousers to his firm legs. The thug could feel the surge of cum pushing through his cock. He needed to be patient. He needed to hold on. He released the buckle and tackled the clasp and zipper on the cop's trousers. Within seconds Marco had released the pressure against Mark's long and slender cock. The cop's trousers were loosened and had been pulled down to his hips. His jockstrap was quickly yanked down as well. The cock now sprung hard and firm to attention. Marco pulled back and looked at what he saw.

"Oh Jesus, mother fucking god…" Marco huffed.

The cop's circumcised cock was everything it should have been, belonging to an officer of the law. It was long, firm and imposing. It was of well-endowed proportions. Marco was both enthralled and impressed. The elastic waistband from Mark's jockstrap held his ball sac down and away from the neatly clipped dark pubic hair. The night air swiveled around the cop's groin, slowly cooling his sweet smelling sweat that had accumulated from the day's events.

Moist droplets of sweat clung to the stems of pubic hair and began to evaporate. Marco pulled the cop's legs further apart as best he could and leaned forward to nuzzle his head further into Mark's cooling groin.

Marco's tongue extended outward to lick the salty sweat around the base of the erect cock. Mark pressed his muscular body against the trunk of the tree. He dug his boot heels harder into the soft earth, allowing him to thrust his lower body forward to allow his captor to be able to probe his tongue into the tight coils of soft pubic hair even further.

"OOOO…God," whispered the cuffed cop. "Hooooo…dear God…"

Marco's right hand moved forward to find the solid and firm cock. He allowed himself the pleasure of slowly clasping his fingers around it. Mark leaned his head back as he felt the fingers of his captor clasp around his hard-on and begin to stroke it up and down, up and down, slowly at first. But then Marco began to accelerate the action, becoming more frantic. Mark felt the sudden sensual experience of being jerked off. Oh fuck, this sensation was so good. If only his hands were free…if only he could allow himself that pleasure to jerk himself off, a pleasure not used in quite sometime by the uniformed cop.

Marco was stroking the cop's cock in a rhythmic movement, feeling his prisoner's throbbing veins pumping with blood. He himself was now pressing the palm of his other hand against his cock, trying to instill the effect that Mark's boot had had a few minutes earlier. It was working. Marco's cock was reacting to the events that were unfolding. The thug felt his own manhood slowly harden. He bit his lower lip as he felt his cock becoming engorged with blood, slowly feeling its natural urge to grow long and thick, pushing against the constraints of his underpants and trousers.

"AHHH…" came the sounds of satisfaction from Mark's mouth.

He moved his head from side to side, feeling an almost ecstatic agony as the surge of cum slowly escalated itself to burst out the tip of his cock.

"OH yes," came the sudden outcry from the cop's mouth as well. "OH yes…"

Marco's hand action had proved fruitful. The captive cop suddenly squirted out his pale white milky cum, splashing out over Marco's grumpy hand. It came out in slurps of almost exacting moments of intense pleasure.

"AHHH…OOO…YES," came the satisfied sounds of the subdued cop.

Marco himself then felt the force of cum spilling out of his cock, quickly moistening his underpants and the slow stain was slowly emerging through his trousers.

Ricardo looked at the clock on the dashboard of the patrol car. How long does it take to cuff a cop to a tree and take his boots off him? He opened the car door and swung himself out of the driver's seat. He stood up into the light of the moon. Ricardo screwed his eyes up to try and look out the area that surrounded him. He spied the tree that he saw Marco and the cop walk towards. He stepped forward and glanced back in the direction of the trunk of the patrol car.

"Don't worry rookie, soon, very soon," Ricardo whispered and returned his attention to the trees in the distance.

He walked off in search of his friend and prisoner.

It didn't take him long to pick up the trail. The faint familiar sound of someone being jerked off was quickly picked up. It was a familiar sound for anyone who was used to it being heard repeatedly every night through the cell walls in the pen. Ricardo followed the sound.

Ricardo's eyes widened as he took in the scene that came into view under the light of the moon.

Mark lay against the trunk of the tree, his head turned to one side. Ricardo could see the cop's chest moving rapidly up and down, his legs spread apart, still with his boots on. Ricardo saw his partner in crime kneeling between the prisoner's legs licking his hand. Ricardo stared transfixed at what he saw and was quick to realize what had happened. The symptoms of rage built up within him. He moved himself forward to the scene.

"Fucking get his boots off him," Ricardo ordered firmly.

Marco responded to the order. He quickly did as he was told. He picked up the right clean boot, pulled up the cop's trousers as best he could and began to untie the lace from the top of it. Once the knot was untied Marco proceeded to pull it through the eyelets, allowing the boot to become loose. Once the lace had been completely removed Marco yanked at the boot. It came away from the cop's foot easily, revealing a white sock fitting in line to the contours of the cop's foot.

"Get the other boot off," came Ricardo's enraged order.

Marco again obeyed. He scurried around to Mark's left boot and again did as before. He pulled up the left trouser leg, untied the knot and then yanked the complete black lace through the eyelets, tugging and pulling at every opportunity. Marco grabbed the heel of the boot and pulled. Again the clean boot came off revealing the white sock, again the seams correctly positioned around the foot, again everything as it should be in Mark's life, correct and proper, at least where his white socks were concerned.

Mark felt the cold winds of the night begin to clear his mind of the events that had preceded these. He slowly shook his head and took a glance into the standing figure of Ricardo. Mark drew back hard. He pressed himself into the trunk of the tree. Was it fear of this guy he was feeling or the fear of guilt of what had just happened?

"Fucking bastard, leave me alone," pleaded Mark through trembling lips.

A reaction of fear or the cold night air?

"I think our officer needs to keep his mouth shut," Ricardo said and stepped forward.

He bent down and ferociously took hold of Mark's right socked foot. Ricardo then took hold of the white sock and pulled it from the toes. The sock slowly stretched before it began to pull away from the cop's foot. It snapped away from the foot and Ricardo held it high as though it was some kind of trophy. The thug held the sock to his nose as if in a defiant gesture. He took a long and hearty snuff of the sock. It was almost like the tradition of smelling blood after the kill of an animal, but in this case it was the smell of a cop's sock that had been encased in a boot, with the seams positioned correctly to a man's foot contours. Ricardo pulled the sock from his face and gazed at his captive. Without a word he quickly rolled the sock into a ball and leaned over the cuffed cop.

"Open wide," Ricardo commanded.

Mark held steadfast and kept his mouth firmly closed. Both captive and captor stared into each other's eyes. It could have been a couple of moments. The captor broke the silence.

"Don't think for a moment that's going to stop me," Ricardo said and suddenly his hand thrust out and grabbed the officer's nostrils, squeezing them tightly shut.

"Try and see how long you can last Officer, ha," Ricardo laughed and was once again in a position of being in control.

His rage now compounded with the element of being in a superior position. He knew that it would be only a matter of about less than two minutes before the cop would need desperately to take in air.

"MMMMPPPFFFFF…" came the muffled protest from behind Mark's sealed lips.

Mark couldn't give in, but what were his alternatives? He began to lash out with his legs as best he could, an action he thought would keep Ricardo back giving him time to draw in another gulp of air. But the cop's energy levels were almost zero at that point. Ricardo was too quick and was able to move aside from the officer's futile lashing out with his muscular legs and came up from the side of the handcuffed cop. It was not even a minute and Mark's urge to take in air got the better of him. His attempt to get his captor away from him wasn't successful. The sweat soaked white sock found its target and was forced into the cop's mouth without hesitation and pushed deep into his throat.

"MMMMPPPFFFFF…" now came the pathetic noises from the captive cop.

"HA, bet you're thinking what a shitty thing that is to do to a poor guy, to gag him with his own smelly sock," Ricardo hee hawed.

If Mark could speak he would have said, "Yeah, it sucks."

"Now to make sure you don't spit it out, we'll tie it in with your bootlace," Ricardo said and drew up the long black bootlace.

He wrapped it around the cop's face, tugging it to ensure that the sock was firmly secured into Mark's mouth. The thug had to use the tips of his dirty fingers to finish off tying a tight knot behind the cop's head. Ricardo pulled himself up from his bound victim to admire his handiwork.

Mark sat, hands cuffed behind him around the trunk of the tree, his uniform trousers pulled down around his ankles, one foot bare, the other socked, his jockstrap still pinning his scrotum down. His boots were lying on the ground, one with a lace, the other without, one of his own socks now pushed into his drying mouth, a bootlace tied tightly around his head to keep the sock contained. Mark was now no more than a victim. Slowly but surely he was losing his own dignity and more importantly, who he was.

"There, now you can shout as much as you like," Ricardo said sarcastically. "Oh, and before I forget, you're best not to struggle too much. You're going to need to conserve your strength and energy. You've got a pretty package to carry tomorrow."

Agent Brooks lay on the double bed in the motel room, his eyes staring straight up, transfixed to the not so white painted ceiling. Brooks was still dressed in his shirt and suit trousers. His polished shoes were neatly placed side by side under the writing desk. His suit jacket was wrapped around the back of a chair. A plate of half eaten sandwiches lay on the bedside cabinet and a bottle of mineral water sat next to them, half full. Brooks had his fingers interlocked with each other and resting across his taut chest. His black tie was loosened from his collar and the top button of his white shirt was undone. His legs were dressed in smartly pressed black suit trousers and were slightly apart as he wiggled his toes in his black dress socks. He had been this way for the good part of the night. His assessment of what had happened to the two cops had only given him minimal information. He was still waiting for the lab back in the city to come up with a more detailed analysis of the blood drops found at the scene of the kidnapping. The agent was deep in thought.

"Oh, what can be happening out there?" he asked himself.

The phone at the side of the bed suddenly rang.

Brooks leaned over and picked up the receiver.

"It's your early morning alarm call Agent Brooks, time is four thirty AM," came the faint voice of the operator.

"Thank you for that," the agent replied.

Brooks replaced the phone receiver and leaned back over. Again he viewed the ceiling. All night he had been pacing up and down the motel room floor seeking out any solution no matter how small as to what the two convicts were up to. He needed to view the maps at the cop station again.

The warm rays of the rising sun, the sudden chirping and whistling of birds, the sound of squirrels running, all would have been reassuring feeling to anyone waking up in the vast wilderness of nature. But for one person it stuck dread. Mark opened his eyes for the umpteenth time. During the night he tried at best to give himself the faint luxury of slumber, but it was not to be. The bootlace tied around his head to stop his sock gag coming out had caused pain, cutting deep into the sides of his mouth. His arms were suffering awful cramps from being pulled back behind the tree and cuffed. His legs open to bare to the elements over the night had also begun to stiffen and were aching from the lack of blood circulation.

"Well, well, Sleeping Beauty has awoken, did we sleep well?" Ricardo asked, standing a few feet away from his prisoner.

The thug was beaming a smile that brought no comfort to Mark. The cop blinked to adjust his eyes to the morning surroundings. He tried to move himself into a more upright position, but the morning dew caused his feet to slip on the grass so he was unable to get a hold to push himself into a more comfortable position. The cop was too tired to make anymore attempts. He slumped back, his head laid against the trunk of the tree.

"MMMMMMFFFFppppllleeease ret reee ro," Mark cried mournfully, trying to say, "Please let me go" through his gagged mouth.

"AWWW, is the poor police officer all hurt and tired?" Ricardo asked menacingly.

Mark stared at his tormentor and narrowed his eyes in a defiant gesture.

Ricardo took two steps forward and allowed his right foot to strike out and slam his prisoner squarely on his firm chest.

"MMMMMMMPPPPPHHHMOTHERFUCKING…" Mark cried out in a muffled tone.

Ricardo bent down and grabbed at Mark's crew cut hair.

"Now, next time you look at me like that it'll be a bullet in your chest and not my foot," Ricardo said threateningly.

Mark bit down hard into his sock gag to try and suppress the agonizing pain from the powerful kick he had just endured. Tears welled up in his eyes. He took long intakes of morning clean air through his nostrils to try and curb the pain. It didn't work as the pain was more intense as his chest raised up and down.

"I never really liked you Policeman Mark," Ricardo stated. "Oh, that's what your boyfriend calls you, isn't it? The one who sucks you off while you're tied to a tree?"

Mark stared through tearful eyes.

"NO! You had to spoil it for me! I was happy to have your rookie buddy to myself!" Ricardo suddenly screamed. "Fucking rookie, all dressed up in his motorcycle uniform and his clean polished boots. His clean face, his firm body, everything could have been just right, but no, you got in the fucking way! YOU, you came back to the house! You fucked it all up for me so I had to make YOU suffer!"

Ricardo released his grip on the cop's hair and stood up.

"You're lucky, I won't hurt you anymore," Ricardo said. "At least for the time being, because you've got some carrying to do cop."

Agent Adam Brooks had stripped himself out of his tailored clothing and stepped into the shower. He turned on the faucet and allowed the water to cascade down his muscular body. He adjusted the water temperature, held his head up, closed his eyes and let the small jets of water hit his face and start to invigorate him. He stroked his crew cut hair, pushing back the water to run down the back of his bull-sized neck. He opened his eyes to find the motel supplied shower gel sachet. He groped with his wet hands at the shelf screwed into the ceramic tiles surrounding the shower unit. The agent grasped at a blue colored sachet and drew it up to his eyes. It was shampoo. He placed it back on the shelf and picked up another sachet. This time it was the shower gel. Despite pulling and yanking with his fingers to open it, it just kept slipping. Eventually the agent put the corner of the sachet in his mouth and pulled. It ripped open without resistance. The blue liquid that came out was quickly rubbed against his wet body. Brooks allowed his hands to explore his taut body, washing the gel all over. He started to wash his scrotum, stroking it gently in his hands, allowing the gel to foam. The falling water was splashing against his sensitive skin. Adam slowly placed his left hand against the tiled wall and with his right hand moved to his penis. He caressed it, drew back the foreskin to reveal the subtle pink color of flesh. He began to masturbate.

Mark felt a sudden slackness in his arms. Ricardo had uncuffed him from the tree trunk. The officer's numb arms fell to his sides. Ricardo came around from behind the tree holding the handcuffs in his hand. In his other hand was the gun.

"Get up scum cop," ordered Ricardo.

Mark gave himself the luxury of a few seconds to try and relax. He knew Ricardo would not hurt him. He was needed to do some carrying. At least that would mean he would be up and walking. But more to the point, to carry something would require having to have his hands and feet free from being tied up. The officer pulled himself up and faced his captor.

"Turn around," Ricardo commanded.

Mark slowly turned on his feet, one foot with a white sock on it, the other without. He was standing. His jockstrap was still firmly tight around his balls. His uniform trousers were still around his ankles. He faced the tree that he had been cuffed to all night.

Suddenly, he felt the back of his head being pulled at. The bootlace that had been used to keep his sock stuffed in his mouth was being pulled free. Ricardo was able with one hand to loosen the knot and eventually pull it away from the officer's head. Mark felt the relief as he pushed out his saliva soaked sock from his aching mouth. It fell to the ground. The cop gave himself the pleasure of moving his jaw around to regain some feeling back into it. Ricardo dropped the bootlace at the captive officer's feet.

"Okay, get dressed quickly," Ricardo commanded; his third command to the cop this morning.

Mark yanked his damp jockstrap back into place covering his now flaccid cock. He leaned down and pulled up his crumbled trousers, tucking his white under vest and uniform shirt into them before fastening them. He secured them in place with his duty belt.

"I need to sit down to get my boots on," Mark said.

The gun pointing at him gave out the motion that allowed him to sit and get his boots back on. One boot still had the lace clinging to the bottom eyelets. Mark began to loop it through the eyelets again. Once completed he pushed his already socked foot into it and began to tighten the lace by yanking it tightly through the eyelets, making sure that at the top of his boot he tugged it tight and tied a knot. He reached for the sock that he had spat out and rolled it back onto his naked foot. Despite the present situation Mark took time to adjust the white sock so that the seams were correct to the contours of his foot. Next the bootlace that had been used to keep the sock tightly stuffed in the cop's mouth was picked up and again Mark weaved the lace through the eyelets of the boot. Once done he pulled the boot onto his socked foot and followed the same procedure as he did with his other boot before tying a tight knot at the top of it.

"UP!" Ricardo said, motioning with the gun up and down to emphasize his order.

Mark did as he was told and pulled himself up. Despite a few creases in his uniform and some grass stains on his trousers the cop didn't look too bad for wear or because of the ordeal he was enduring.

"Okay, back to the car," Ricardo said and again Mark did as instructed.

He walked past his abductor. Ricardo turned and was quick to follow his prisoner through the woods toward the patrol car.

Adam Brooks stood back and viewed the maps pinned to the wall at the cop station. There was a sudden knock on the office door. Brooks turned around and saw Alma standing in the doorway.

"Ah, the very person I was looking for," said the FBI agent.

Alma gave back a puzzled look.

"Come in, come in, I need your knowledge," Brooks said in an excited sounding tone.

He extended his hand out to invite Alma into the office.

Mark made his way back to the patrol car; leaning against it was a badly bruised Marco. No doubt Ricardo needed to make a point and Marco had become the punching bag for the duration of the rest of the night.

"Okay Officer, open the trunk," Ricardo ordered and kept the gun pointed at his prisoner.

Mark moved to the back of the patrol car. He took notice of the hole in the trunk, a bullet hole? He pushed the trunk lock. The lid of the trunk opened slowly.

Mark was not prepared for what he saw.

Chris lay on his side, his hands still tied behind his back with rope. A bruise congealed with blood was visible on the side of his forehead.

"What the fu…" Mark began but didn't finish his sentence.

He was having a sudden surge of different emotions, surprise, fear, anger, and one of hope. Could his handsome rookie still be alive?

"Now, now, you'd think that I would let a beautiful specimen of rookie cop go to waste?" Ricardo asked cynically.

Mark looked back down at the bound rookie. He suddenly realized what the bullet hole was, a hole to allow someone to breathe. Mark bent forward to check his rookie. Chris was making faint sounds of breathing. There was hope. My God, all this time the poor kid had been locked in the trunk of the car Mark thought. No doubt the two thugs had even kept him in there overnight. It amazed the senior officer that his rookie was still alive. But after the speech that Ricardo had given the night before about Chris, Mark wondered for just how long the rookie would be his.

"Okay cop, get him out, you've got a mighty big load to carry," Ricardo ordered.

Alma was escorted to the wall where maps of varying sizes showed Ridgemount and its surrounding area pinned up. Agent Brooks stood beside her and he too glanced at the maps.

"Alma, how long have you lived in Ridgemount?" Brooks asked, his eyes still peering at the maps.

"All my life, born and bred, except when I went to police training," she replied proudly.

"So would you know a lot about the area?" Brooks asked.

"Absolutely, north, south, east and wet of this town and all around it," Alma said.

"Good, very good," Brooks continued. "Now, looking at the maps here I can see some places that seem to have been abandoned in the not so long ago. What happened?"

"Progress I'd say," Alma replied. "Ridgemount, like any other town had to move on with the times."

Brooks gave a knowing nod.

"So stop the rot before it sets in," the agent said.

"Exactly," she proudly smiled.

"Well, that helps us," Brooks said. "I would assume that our convicts and hostages with one of them injured are going to be looking for somewhere to hide out and plan their next move."

There was a knock on the office door and through the pane of glass on the door both Brooks and Alma saw Officer Andy Rudd. The cop's face had a story to tell.

Brooks waved him in.

"Just got the results back on that blood sample," the cop said and Alma's eyes lit with nervous anticipation.

Rudd handed a slip of paper to Brooks.

"We matched the blood against the prison databank and it isn't either of the convicts, it looks like one of our guys got it," came the sullen statement from the young officer.

Alma's eyes suddenly lowered.

"I would ask you to define "got it" Rudd," Brooks said and began his pacing up and down the office floor.

"Firstly, we can say that whichever officer it is, is injured, not dead," the FBI agent said. "The blood on the carpet floor is far too small an amount to indicate anymore more than a severe blow to some part of the body. I would take a guess and say the head. Secondly, if the officer was killed why would they take him? He would be nothing more than excessive baggage, slow them down. Why not leave him as a sign for us to say that they mean business, a threat to what they could do to the one remaining officer they hold?"

Alma and Rudd both looked at the FBI agent and began to realize that there was still hope for their guys.

"So what's the plan?" Alma asked.

Brooks gave Alma a wink.

"Good, okay, I see we have a few abandoned places that could be used as a hideout, but I have my doubts about their suitability," Brooks said.

Rudd gave the agent a confused look.

"Well, they're not looking for a Comfort Inn, just somewhere to lie low," Officer Rudd said.

"Absolutely right Officer Rudd, I can see we have a drive-in, a mine, and a small hotel, all abandoned," Brooks said. "They would have dumped the patrol car and continued on foot. Now, my reckoning is what would their reason be to go to a deserted drive-in? A big open space where there's nowhere to hide? What reason is there to go there?"

Rudd shrugged his broad shoulders.

"A deserted mine…good place to hide out but also a place where you can get lost in the tunnels, a place with only one opening," Brooks surmised. "No escape if ambushed, a place that can be as enclosing as the bars of a prison?"

"That leaves only the motel," Rudd said.

"It seems almost too simple a solution, but I suppose we start somewhere and the motel it is," Brooks said in an affirmative voice.

"Get him out," Ricardo ordered.

The thug was standing next to Mark, both of them viewing the unconscious figure of Chris, wrists bound behind him lying in the trunk of a police car. Mark leaned forward. He clenched his teeth as the pain from the kick he had received from his captor earlier was still agonizingly painful. But, despite the pain he had to get his rookie out of the trunk. As long as Chris was breathing Mark felt that there was a chance of getting help for him. He gently pulled at one of Chris' strong arms and slowly eased him out of the trunk.

"You be careful with him," Ricardo ordered, a strange request Mark thought.

Mark nodded as he lowered himself to take the muscular rookie over his shoulder. Ricardo gazed over at the bruised Marco.

"Get the bags out of the car cock sucker, ha, ha, ha," Ricardo said and laughed evilly.

Marco opened the back door of the patrol car and pulled out the bags containing the hostage's clothes and shoes. He pulled the bags over his shoulders. It looked like both he and Mark would suffer the consequences for their actions from the previous night by being made to carry heavy loads.

Mark slowly pulled himself up with Chris now securely slung over his shoulder. The smell of the rookie's leather boots close to Mark's face lingered around his nostrils. The buckle from the rookie's belt pressed deep and hard into his shoulder blade. With that and the constant throbbing pain from his bruised side Mark knew he was going to find it difficult to walk. But there was no alternative. With the thought that Chris could now recover from his wound Mark felt that other possibilities could indeed come to fruition, like being rescued.

"Where are we going?" Marco questioned Ricardo.

Ricardo viewed the motley band around him.

"We're fucking going to get ourselves a bath," Ricardo replied.

It was at least an hour later since they had left the patrol car and the convicts and hostages were now walking through the woods to a destination known only to Ricardo. He had produced the gun from his waistband and again began to exert his authority with it. His temper was near the breaking point; his emotions were raw with anger. The convict seethed as he watched Mark trying hard to keep his balance while trampling through the undergrowth. Grass, wet with morning dew was clinging to the cop's boots, branches were sticking hard and sorely into his sides, persistent pain was pressing down on his shoulder from the weight of Chris gradually becoming unbearable. The relentless pushing and stabbing of the gun barrel into the small of his back was annoying beyond words. Despite being obscured by the trees, the rising sun was beaming hot and hard on the band of convicts and hostages.

Marco's prison issued footwear might have been suited to the hard concrete floors of his walled confinement, but the wet slippery grass was making his headway extremely difficult. The two large gym bags were slung across his shoulders and were adding to his discomfort and the stinging soreness from the bruises Ricardo had dealt him the previous night would take time to heal. He stumbled on, thinking, when would it end?

Ricardo was taking great pleasure in walking behind his prisoners and fellow inmate. He held the gun firmly in his hand. At every opportunity he would poke it hard into Mark's back, making sure that it was becoming an annoying hindrance. This was the convict's way of punishing the officer for his actions, continuous persistent annoyance. It reminded him how whilst in solitary he was himself beaten by the prison guards. This was in some way a form of retribution. It was payback time.

The small motley band made their way through the woods, each of them in their own thoughts. It was approaching lunch time when Ricardo blew a quick sharp whistle. The group froze in their tracks. Both Marco and Mark were hoping this would be a chance to rest. They both turned to gaze at the convict with the gun.

"I think I smell a bathtub," Ricardo whispered to the facing group.

Marco and Mark gave puzzled looks.

"We've got ourselves a roof over our heads," Ricardo whispered again, though in an excited tone.

Mark's police intuition suddenly kicked in. Why he had been asked about signs on the map, where they had been walking toward. It was the abandoned motel.

Agent Brooks found himself surrounded in the office with a handful of uniformed patrol officers.

"Okay, this isn't exactly Sherlock Holmes, but damned near," the FBI agent said and the officers looked at each other. "Okay, the consensus is that we're looking at a disused motel. It seems that our captors and captives are going to need a relatively safe house to plan their next move and to rest."

The office door opened.

"We found the patrol car," came an excited rookie's voice.

"Where?" Brooks asked in a calm and collected tone, as he was almost certain of the answer.

"Off the west highway," the rookie responded.

Brooks gazed up at the maps.

"Well, well, the net tightens and closes," the agent said, sounding almost concerned now.

"What do you mean?" Alma asked.

"Well Alma, if our deductions are correct I think we might have a standoff very shortly at somewhere called Ridgemount Bar and Rest Motel," Brooks said.

The trees of the woods began to slowly give way to open space, something Ricardo was none too pleased with. This could be an opportunity to be spotted. The group stood just short of coming out of the woods. In front of them was a small open space of flat grassland.

Ricardo took a long look ahead and gave himself a smile. Just beyond the flat grass was the distinct impression of something manmade. The thug narrowed his eyes to focus better. Again he beamed a smile. Something had indeed caught his eye.

"Where to now?" Marcos asked.

He was feeling the straps of the bags cutting hard into his shoulder blades and he was becoming tired and agitated.

"There," Ricardo said and with a long arm stretched out extended a finger and all eyes followed it.

In the distance could be seen the distinct outline of a roof of a building. Dilapidated by the looks of things, but hopefully a good place to take cover Ricardo thought. The only problem being would be the quick run across the short distance of open ground to get there.

"Okay Mr. Police officer, lets see you get across in double time," Ricardo ordered.

He dug the point of the gun into the small of Mark's back. The thought of shelter and maybe, just maybe, a chance to rest and the recovery of his buddy from his injury were paramount in the officer's mind.

Mark adjusted the slump figure over his shoulder and whispered, "Okay buddy, we'll get you alright, just stay with me."

"STOP YOUR WHISPERING!" Ricardo burst out loudly. "Now get going!"

Another prompt from the end of the gun barrel into the officer's back and Mark knew that he would have to get across the opening. Thankfully the officer recalled his physical training back at the police academy. One part of the training was the ability to safely carry a person. The training would now come into play. Mark glanced out at the open space and moved his partner until he was in a more secure holding position on his shoulder. He then moved forward.

Ricardo wasn't sure what happened the next moment. He had the gun sticking in the hostage's back. The next thing was the sound of boots stamping heavily down on the grass. Mark was taking quick and long strides out into the open, adrenalin pumping into his long muscular legs, his training taking over, a goal set in his sights, objective: to get his buddy to safety.

Ricardo reacted to the scene before him.

"Marco, come on, follow him," Ricardo commanded.

Marco shrugged himself down and with the bags still slung across his shoulders he stumbled out into the open, quick to catch up with the fast paced police officer.

Ricardo took a quick glance behind him and then looked in front of him. He shot out from the last remaining cover of trees and ran as fast as he could. They were all running toward the manmade structure.

Agent Brooks unlocked his car and got in. He swung the seatbelt across his well tailored suit and locked it in place, securing himself to the driver's seat. He gazed down at his feet encased in highly polished black lace-up ankle boots. He checked them for scuffmarks, none were present. He then checked himself in the rearview mirror, adjusted his dark silk tie and maneuvered himself so he was sitting comfortably in the car seat.

"Okay, let's put this to rest," he said quietly to himself.

He turned the ignition key and the car came to life. He allowed the automatic gears to adjust and he put his foot down on the accelerator. The car moved away from the parking bay outside the police station. Destination: Ridgemount Bar and Rest Motel. Alma gazed through the blinds from the office to see the car drive away and gave a reassuring nod of her head.

The convicts and hostages were standing outside the two story dilapidated clapboard house, a sign calling it "Ridgemount Bar and Rest Motel" lay on its side with one end still screwed above the front door. Ricardo stepped up to the main doors and twisted the door handle. It turned in his hand but there was no sound to indicate that it was opening. He pushed against the wooden door and still it would not budge. He put his shoulder against it and gave another push, nothing. He turned and faced Mark, still carrying his injured buddy.

"Come on Policeman, lets see what you can do," Ricardo said and waved the gun at Mark. "You look as though you've been to the gym a few times. Let's see if your shoulders are as good as those running legs of yours."

Mark gazed at the doors and sized them up. He then bent down to allow his unconscious fellow officer to slide off his shoulder and lay gently against the wall of the motel.

"I don't think a shoulder is going to help," Mark said, assessing the situation. "I think a good strong kick is what's needed."

"Like a drug bust hey officer?" Ricardo commented, giggling. "Just busting right in..."

"Yeah, just like a drug bust," Mark replied as he pulled up his right muscular leg and let it aim for the door.

It connected with the sole of his boot. The door shook but remained firm. Mark stood back and again looked at the door. Within a few seconds he kicked at it again, this time though he targeted a different part of the door. He threw another powerful kick. The aim of the officer's boot was just next to the door lock and this time it hit home. The wooden door opened, taking with it a cascade of splintered wood.

There was a sudden sound of clapping hands. Mark turned to find the source of the sound but was met with the hard butt of a gun hitting him. The officer staggered. He tried to find something to grab hold of but his knees buckled beneath him and he saw the ground come towards him...then there was blackness...

His vision was blurred. It took Mark a few times to blink and adjust, but slowly the officer began to make out things. The beams of light shooting through the gaps between the wooden boards and planks that had been haphazardly nailed against the windows were sufficient enough to make out where he was. It was room that had seen better days when used by guests. Trying hard to recollect the past events Mark could only come to the conclusion that he was now in one of the rooms in the motel. He moved his head and a blinding pain shot across his forehead. He tried to relieve the pain, but that was when he realized the severity of his actual predicament. He was pinned down in some way. Despite the pain the police officer slowly raised his head and allowed his eyes to gaze.

"What the...fuck?" came from under his breath.

The scene that presented itself would not have looked out of place in some gothic horror book or film. The officer had been tied down to a wrought iron bedstead that, like the room, had seen better days. A mattress was the only form of comfort and it reeked of urine, sweat and God knew what else that had taken up residency in it. Mark looked down the length of his body. Lengths of rope cut across his body securing him tightly to the bed frame. Mark carried on looking down his body towards his legs and feet. His legs had been bound together above the knees as well as being tied tightly down. His feet were also bound together and the excess rope had been used to pull his feet tightly down to the bottom of the bed. They were securely tied off to the footboard. Mark's arms were tightly cuffed behind him, the ropes and his muscular frame posed a problem. His well toned body was pressing down on his arms and cuffed hands, pushing them deep into the soiled mattress. There was no way he could try to either relieve the acute soreness or even attempt to free himself. He had come this far. Why would it be any different? He was still a prisoner.

The young rookie cop lay on the double bed. Chris was still out of it, but his breathing was becoming more regular and a few audible moans from his lips drew attention, but from the wrong person. Somewhere in an adjacent room the sound of running water could be heard. The sound was coupled with someone humming a tune. Chris was still tied at the wrists, but now his booted feet had been tied together as well. He lay on a double bed the same kind of design as the one Mark was bound to, except Chris had been given the privilege of a double while his buddy was suffering on a single. Ricardo knew who his favorite was.

Ricardo finished humming his tune and stepped out of the shower. He grabbed the threadbare towel and wrapped it around his lean torso. He took a glance in the cracked bathroom mirror, gave himself a wink of the eye and walked out. He felt satisfied.

"Hey there…" he said and stopped in mid sentence as he came into the bedroom, realizing his prisoner would not hear him.

He gave himself a moment to reflect, a young handsome officer of the law, bound hand and foot, his prisoner. Chris lay on his back, deep in some unconscious void. Ricardo was deep in thought. Maybe it was the time to make his move. It was just him and the rookie after all.

A sudden thought hit Ricardo and slowly he approached the foot of Chris' bed.

The air was still and the outside was silent, no sound save for the regular breathing of the captured rookie cop and his captor. Ricardo took a long slow intake of air and peeled away the towel from around his torso. He stood lean and firm, his dick swelling with blood, slowly becoming erect. The towel fell to the floor. Ricardo touched his dick and began to slowly stroke it. He looked down at Chris lying on the bed, bound hand and foot, defenseless, vulnerable, and available. Ricardo's blood surged through the pulsating veins of his dick. The convict released his hold on his dick and grabbed the heels of the rookie's boots. He slowly pulled the unconscious rookie down the bed. It was only a matter of inches before Ricardo stopped. He lay the booted feet down and frantically loosened the cord that bound them together. Once he reckoned the cord was loose enough, but still held the feet together he raised the boots again and squeezed his dick between the soles of the shining footwear. Ricardo pushed his dick in slowly, allowing the growing erection to move up the sides of the smooth boots. Once he felt he was comfortably slotted in Ricardo began slowly allowing his sexual desire to take over, allowing the erection to increase in length as well as girth. Ricardo's grip tightened on the shiny black Dehner boots as his erection then began to throb uncontrollably. He pushed backward and forward as his foreskin rubbed against the black smooth leather. His thighs slammed against the soles of the boots back and forth as he gazed down and watched dribbles of pre cum slowly leak from the sensitive dick. So long he had wanted this, so long. He bit down on his lower lip as he slammed himself hard against the soles of the boots. Ricardo felt the rush of cum shoot out and splat hard against the young rookie's black boots. It was almost as though Ricardo was creating a ritual, a ritual where he was marking Chris as his property, his God given right to own and use the rookie as he wanted.

Under Ricardo's orders Marco walked around the corridors of the motel. He was in search of anything useful they could use. At one time the place was a huge house. Remnants of a grander, more opulent bygone age showed through. Marco slowly went from room to room, once large rooms, but now partitioned into smaller rooms. The more rooms the more money, but not anymore. Obscure floral patterned wallpaper from an age when it was visually acceptable was now peeling away with dampness and rot. Strips of carpet now threadbare were exposing the wooden boarding underneath. The wood was warped and splintering. The smell of rot and staleness stayed constant in the air.

Marco's investigation of the decaying building had not only led him into various bedrooms, but through a labyrinth of hallways, staircases and cupboards. He had discovered what was once the janitor's office and store. Here he found the rope and following Ricardo's orders he had used it to tie up the knocked out Mark down to the bed frame. He then gave a length of the rope to Ricardo who insisted that it was to tie Chris' booted feet tightly together. No escape for either officer. Ricardo was insistent that both cops be held separately, away from each other, in different rooms. Marco had carried Mark to a room where he tied up the officer and let him slumber in unconsciousness. Ricardo had taken it upon himself to keep the young rookie Chris to himself. He carried the rookie to another room where his frustration would become apparent after the shower. Marco returned to the room where Mark lay bound.

"Well, what are you staring at?" Mark questioned the thug between gritted teeth.

The officer suddenly tried to struggle, to push himself up and try to free himself in a sequence of tugging and pulling. But it was a pointless maneuver. The ropes held and nothing more was achieved than severe pain in the head. The ropes cut deep into the fabric of Mark's uniform, tightening against his body. He slumped back into the soiled mattress.

"Sorry about this," Marco said and raised his head slightly in acknowledgement that it was his handiwork that had Mark bound so securely.

In a sympathetic voice Marco then said, "I think your buddy is coming around, he's been making moaning sounds.

Mark allowed himself a long exhale of breath. To know that Chris was coming out of his unconscious void was clearly a relief. But still it was uncertain if there was any permanent damage to the young rookie.

"Where is Chris?" Mark asked.

The look in Marco's eyes told the bound officer what he needed to know.

"With Ricardo isn't he?" Mark asked in confirmation.

The bound up officer bit down on his lower lip.

"What the fuck is he going to do with him?" Mark asked miserably.

Again the officer struggled, tugged at his bindings, trying his damndest to get loose from the ropes. But it was futile.

Marco pressed his hands down on the officer's chest to prevent Mark's limited movements.

"Relax," Marco said in a calm voice.

Mark lowered himself into the confines of the mattress, defeated again.

"Don't struggle, you'll hurt yourself," Marco said, sounding concerned.

"Oh yeah, as if I haven't been already," Mark seethed. "FUCK, I've been knocked out, tied up, told to dance, a gun stuck at my head, made to walk with my buddy on my back and then slugged again by your fucking…"

"No, no, it wasn't Ricardo that hit you, it was me," Marco said and Mark gave out a puzzled look at his captor.

"Ricardo told me after he beat the crap out of me that when we found somewhere safe he would finish you good and proper," Marco explained. "He was fucking jealous man, of me and you, sucking off and all. He was going to shoot you there and then. I had to grab the gun and hit you with it, just to distract him."

Mark considered what Marco had just said and then had a thought.

"I suppose I should say thanks, but if you untie me I might be able to help you if and when we're either caught or found," Mark said. "I can say you tried to help us, which would be even bigger thanks."

Marco pulled back from the tied up officer.

"You think that I want to end up in the penn again?" Marco asked. "Man, think again. This is my last chance at freedom. If I get caught I'll end up in a cell forever. You cops are all the same. You all stick together when your own kind are in trouble. What chance do you think I've got?"

Mark stared at his captor and realized he was right. He had participated in the abduction of two police officers, assaulted those officers and even raped one of those officers, if one chose to see it that way. Yes, Marco was indeed in a shit-load of trouble.

Chris blinked. He made a slight movement. Something wasn't right. He tried again to move, but nope, still unable to. The rookie then moved his head. That seemed okay, but it sure was mighty sore. He instinctively tried to raise his right hand to find the point of pain on his head but something prevented him. He again tried to move both hands, nothing doing. He raised his head and gazed down at his feet. The rookie's eyes widened when he saw that his ankles were loosely bound together. He tried to move his feet but the only sound was the leather of the boots rubbing together. Chris gave out a few quick breaths as he surveyed his predicament.

"Well, well, look who's awake..." Chris heard someone say.

The rookie gazed up and saw the silhouette of Ricardo. Suddenly, everything started coming back to him...

Chris watched as the tall figure of his captor came into clear view. The thin streaks of light beaming through the wooden planks nailed secure against the window frames illuminated the tight torso and firm muscles of Ricardo.

"Well, well, the sleeping rookie has awoken," was Ricardo's sinister sounding comment.

It took some time for Chris to piece together the fragments of events that had happened before this bastard cracked him across the head with the butt of a gun. But soon, a shaft of light hit the face of his captor and Chris' puzzled memory suddenly snapped back into place. The coming back home, being captured, tied to a chair, made to dance and finally hearing the words, "Do as you're told rookie," before the slug across his forehead rendered him to a void of darkness, until now.

"FUCKING CUNT," came the loud expletives from the rookie's mouth.

"Temper, temper young officer, I don't think you're in any position whatsoever to be calling me names," Ricardo chided the rookie, wagging a finger in a mocking gesture.

Ricardo then moved toward the rookie and sat himself down on the side of the double bed. Chris tried to move himself away but trying to he dug the heels of his bound Dehner boots into the fabric of the mattress. Trying to get some leverage was an exercise in futility.

"Now, now Chris, don't think that moving away from me is going to help," Ricardo said mockingly.

Chris knew he was in no position to fend for himself. With his wrists bound behind him, his feet tied together, a pretty sore head and being held somewhere he didn't know the rookie realized he was up shit's creek without a paddle.

"What the fuck do you want?" questioned the tied up rookie.

Ricardo simply looked into Chris' eyes.

"Chris my friend," Ricardo said and gave the gesture of open arms and a smile that the rookie took not to be at all welcoming.

Ricardo knelt down on the bed next to the bound officer. Again Chris tried to pull himself away, but to no avail. Ricardo allowed his fingers to touch the leather of his captive's boots, feeling the dried cum stains made earlier, giving a knowing smile to himself.

"Now my pretty rookie, let me put a proposition to you," Ricardo said and his fingers continued to weave around the leather boots.

Chris looked down at his boots and took a more intense gander at them. Even in his profession he could work out what were cum stains and what were not.

"You fucking cunt, mmmmmfffffff…" Chris began but a sweaty hand was quickly clamped across the rookie's mouth.

Ricardo placed his forefinger against his lips to tell Chris to be quiet.

"Chris, please shut-up, or else your cop buddy Mark may get hurt," Ricardo said.

The young rookie suddenly realized that it wasn't only him that was in this crazy scenario being held against his will. There was someone else, someone, who looking around the room was not there. Chris knew that he was at the mercy of this man. He also knew that he was at his beck and call. Where was Mark???

Chris nodded his head in agreement to be silent. The sweaty hand moved away. Chris took a slow intake of air.

"Good Chris, that's what I like, a cop who knows when to shut their pretty mouth," Ricardo said and stood up from the bed.

He gazed down at his captured prize. My God Ricardo thought, but this rookie was beautiful. The gods had really been smiling when they created him.

"Okay Chris, I want you to make me cum," Ricardo said, saying it in an almost endearing fashion.

The rookie's face went white.

"Don't think for a fucking second that I'm going to suck you off you fucking bastard," Chris ranted and the sudden hard slap across his handsome face was very to the point. "UHHHFFFFF!!!"

"Chris, do as you're told and you and your partner might get through today," Ricardo stated and the hard slap had also made his hand sting with pain.

"What's to say you haven't done him in already?" came the rookie's quick retort.

"Well, why don't we arrange a little get together shall we?" Ricardo asked snidely.

Chris suddenly felt himself being pulled off the decaying mattress. The heels of his Dehner boots hit hard the warped floorboards and fraying carpet. The rookie was maneuvered by his upper arms into an upright position. He wanted to cry out for help, a possibility indeed, but still tied up and with no sign of his partner he could not risk it. He would have to play along, at least for now. The thought of his captor's prick in his mouth was something he did not even want to comprehend.

Then, holding Chris tightly by his upper arms as he got him balanced on his tied up booted feet Ricardo said, "Now you stand there like a good rookie and don't try and move, though the way you're all tied up you won't be going far, ha, ha..."

Chris looked miserably straight ahead, the feel of the thug's hands squeezing his upper and muscular arms making him feel awful and helpless.

Ricardo stepped back into the bathroom and came out with Chris' sport bag. The convict unzipped the bag and threw the contents on the bed. There was a variety of clothing, t-shirts, jeans, sneakers, loafers and police issued shirts and footwear.

Chris recognized it being a mixture of both his and Mark's items. Fuck, they had ransacked their wardrobes and cupboards back at the house.

"Got some good stuff here rookie," Ricardo stated. "Let me see what's good to wear.

With that the thug allowed the threadbare towel to unloosen and fall to the floor. Chris took in the scene before him. Ricardo's semi erect circumcised cock was smooth with a cluster of dark pubic hair surrounding the base. It was still damp, either from sweat or the water from the shower. Ricardo continued to rummage through the clothes and footwear, knowing that his captive was intently looking at his dick. A small wry grin showed on Ricardo's face.

"Not bad is it rookie officer?" came the boastful comment.

Ricardo pulled up a dark t-shirt and placed it against his lean torso.

"Perfect fit, I think," he said.

Chris recognized the t-shirt as one of his best. He watched as the convict stretched it over his head and let it slide down his upper body to fit neat and tight. Chris tried to shift his weight from one leg to the other, as he was feeling the onset of a cramp. But with his feet still tied together and to achieve any form of relaxation to ease the pain was just minimal.

"All in good time Chris, just be patient, we'll see your buddy soon," Ricardo said and continued to look for some trousers or jeans. "If you try to go walking on those tied up booted tootsies of yours you really could do yourself some damage."

Agent Brooks had slowed down to almost a crawl as he viewed the map lying on the front passenger seat, glancing out at the quiet lonely road ahead.

"Almost there," he murmured and with that being said the FBI agent shot a glance at a roof coming into view.

He drew his car off the road and parked to the side. Brooks released himself from his seatbelt and instinctively adjusted himself in the rearview mirror. He gave his black tie a small tug to place it back into position against the pressed material of his shirt. He then gave himself a deep intake of air.

"Well, its all or nothing," he said softly.

The car door opened and Brooks' black ankle length lace-up boots hit the ground with a crunch. He drew himself up from the opened car door and immediately checked his gun holster. The gun was in place. He slowly closed the car door and keeping himself down headed towards the motel.

Ricardo had finished dressing.

"Well, what do you think?" he asked and stood back, allowing his handsome prisoner to view him newly clothed.

"You know that somehow when this is all over, I swear that someone will get you for this, and get you good," came the words through Chris' clenched teeth.

"Okay, okay, you had your say, but its time that you meet your friend and say hello," Ricardo said and reached over to grab the gun lying on the dilapidated dressing table.

He grabbed Chris' upper arm tightly.

"Okay rookie, start hobbling," Ricardo ordered and gave out a snicker.

Mark gazed up at the decaying ceiling above him as thoughts were spinning and spiraling. He was trying very hard to comprehend what had taken place and more to the point, what was to happen next. Suddenly his thoughts were pushed to the back of his mind as he heard the door to the room he was in creak slowly open. Mark lifted his head and tried to adjust his eyes to what he could see. It was a man dressed in the standard associated with the FBI. He wore a dark suit and tie and well-polished footwear.

Agent Brooks stood silhouetted in the doorway, gun in one hand, his forefinger against his lips to tell Mark to be silent.

Mark knew that rescue was finally in sight. The officer gave a slight smile, but his training as a policeman told him it wasn't over until the bad guys were locked in handcuffs.

Brooks offered a slight nod to the tied up officer, wanting to know if anyone was in the room. Marco had taken his leave and had continued his investigation of the motel and surrounding area. The thug had left Mark in total isolation, until now. Mark shook his head and Brooks stepped slowly into the room, the gun now held in both hands, lowered, but ready to pull up in an instant.

Brooks gently eased himself towards the bed, the soles of his ankle boots slowly pressing down on the damp threadbare carpet. His boots made small creaking sounds against the wooden floorboards beneath the decayed carpet. The agent continued his movements toward the captive cop.

"You okay?" the agent whispered.

"Fuck, am I glad to see you," Mark whispered, sounding relieved.

Brooks was now next to the bed and viewed what was ahead of him, a police officer bound hand and foot, secured tightly to the framework of the bed, a lousy and unlawful thing at the same time to do to an officer of the law.

It was the sudden sound from outside the room that diverted the FBI agent's attention. Brooks stepped back from the bed and quickly scanned the room for a place to hide. The only place he could see for hiding was behind the room door, so the room door it was.

Outside the room in the hallway came the bound figure of Chris hobbling and being forced to take small hops and steps on his bound booted feet. Ricardo had a firm grasp on the rookie's left arm, maneuvering him toward the room where Mark was, in his other hand the gun still being held.

"Hey, we'll be seeing your friend soon," chuckled Ricardo and squeezed the rookie's arm tighter.

Ricardo and Chris then turned and they were in the room. The sunbeams were now at the utmost. They shined bands of light illuminated the entire room. Both Ricardo and Chris stumbled into the room. Mark gave out a long sigh of relief. Despite his partner standing tied hand and foot he was okay.

"Fuck, Chris, are you okay?" Mark asked, tears choking him.

"He couldn't be better," Ricardo replied sarcastically.

"Yeah, doing just dandy," the rookie responded, sounding defeated.

"I'll be the judge of that," came a disembodied voice.

The room door slowly moved and from behind it came the formidable figure of Agent Brooks. Ricardo positioned himself so that Chris would now be used as a shield. He slid behind the rookie and held his arm tight, the gun pointing at Chris' back.

"Who the fuck are you?" Ricardo asked angrily,

"Guess, FBI," Brooks responded, the barrel of his gun pointed towards Ricardo, but Chris' muscular bulk hid the convict well.

The rookie suddenly found himself being turned on the spot and now facing not only the FBI gun but the gun Ricardo had as well, pressing it now into his side. Fuck, he was in a no-win situation.

"Okay, let's look at this logically," Brooks said in a calm sounding voice.

But he wouldn't be doing much looking anymore into logic, as the agent was about to find out. What happened next could have almost happened in slow motion. The sudden emergence of Marco from out of the closet next to the where the agent was standing behind the door, holding a lengthy two by four brought it down hard on the back of Brooks' shoulder, causing the FBI agent to drop his gun. Brooks turned around quickly to face Marco but he was too late. The thug hit the agent hard with a curled fist straight across the jaw. Then Marco's body pushed the agent to the floor. Adam Brooks fell onto the damp, filthy floor on his stomach, his jaw reeling from the blow he had just been dealt. Then, he felt his arms being pulled up hard behind him as Marco's knee dug hard into his back. Adam Brooks clenched his teeth in pain…then a voice.

"Well, well Chris looks like we got someone else to watch us," Ricardo said, squeezed the rookie's arm and Chris realized with a sick feeling of dread what was going to happen next.

Adam Brooks felt himself being pressed down hard into the soiled carpet. The smell of rotting wood seeped into his nostrils as his face was held down by strong hands.

"FUCKING CUNT, you FUCKING BASTARD!" Chris reeled and Agent Brooks tried to access the rookie's situation above him.

Now he was being held down by two perpetrators. The agent was in no way able to move and even at least try to get free. He found himself totally at their mercy. He then felt his hands being forcibly pulled behind him.

"HOLD THEM THERE WHILE I TIE THEM," he heard a shout.

Adam Brooks then felt the coarse texture of rope being wrapped around and around his wrists. The rope bit hard into his skin and was yanked tight at every possible moment. The agent could feel his skin almost immediately becoming sore as he tried to somehow twist and turn in the hopeful gain of getting some slack in the bindings of his wrists. It wasn't happening however.

"GET HIS FEET TIED AS WELL!" Ricardo barked.

Chris watched the scene before him and his eyes widened as he watched Ricardo and Marco working in unison to subdue the FBI agent. The rookie was in no position to help. All he could do was watch from his standing position bound and helpless. Marco grabbed the FBI agent's ankles, bent his legs up and began tying a length of cord around them, again tightening the cord as he went. A few minutes passed and then the suited and booted agent lay on the floor, securely tied hand and foot.

Alma gazed up at the clock on the wall. It was fast approaching the appointed hour. She held a mobile phone in her sweating palm. It was a mere few minutes before she would press the button she had been instructed by Brooks to use. She sat on the side of a desk. Around the office was a group of uniformed cops, some of them looking at her, others trying to talk to one another, but all were knowingly waiting for the appointed time.

"Do you think this will work?" asked a seasoned officer.

"Well, let's see shall we?" Alma replied and allowed her thumb to press the designated number on the mobile phone.

A series of numbers suddenly appeared. They backlit for a few moments and then the word "Calling" came into view. Alma placed the mobile to her ear and waited.

Agent Brooks was now himself like Chris and Mark, totally incapacitated. Ricardo and Marco gazed down at their new bound addition. Both captors' chests were rising up and down rapidly, them taking in sharp intakes of air, results of their actions tying up the federal agent.

"Where the fuck did he come from?" Marco asked in between taking gulps of the stale air.

Brooks suddenly felt a hard kick to his side.

"OOOFFFFF…" he muttered.

"SO WHO THE FUCK ARE YOU, YOU SHITFACE ARSEHOLE?" Ricardo thundered.

Brooks remained silent until a sudden vibration in his trouser pocket urged him to speak out, "I'M A FEDERAL AGENT OF THE UNITED STATES GOVERNMENT!" The timing of the phone vibration could not have been more precise.

"Okay arsehole, you don't have to shout about it," Ricardo responded. "Best thing is to shut you up good."

Brooks immediately took this comment as to mean he would be getting a bullet in the head. He tried to struggle, but he had been bound too well to make any significant effort to escape. Instead he felt his head being pulled up by his short hair and the hard rough texture of a cloth gag being pushed against his closed mouth. The FBI agent tried his best to keep his mouth closed, but another sudden kick into his muscular torso gave the desired effect and the agent opened his mouth to let out a sound of excruciating pain. But the sound was not to be as the rag was pushed violently into his craw. It cut off any sound of agony. Brooks again tried to struggle against the bonds that bound him but it was for a reason…

Alma pulled the mobile from her ear. No answer, but it did ring. She gazed at the assembled group of law enforcers.

"Okay, let's get moving," Alma commanded.

The office door swung open and an eager group of uniformed men and women emerged. Determination was written plain and simply across their faces.

Brooks lay still. There was no sense in getting another kick to his body. A thin strip of toweling material was wrapped around his head to keep the rag secure in his mouth. He felt the strip being knotted a couple of times tight behind the back of his head. The agent allowed himself to be physically handled by the two escapees, he had to. It was all part of the plan. Wrists behind him, ankles bound together, now gagged…he was now in no position to do anything but wait.

Throughout the FBI agent's ordeal both Mark and Chris could do no more than be spectators. Mark could do no more than move his head up, as the ropes still held him secured to the iron framed bed. Chris was still standing, balanced on his tied booted feet, but the tight bindings around his wrists and ankles were now beginning to take their toll.

"Okay Chris, looks like we've got ourselves another guest," Ricardo boasted and squeezed the rookie's arm again.

The thug was now dressed in a mixture of both the cop's clothing, a dark tee shirt belonging to Chris, a pair of jeans that looked as though they belonged to Mark and a pair of deck shoes. Ricardo moved around to stand in front of the rookie.

"Chris my rookie, you look as though you need to rest those legs of yours," Ricardo said. "Why don't you bend down?"

Marco took a step forward and said, "Ricardo, we got to move on, we can't stay here. If this fucking secret agent found us who's to say he hasn't got backup outside or on their way?"

"FUCKING HAVE PATIENCE GODDAMNIT," Ricardo roared.

It was becoming obvious that Ricardo wanted more than just shooting his cum onto a pair of highway patrol boots. Knowing that his partner in crime had the privilege of touching the flesh of an officer Ricardo would be damned if everything was to finish in a disused hotel too soon.

Brooks felt two sets of arms pull him up onto his knees. His kneecaps suddenly had his weight digging hard into the solid floorboards. Excruciating pain would soon develop.

Ricardo shot a glance at Chris. The rookie was still standing, bound, though he was beginning to show signs of exhaustion. His eyelids were now closing and opening. He was swaying from side to side. Mark, still bound to the metal frame of the bed could only raise his view to the scene before him. Something told him that the end was in sight, but what was that ending going to be?

"Before we go I want to finish something…" Ricardo said.

The thug stepped up to the standing rookie.

"I'm not finished yet Chris…" Ricardo said and began to unbuckle the rookie's belt.

The situation seemed bleak. Agent Brooks had let his guard down for a few seconds and for that he was now a prisoner himself. He viewed his surroundings, a motel room, peeling wallpaper, damp stains virtuously everywhere. The stained carpet, warped floorboards, the buckled strips of the blinds was all moldy looking. The wooden planks nailed haphazardly across the windows to keep people out, or in this instance to keep FBI agents and kidnapped cops in.

Brooks' dilemma was just as bad as the motel room décor. He tried to move himself but both convicts had learnt the skill of rope tying pretty well it seemed. After he had sat on his kneecaps his wrists had been crossed and bound, tied tight to the wooden slats that made up the back of the chair he was now seated in. With thin blinds cord his ankles were also tightly bound together, additionally they were bound to the cross-support of the two front legs of the chair. The two thugs were obviously making sure that their new captive didn't get away. Ricardo and Marco had finished off securing their new prize by wrapping additional cord around the FBI agent's torso, tugging it as tightly as possible, binding him to the back of the chair. The agent was bound to the extent of not being allowed to breathe properly. This ensured he would not be going anywhere for quite some time, if at all. His mouth was completely filled with a rag tied securely in place with a strip of bed sheeting, of which the faint odor of piss was present. Brooks jerked violently at his bonds but it did nothing but cause severe pain in his wrists and ankles and the blind cord cut deep into them, causing the agent to bight into the handkerchief, trying to dull the pain. The only sounds were of Brooks drawing large intakes of stale air through his nostrils and the sound of the wooden chair creaking under the suited agent's firm body. His ankle length boots made a sound as they rubbed together whilst he tried to loosen the cord around them. But for all his experience as an FBI agent his superiors had never prepared him for this sort of situation, well, at least not this type anyhow. Again he gave another violent jerk at this confinement, but it was not to be. Agent Brooks realized he had been caught, hook, line and sinker.

Ricardo began to slowly loosen the rookie's belt. Tugging at the black leather, yanking at the metal buckle, he stared into Chris' eyes.

"Please don't do this," Chris whispered pleadingly through trembling lips.

"There's nothing you can do to stop me rookie," Ricardo whispered in reply.

The rookie's belt was now completely unbuckled. Next, Ricardo would unfasten the uniform trousers.

"Marco, make sure our secret agent gets a good view of what's about to happen to my rookie here," Ricardo said.

Brooks still lay bound. His mouth was becoming dry due to the dusty dirt-ridden rag that had been roughly stuffed deep and tight and bound into his mouth. The toweling strip served well, holding the gag securely in place, knotted tight behind the agent's head. Suddenly, a pair of hands grabbed the agent by his arms and yanked him off the chair he had been tethered to. The ropes that had held him to the chair were undone and he was pulled up. Marco positioned Brooks against the far wall on his bound up feet. The agent tried to take in the scene before him as he was pulled up and then balanced. He observed his surroundings, assessing the likely possibilities of escape or rescue, a slight chance that his plan that he had discussed in the police station car park with Alma was now in action. The consequences would be either failure or success.

"Please don't do this to me..." came another pitiful request from Chris.

"Stop your fucking whining, Jesus, you're like a fucking baby," Ricardo spat in the rookie's handsome face. "Don't you know that it's time for you to accept what's coming to you?"

Mark watched helplessly as his partner was being traumatized. The superior cop had also come to realize that this had been Ricardo's plan all along...to capture the rookie and make him his own.

Chris' eyes began to well up with tears. He was beginning to break. This was the final injustice for a rookie cop, the certain knowledge that he was going to be raped.

The rookie's belt was yanked open. Ricardo fingered the top of Chris' uniform trousers and unfastened them. He then grasped the zipper and slowly began to tug at it. Chris kept closing his eyes to prevent the tears from slowly streaming down his cheeks; it was only a matter of time.

"Have you ever had a thick cock in your hole Chris?" Ricardo whispered lustfully.

It was at that moment that the rookie could no longer hold back. The warm sensation of tears trickled down his cheeks.

"Hey, hey, buddy, I'll be gentle with you, don't fret," Ricardo chuckled and wiped a tear from Chris' handsome face.

There were a few moments while Ricardo stared into the tearful eyes of the youthful cop. He then took his gaze and looked down at the bound figure of Mark. Again, it was that look of Ricardo's that spelled unforeseen trouble for the cops.

"Look, I got an idea that will make it easier for you," Ricardo said, squeezing Chris' arm again as he spoke to the captive rookie. "Why don't you suck your partner's cock?"

A sudden and deafening silence consumed the entire dingy room. Chris swallowed a silent gulp.

"Oh didn't you know? Your partner here," Ricardo began, waving an accusing finger at the tied down figure of Mark. "He isn't all he seems to be. He likes being sucked off, good and plenty, by Marco. They really enjoyed themselves."

"YOU FUCKING BASTARD!!" reeled Mark as he began struggling against the tight ropes that held him to the bed.

The cop's frantic thrashing and tugging at his bindings did nothing but intensify his anger at Ricardo.

Chris watched Mark feverishly twist and turn in all ways possible, trying anyway anyhow to break free, but it resulted in no more than the cop exhausting himself. Mark fell back into the mattress throwing out a groan of defeat. Chris knew that it was now only a matter of time before the final insult to an officer of the law, that degrading ritual of being fucked by a convict on the run would happen. The rookie felt his bunghole twitching and contracting.

Ricardo grabbed the waistband of Chris' trousers and with a swift yank pulled them down as far as the top of the rookie's boots. Chris' uniform shirt tails fell to cover his white briefs that held his dick and balls. Ricardo lifted the front shirt tails and bent his head down slightly.

"Let's see what's down here shall we?" Ricardo snickered.

Ricardo grasped the elastic waistband of the cotton briefs and pulled them down, again, as far as the top of the rookie's boots. Ricardo took in the scene before him. There was still a few seconds. Brooks gave a feeble sounding groan from behind his gag, trying to somehow distract Ricardo from violating the poor handsome rookie anymore, but there was nothing doing it seemed. Ricardo was transfixed, mesmerized by the manhood that was now in front of him.

"Well, well Chris, I see that your father and mother blessed you well," Ricardo said tauntingly to the rookie. "Let's see if that cute arse of yours is just as appetizing shall we?"

Ricardo maneuvered himself around to the back of the bound rookie. Chris looked desperately and helplessly over at Mark. Ricardo gave a small thin smile as he lifted the rookie's shirt tails at the back to reveal two firm muscular butt cheeks.

"Oh baby, I think we've hit the jackpot with this one," Ricardo chuckled.

The thug pulled himself straight up and grabbed hold of the bound up rookie's shoulders.

"Okay, let's get you into position shall we?" Ricardo asked and Chris felt the firm clinging hands of the convict pushing him nearer to the metal framed bed.

"There, that should do it," Ricardo said and stood back from the scene of a tied down cop and his rookie standing bound hand and foot over him.

The scene was set for Ricardo's warped mind.

"Okay Chris, those arse cheeks of yours are going to be spread wide open to take my big fat cock up your arsehole," Ricardo stated. "I'm going to have to untie your pretty booted feet. Now don't try anything. I've still got your cop buddy there and Mr. FBI all tied up. Try anything and they might just not make it."

Again Chris looked desperately at Mark. Mark felt totally helpless not being able to help his buddy out of the predicament Ricardo had him in. Ricardo then knelt down and picked at the knot that bound Chris' feet securely. In a matter of moments the rookie felt the rope slacken around his ankles. Ricardo pulled the rope away and Chris felt the sensation of feeling suddenly begin to slowly seep back into his feet.

Marco watched as Ricardo positioned Chris next to the bed and then untied the rope around the rookie's feet. Ricardo was acting as if he was the puppeteer and Chris was his puppet. Time was ticking away. They had to start making their escape. Marco bit down on his bottom lip. His nerves were getting the better of him at this point.

Chris stood now with his legs slightly apart. His blood circulation was slowly returning to his numbed feet. His uniform trousers and white briefs were still down around the top of his boots, humiliating.

"Okay Chris, now, lets get your buddy ready for some action," Ricardo said, released his grip from the rookie's shoulders once again and leaned over the tied down figure of Mark.

"Time to see what you're made of cop," Ricardo said and grabbed the cop's zipper on his uniform trousers, pulling it slowly downward.

Mark began to squirm and wriggle, trying to stop the convict's fingers from pulling down his zipper, but it was a pointless exercise.

Once open Ricardo's fingers probed for Mark's cock and he was able with some slight difficulty to yank it out from the safety of the cop's jockstrap. Chris looked helpless as Ricardo asked him if he thought he could suck his partner's cock.

"MMMMFFFFFFF..." Brooks again attempted at a distraction.

"FUCKING SHUT UP!" Ricardo roared and took three large strides across the room.

The punch was quick and precise, catching the FBI agent squarely in the jaw. Adam Brooks, with no means to stop himself falling, crashed to the floor.

"MMMMMFFFFFFFF...FUUUUCCCKKKKIINNGG..." the agent protested through his gag.

Brooks was stunned by the blow. He needed to regain his senses. Time was running out...to a conclusion.

Ricardo turned his attention back to Chris and again with three strides he was directly behind the rookie.

"FUCKING BEND OVER AND SUCK HIS DICK," Ricardo screamed his command.

Chris felt the back of his neck being grabbed and roughly pushed down toward Mark's flaccid cock.

"NOOOOOO...PLEASE NO..." Chris panted.

Ricardo feverishly unfastened the trousers that once belonged to one of his captives and let them drop around his ankles. He next pulled down the boxers he was wearing. Already the veins in his dick were pumping with blood, engorging it, making it thick and solid. The thug was ready to penetrate. And what he wanted to penetrate was a handsome young rookie.

The sound of saliva being spat into an open hand filled the air. Ricardo moistened his long shaft of manhood, smearing the spit completely over the foreskin, ensuring that it would glide hard and forcefully into the rookie's tight hole.

"Now, let me get my hard dick all nice and moist and stuffed into that tight hole of yours rookie," Ricardo commented subtly.

Chris shot a fear filled glance at Mark on hearing this. Both cops were in a no win situation.

"Hey cop, better get that cock of yours rising," Ricardo stated meanly to Mark. "I want this rookie sucking hard while I fuck his handsome brains out.

Ricardo's hands smacked hard on Chris' bare cheeks a few times before slowly forcing them apart and revealing the young rookie's hole. Chris clenched his teeth in a mixture of fear and outright anguish.

"Oh boy, that arsehole is begging to be fucked!" Ricardo chucked and grabbed a handful of one of Chris' ass cheeks, giving it a hard jiggle.

The thug positioned his erect and towering cock and began to slowly push forward. Chris' handsome face scrunched up in total fear. Ricardo allowed his hardness to slide with the help of his spit between the rookie's firm and opened cheeks. The young rookie then felt the tip of his captor's wet cock press against his tense muscles that kept his hole firmly closed.

"OH GOD NO..." Chris pleaded to Ricardo and the others in the room.

Ricardo leaned over to Chris' left ear and threateningly said, "Best you start relaxing rookie." Again Chris gave an anguished looking glance at his tied down buddy. Mark stared helplessly up at his young mate. Both men knew by their expressions that they would have to succumb to Ricardo's twisted mind.

Chris drew in gulps of air, trying hard to somehow relax. The pressure of his tormentor's cock was pressing hard to penetrate now into his asshole. It

144

was becoming unbearable. He had to relax, had to allow this bastard to violate him, allow him to take away the last remnants of a cop's dignity.

"Hey cop, are you getting a stiff dick ready for this rookie to suck?" Ricardo asked Mark. "If you don't, I might just have to hurt someone."

The police officers recognized the threat in Ricardo's voice. They had both suffered his torments enough already to know he meant business.

Mark lay on the bed, securely bound, his cock exposed, lying dormant on the fabric of his uniform trousers. He had to relax and allow his raging emotions to be subdued. He closed his eyes and tried to find something in the deep recesses of his mind, something to focus on. He had to concentrate on something sexual that would trigger the ability to get an erection. Slowly, images began to form in his mind of being handcuffed to a tree and then being sucked off by a convict. Mark was beginning to feel arousal in his cock.

The beaten FBI agent raised his head as best he could to try and view the torturous scene beginning to unfold. His eyes widened as he was just able to see Ricardo forcing his cock into the poor young rookie's ass. He tried again to work the ropes that held him, but nothing gave. He was totally immobilized. The agent's only hope was the plan he had come up with using the mobile phones. If Alma rang his phone and didn't get an answer from him then she and the rest of the division were to get to the scene, pronto. Adam's mobile did ring on vibrate mode and shouting at his captors earlier covered up the slight sound. Ricardo and Marco were none the wiser. Adam was now hoping that Alma was fast making tracks to the hotel, but time was running out... especially for the poor handsome young rookie.

Events that had taken place in the room could not have taken more than twenty minutes, but it was twenty minutes too much for Marco. He was becoming increasingly uncomfortable. Droplets of sweat began to form on his forehead. He felt as if the room was closing in, becoming almost a cell. He would not feel okay until he and Ricardo were back out on the road. Like Mark, he needed to distract his mind. Ricardo was too fixated on the young cop to pay any attention to his verbal ramblings of getting away so he glanced down at the FBI agent lying at his feet. Adam Brooks was beaten and bound and gagged. Marco then remembered what Ricardo said, to make sure the agent could clearly see what was happening to the two cops. Marco bent down and grabbed the suited agent's bound feet. This would allow him to calm down momentarily at least.

The line of patrol cars, five in total, slowly came over the hill. The roof of the motel came into Alma's sight. Now she needed to locate Brooks' car. A quick scan of the surrounding territory and Alma was able to make out the metallic glint of the FBI agent's car roof. A radio message from her to the other patrol cars and the convoy slowly drew up behind the car. Alma gazed out and began to bight her lower lip. She felt that the end was soon to come. She raised the car radio mike to her mouth and said, "Okay, outa sight guys."

"OOOOOOOO…FUCK…you bastard…" came the pitiful outburst from Chris' mouth.

Ricardo in turn gave out a long gasp of air from his lungs as his cock slowly pushed aside the walls and muscles around the rookie's shit chute. The long thick cock pushed deep into Chris' hole.

"OHHH MOTHERFUCKER, SWEET JESUS," Ricardo moaned ecstatically. "YOU'RE SO FUCKING GOOD AND TIGHT."

Chris squeezed his eyes shut as he felt the long hard erection pushing its way into him. Ricardo's hands firmly gripped the young cop's shoulders on either side to steady himself and he then began to thrust back and forth. The thug's muscular thighs slapped against the firm cheeks of Chris' ass.

"OH GOD MARK, I'M BEING FUCKED HERE LIKE SOME CHEAP ASS WHORE…" Chris swore angrily.

Mark opened his eyes and watched intently and with woe as Chris was being fucked. He watched as Ricardo beamed an expression of sheer pleasure and satisfaction through gritted teeth as he thrust deep into the rookie's hole. Mark felt a mixture of emotions surging through him. He felt outright anger and hatred at Ricardo and Marco for all they had done since capturing him and Chris. He felt helpless at not being able to prevent this awful indignity that was happening to Chris…his rookie. And mostly he felt revulsion, revulsion over this entire situation. But then the cop felt something else, he felt something stirring. His dick was betraying him by getting hard. It was slowly rising, the blood surging into its veins, forcing it to rise. And it was rising in front of the eyes of poor being fucked in the ass Chris. The images that Mark had allowed to come to the forefront of his mind now became clear as day. They were images that Mark had hoped and prayed would never surface again. The cop realized with total dismay that he was in a no win situation to avoid the inevitable. His erection was at the point of no return.

Chris was now feeling the emotional and physical onslaught of being horribly violated and now in front of him his friend, his mentor, his best buddy was slowly getting an erection. Ricardo leaned over to see Mark's hard-on grow.

"Hey rookie, looks like you got some blowing to do," Ricardo laughed and pushed the back of Chris' head forward, directly onto the erect cock.

The swift action from Ricardo took Chris by surprise and the rookie's attempt to shout out was cut short as his partner's engorged cock was stuffed unceremoniously into his mouth. Mark felt the warmth of Chris' mouth enclose around his cock. Ricardo didn't release his grip on Chris' head; instead he started to push it up and down. Chris began to gag instinctively as the cock found its way deeper and deeper into the back of his mouth.

"There you go rookie, get your buddy all excited, get him to shoot into that pretty mouth of yours," Ricardo said relentlessly, fucking deeper and deeper and harder and harder into the rookie's asshole.

With Chris now bent in a doubled over position Ricardo pushed the young cop's head onto Mark's firm erection while fucking him from the rear at the same time, almost attaining a perfect synchronization in both actions.

Brooks felt Marco grab his bound feet and he was dragged to the middle of the room. Suddenly, the FBI agent felt himself being rolled over onto his side. It was a bad move because something small and oblong fell from his pocket. It was a mobile phone. Marco's eyes lit up when he saw it. The convict picked it up and stared at the small screen.

"FUCKING BASTARD!!" Marco shouted.

Brooks then felt the stabbing pain of a foot slammed into his chest.

Ricardo turned his head to see Marco holding the mobile phone. Marco held the device up so Ricardo could see it clearly.

"This fucking bastard may have sent a signal," Marco said.

"How the fuck could he?" Ricardo asked bluntly. "He's all tied up."

"I fucking don't know, but we've got to go," pleaded Marco.

"NOT TILL I'VE FINISHED FUCKING MY ROOKIE!" Ricardo shouted and with that he turned back to the chore at hand.

His rookie??? When Chris heard that he wondered what was to become of him.

Marco glanced down at the bound FBI agent and a feeling of uncertainty took hold. The thug raised his right foot and slowly pressed it down onto the side of Adam Brooks' face. He pressed down good and hard.

"MMMMMMMFFFFFFF!!!! MMMMMFFFFFFFFFF!!!!!" the agent reeled as he felt the rough sole of a shoe being pushed hard against his cheekbone.

Adam Brooks was in no state whatsoever to offer any resistance.

"Who the fuck were you phoning?" Marco asked and pressed harder into the agent's face.

The thug dropped the mobile phone on the floor in front of Adam Brooks' face and allowed his left foot to come down hard on the device. The phone broke and splintered into various pieces. The agent could only give a slow moan from behind his tight gag.

Marco released his foot from the side of Brooks' face and promptly threw a hard kick into the suited agent's torso. Brooks felt a sensation of vomit swimming up from his much wounded stomach to the inside of his gagged mouth. The sudden fear of choking became prevalent.

The motel was surrounded by police. Alma surrounded herself and conversed with a small band of uniformed men. The choice was not simple. It was either charge in or stand off and negotiate. In either case someone could get hurt…or killed. All eyes were on Alma.

"We go in," she said through clenched teeth.

The majority of cops around her gave a smile. They were ready to fight to save their own.

"We're going to have to go in without knowing where they are," said one of the cops.

It was true despite the hotel being small. There were rooms, attic, basement and any other numerous places where they could be. Alma gave herself a moments thought.

"Time is not on our side, we go in and split up," she said. "That way we cover more rooms. Surprise will have to be our only advantage."

Ricardo's deep thrusts were now becoming more and more frantic. The sounds of flesh against flesh became more rapid as his hips slammed into the back of Chris' ass cheeks. He was fast approaching shooting his load into the rookie. Mark too had succumbed to his sexual desire. Within a day his cock had been twice delivered into the mouths of two different men…and both times there was an inner voice telling the cop to allow it to happen. What was going on within his mind? Why was his body responding in this way? These were the questions that suddenly paled in the recesses of the cop's mind as he was fast approaching shooting his load into Chris' moist mouth.

Alma and her band of officers slowly moved up to the recently broken wooden door of the motel. Firearms were at the ready for whatever was beyond it. One by one the officers stepped into the motel. Silent hand signals were used between them, showing what needed to be done. A thorough search of the building was in order. The officers split into groups and slowly fanned out into different directions. All they needed now was some sort of sign that would tell them that this was where their cop brothers were being held. It would not be long for confirmation.

"OH FUCK ROOKIE, I'M FUCKING GOING TO SHOOT MY LOAD!" Ricardo shouted and Chris whimpered miserably around Mark's cock lodged in his mouth.

It was all that Alma and the cops needed. They honed in on the shout and made their move.

Ricardo's face creased up in total ecstasy as he felt his juices explode from his dick and into the young rookie's hole. A few seconds later and Mark was only able to bight down hard on his lower lip as he felt himself shooting his cum into the rookie's mouth. The cop turned his head away, to hide the expression of satisfaction. He could not have his face seen like this, especially by poor Chris.

"OH FUCKING BEAUTIFUL," Ricardo cried ecstatically.

The thug felt himself slump onto the back of his victim. He wiped his forehead against the rookie's shirt, drying off the beads of sweat that had accumulated there. His hands were still clinging hard to Chris' shoulders.

"OH Chris, you are mine from now on you fucking rookie pig," came the elated and exhausted voice of Ricardo.

The convict pulled himself up from the soiled shirt and stood still for a few moments as he took in long breaths. It was a matter of seconds before he slowly pulled his spent cock away from the rookie's backside and released his grip from his shoulders. Ricardo grabbed one of Chris' shirt tails and wiped his cock clean…another humiliation, another sign of hatred against cops.

"Fucking bastard…" Chris whimpered as his mouth came off of Mark's cock, his craw dripping cum as well as his asshole.

What happened next was total mayhem. The door to the room was suddenly sent flying. It was wrenched from its hinges. Uniformed cops marched in, guns at arms length, straight out and pointing. Sudden shouts of commands "GET BACK" and "ARMS ABOVE YOUR HEAD" quickly echoed around the four walls of the motel room.

Marco instinctively raised his arms above his head and stepped back from the choking FBI agent. An officer was quick to pull the gag away from Brooks' mouth. The agent allowed a pool of vomit to be released from his craw and pour onto the wooden floor.

He then felt himself being untied by a couple of police officers. The agent felt relief as the binding ropes around his wrists and ankles were slowly loosened and he was able to eventually pull free.

"So the cavalry has arrived, pity it wasn't in the nick of time hey rookie?" came the comment along with a wry and mocking grin from Ricardo.

Alma entered the room and took in the scene before her. It did not take long for her to realize what had taken place. She was immediately taken in by the young rookie, him standing with his head lowered, his trousers down around his ankles.

Chris felt his wrists being slowly untied. The rookie's hands felt numb, void of any sensation. He felt exposed. When he raised his head he gazed slowly around. It was Alma that his tear stained eyes focused on. She gave a nod, a nod that gave the signal that this bizarre chain of events had come to an end. When Chris' wrists were free his arms slowly dropped to his sides. He stood there in plain sight for the occupants of the room to see the indignity that he had suffered. The rookie began to tremble. He tried to grab his trousers and underwear and pull them up, but he couldn't, seeing as he was drained of all things emotional and physical. He stood as though like a small boy, hurt and alone. An officer leaned over Mark with a pocketknife he had pulled out and began sawing through the tight ropes that held the officer down on the metal bed frame. Mark could not wait for as soon as the bindings loosened he began to twist and turn vigorously. He raised himself up as his feet were being cut free from the metal framework. He could feel his ankles slowly coming loose from the ropes that bound them. It was now only a case of his wrists being unlocked from the cuffs. The cop took a glance down at his open trousers, his cock no longer hard and erect. A sudden surge of confused feelings and emotions enveloped him. Chris had swallowed his cum. What did that mean? How was he supposed to feel about that? A few moments later and his wrists were free from their metal bindings. Mark quickly pushed his cock back into his uniform trousers and zipped up. He took a quick glance around the room but all attention was focused on Chris. Mark rubbed his swollen wrists, trying to kick-start the blood circulation, but in the back of his tortured mind, something stirred…

"Okay guys lets clear this mess up and make sure we read these scumbags their rights," came a female voice.

Alma had taken the initiative, trying to divert attention away from the young rookie.

She walked over to stand in front of Chris. She raised her arms to hold him. The rookie slightly raised his head, but it was too much for him and a sudden rush of emotions took hold. He clenched his fist tight and allowed himself to swing around and throw a punch. With all the pain and anguish behind it, the punch landed squarely into the face of Ricardo. It struck straight, a cracking sound of bone confirmed that the thug would not have much of a straight nose in the future. Ricardo fell back against the wall. With his hands cuffed he had been unable to protect himself from the fist. He shook himself and droplets of blood from his now very broken nose dripped to the floor. Chris stared long and hard into his tormentor's eyes. No way would he ever be this thug's rookie. Ricardo gave back a slight grin. It could have lasted a few minutes, but in actuality it was no more than a few seconds. Two officers grabbed Ricardo by his arms and began to march him out of the room. Ricardo did not put up any resistance. He reached the door, a cop started reading him his rights and he turned and gazed into Chris' hurt eyes.

"See you soon rookie," he said and leered.

Chris felt his stomach turn as Ricardo was led out followed by Marco, hands cuffed behind him as well. A quick glance at Mark from Marco was not reciprocated. Mark did not know what he felt for Marco. He was, at that moment, confused, but more compelling were the inner demons within himself that were slowly taking hold…

He and Chris looked blankly at each other…

A few days later a patrol car drove up to the small house where two police officers had once lived. The doors and windows were securely locked. The house was now empty. The real estate agent would be along later to value the property.

Alma pulled up and got out of the car, her hands on her hips. The passenger door opened and a smartly dressed FBI agent got out and joined her.

"Well, its over," said Alma.

"Give it time, I'm sure the guys will get through it," Adam Brooks said and stared down at his well polished shoes.

"Will they ever come back here do you think?" Alma questioned.

"Who knows? I hear once they've had some therapy and some time off to get over it they'll be back on the force," the FBI agent said.

Alma glanced at Adam Brooks.

"And what happens to you?" she asked.

"Back to the office I suppose and hang around for the next case," he replied. "Though I've got to write up this one, which will take some time."

"So, can I get you a beer then?" Alma asked.

Brooks gazed at the female police officer.

"I don't see why not," he replied. "Maybe we can talk about where your future is headed."

A grin passed both their lips. They got back in the patrol car and turned away from the house, back in the direction of Ridgemount.

A Boner Book

ABOUT THE EDITOR

Christopher Trevor was born in July 1963 and grew up in New York City. As soon as he was old enough to know how he began writing fiction and has been writing gay erotic/fetish stories for the past ten to twelve years at this point. He became an avid reader as well from the time he knew how and reads everything from fiction, to non-fiction to biographies of interesting and unusual people, people who have made a difference or who have paved the way for others. Christopher attributes his writing artistic inspiration to artists such as Etienne, Tom of Finland, Tagame,
The Hun, and most notably Joe T, who Christopher has had the pleasure of speaking with and even meeting over the last few years. Christopher states, "Joe T encouraged me to write about my fetish because I was embarrassed about it at the time. Joe T said that when we are embarrassed about something that makes it even more enticing somehow." Christopher totally agreed and never stopped writing in this genre. Erotic writers who inspired Christopher Trevor were: Tom Shaw (author of "That Day at the Quarry), C.S. White (author of Big Sur), Larry Townsend (author of countless erotic novels), and Mason Powell (author of the classic story "The Brig.")

Christopher discovered that not only did he enjoy writing erotic tales but that after his first bondage experience he had a genuine flair for it. Writing to erotic oriented magazines about his first bondage experience truly opened the floodgates for Christopher where this style of writing is concerned. Christopher thanks the handsome and muscular "Greg" for that experience way back in time. Christopher took "Creative Writing" courses every semester during his high school years and while other friends of his stopped writing what they loved to write about as time went on Christopher never let a day go by when he didn't write something... "I feel that if I don't write every day I will die," Christopher has said many times over.

Foot fetish stories and all things related; spanking fetish, erotic shaving, muscle bondage, tickle torture, and hardcore stories are just a few of the areas of gay eroticism that Christopher enjoys writing about and inspiring in others as well. As one internet buddy said to Christopher where the black socks fetish is concerned, "Until I started talking with you I never gave a thought to my socks when I got dressed for work in the morning. Now when I pull my dress socks on every morning I get a chill up my spine."

Christopher is proud of the erotic effect he has on people...

Christopher Trevor is also the author of:

The Executive Guide to Foot Fetishism and Office Discipline

    1-887895-36-1

Executive Ties That Bind

    1-887895-37-X

Don't! Stop! That Tickles!

    1-887895-31-0

The Taming of Dominick

    1-887895-45-0

Timmy and The Hong Kong Tailor

    1-887895-30-2

Love, Torture and Redemption

    1-887895-32-9

Timmys Ticklish Trials

    978-1-887895-74-3

The Gym Instructor

    978-1-887895-44-6

Milked

978-1-887895-66-8

Erotic Street Blues

978-1-887895-97-2

The Abusive Wager

978-1-887895-04-0

Terry's Appointment and Other Tickling Stories

978-1-934625-08-8

The Military File

978-1-934625-21-7

Quirks

978-1-934625-24-8

Timmy and the Evil Dr. Vonvellicator

978-1-934625-42-2

Blackmail

978-1-934625-47-7

Tickled Kink

978-1-934625-49-1

Humiliation

978-1-934625-58-3

Discipline

978-1-934625-07-1

Revenge

978-1-934625-60-6

Taking Liberties

978-1-934625-65-1

Look for them where you bought this book, Amazon.com or
TheNazcaPlainsCorp.com

www.ingramcontent.com/pod-product-compliance
Lightning Source LLC
Chambersburg PA
CBHW070757280626
47162CB00016B/1403